"Let me go!"

"Give me that pouch."

"I'll die first!"

"Don't tempt me," he grunted.

They scuffled, finally falling to the ground as they became locked in a stubborn duel. Screaming, she fought him, but he had suddenly developed the strength of Goliath. He had the leather packet almost in his fingers when she wriggled from beneath him.

Swearing, he caught her arm and jerked her back.

"See how you like this!" she grunted.

He quickly sidestepped her trouncing knee and flipped her around so that her back was to him. He barely escaped the ferocity of her teeth on the back of his wrist as he fought to control her. When his hand brushed against her breast, she froze. The funniest feeling came over her. It was almost a pleasant diversion.

She suddenly screeched with fury and hurled herself at him.

"Give up, McDougal. I'm gettin' those damn papers!" he shouted.

"Never, never, never, *never!*"

PROMISE ME TODAY

Lori Copeland

FAWCETT GOLD MEDAL • NEW YORK

A Fawcett Gold Medal Book
Published by Ballantine Books
Copyright © 1992 by Lori Copeland

All rights reserved under International and Pan-American Copyright Conventions. Published in the United States by Ballantine Books, a division of Random House, Inc., New York, and simultaneously in Canada by Random House of Canada Limited, Toronto.

Library of Congress Catalog Card Number: 92-90604

ISBN 0-449-14751-7

Manufactured in the United States of America

First Edition: December 1992

Houston, Texas: July, 1864

"Best lookin' herd of beef I've seen this side of the Colorado!" A. J. Donavan knocked the dust from his hat, then pitched it onto the bar. Texas Longhorns were a scroungy-looking lot, but this herd seemed superior.

The overhead fan in The Silver Slipper labored to stir the midday heat as Donavan signaled to the bartender for a shot of whiskey. Turning to the cowboy standing next to him, he asked, "Got any idea who owns the herd?"

Ealy Moore thought about it for a moment, then had to admit that he didn't. "Nope."

Ealy had seen the twenty-five hundred or so head of steer being led into the south holding pen late that afternoon. Right fine-looking animals, wearing a brand out of the panhandle of Texas, but he didn't know who owned them.

The bartender eyed the cattleman curiously as he set

a shot glass of whiskey in front of him. "You in the market for beef, stranger?"

"I'd be damn interested in buying that particular herd," A.J. admitted. Tossing the whiskey down, he motioned for another one. He'd been on the trail for over a month now, and he was dry as a bone.

"Don't guess it would be too hard to find out who owns the cows." The bartender lifted the bottle to fill A.J.'s glass again. "My guess is they belong to one of those drovers who was in here an hour ago."

"Know where the men went?"

"Said they were going over to the hotel for a bath and a shave, then they were gonna get roaring drunk—"

The bartender's voice faded as a shadow suddenly fell across the doorway of the bar.

The men looked up to see three sisters standing in the doorway, their hands resting lightly on the crosses they wore on gold chains around their necks.

Taken by surprise, the men stared back at the nuns, aware of the reverent hush that had suddenly enveloped the room. A.J. would later recall that the nuns were young and exceptionally pretty. Not remarkable, but it was noteworthy to find such rare beauty hidden beneath dark habits.

The sisters remained in the doorway, their gazes moving slowly about the room, pausing momentarily on the table where four men with cigarettes dangling from the corners of their mouths were engaged in a game of jacks high.

As they spotted the women, the men quickly folded their hands and crushed their smokes.

A fly droned idly overhead as the sisters entered the bar. Moving with somber dignity, they glided across the room, their black habits brushing quietly along the wooden floor. The saloon was nearly empty this afternoon. The earlier drinkers had gone about their business, and the evening crowd wouldn't be in for a while.

The air in the room grew closer as the silence stretched. The men stood, glasses posed in midair, watching as the women approached.

Pausing in front of A.J., the middle sister said, "I understand you are interested in purchasing our cattle." Her voice was soft and lyrical, befitting her calling.

A.J. straightened, trying to collect his rattled thoughts. "Er . . . those your longhorns, ma'am?"

The sister smiled. "Yes, sir, they are."

"Well . . . yes, ma'am. I'd be interested . . . Sister . . . ?"

Sister's eyes lowered submissively. "Sister Anne-Marie."

"Pleased to meet you, ma'am . . . er, Sister." A.J. hurriedly wiped the dust from his hand, then extended it to her. "A.J. Donavan's my name."

Sister bowed her head submissively. "Mr. Donavan."

"Pleased to meet you, Sister. You say you want to sell your herd?"

Sister Anne-Marie lifted her eyes, and A.J. encountered the most uncommon shade of jade green that he had ever witnessed. *Exquisite.* The term was fitting; still it fell short of the breathtaking beauty that lay in the emerald pools.

"The cattle are a gift to our mission," Sister explained.

Glancing at the two other sisters, A.J. was startled

to see the same emerald likeness staring back at him. The women must actually be sisters, he thought fleetingly.

"A gift?" he repeated, surprised that women would be in charge of such a large herd.

The sisters bowed their heads, murmuring softly in unison, "Praise be to God." Sister Anne-Marie continued, "If it were not for the kindness shown by others, our mission could not survive."

Unable to contain his curiosity, the bartender asked, "What mission is that, Sisters?"

"Our Lady Of Perpetual Grace," Sister Anne-Marie replied.

The bartender frowned, shaking his head. "Don't believe I've ever heard of it." He agreed with the grace part though. He'd never seen three women better endowed with comely grace, even if they were sisters.

"It is but a small, inferior mission," the nun conceded humbly.

"I don't understand, Sister, if the cattle are a gift—"

"A gift we cannot keep," the sister acknowledged. "We have no means to care for such a large herd. Our mission is small, and our funds are meager. With the help of some very kind hombres, Sister Amelia, Sister Abigail, and I have managed to bring the herd here to sell. Our order is small, sir, and the money we receive from the sale of the cattle will help see us through the coming winter."

A.J. glanced at the two sisters, and they nodded gravely.

"They're fine-looking animals," A.J. admitted. "How many head do you have? Twenty-five, twenty-six hundred?"

"No, sir. Only twenty-four hundred and eighty-six head," Sister Anne-Marie said. "We began the journey with twenty-five hundred, but we suffered losses along the way."

Sister Abigail reached out to lay her hand upon Anne-Marie's arm. "Still, we have been most fortunate, Sister. The Lord has smiled upon us, for we lost only fourteen cattle in all."

Sister Anne-Marie nodded, looking repentant that she had sounded ungrateful. "Of course, Sister. We have been most blessed."

"You must have had good grass and water along the way. The cattle appear to be well fed," A.J. noted.

"The Lord smiled, Mr. Donavan."

"Well, ladies." A.J. was ready to buy the cattle, providing the price was right. "If you're willing to sell the longhorns at market price—"

"Oh, no, sir." Sister Anne-Marie stopped him. "We couldn't do that."

Now as fine as those cattle were, A.J. would have to think about paying above market price for them. He'd like to have the herd, but he wasn't about to be fleeced, even if the women were nuns. "Well, they're mighty fine-looking cattle, ma'am, but I couldn't pay above three dollars a head—"

"It would only be fair if we sold the cattle for a dollar a head below market price," Sister insisted.

"A dollar below market price?" A.J. repeated, certain he'd misunderstood.

"Below market price," Sister stated again firmly, and Sister Abigail and Sister Amelia nodded in solemn agreement.

"Mr. Donavan, it is imperative that we sell the cattle and return to the mission as quickly as possible,"

Sister Anne-Marie confided. "The vaqueros who have so kindly helped us bring the cattle to market have families who need tending, and the return trip is long and arduous. Even if we leave before sunset, we shall travel for days before we reach home again. Since it is we who find ourselves on the horns of this dilemma, it is hardly fair to ask you to pay market price." Sister Anne-Marie looked at Sister Abigail and Sister Amelia, and once again they nodded their full agreement. "If you want the cattle, the herd is yours for a dollar a head below market price."

"You're sure? A dollar a head below market?"

"We are quite certain," Sister Anne-Marie said. "If we are able to start back to the mission within the hour, the sacrifice will be a small one."

"Sister," A.J. extended his hand, "you just made yourself a deal."

Sister Anne-Marie smiled. "May God richly bless you, Mr. Donavan, as He has so richly blessed us."

"If you'll wait right here, it'll only take me a minute to go to the bank and get your draft—"

"Cash," the sister corrected. "Cash would be most suitable."

"Cash it'll be." A.J. had excellent credit at the bank, and it wouldn't take him fifteen minutes to have the money.

Reaching for his hat, A.J. motioned to the bartender. "Get the sisters a glass of sarsaparilla while I'm gone."

The sisters looked at one another, their eyes silently condoning the small stimulation. A glass of sarsaparilla would be refreshing.

The clock on the wall slowly ticked away the minutes as the sisters sat at a table near the doorway, sipping their sarsaparilla.

The men had all drifted to one corner of the bar, trying to look inconspicuous until Donavan returned with the money.

Exactly fifteen minutes from the time he had left, A.J. entered the bar again.

The sisters quietly rose as he hurried toward their table.

"Here you are." He pressed a large brown envelope into Sister Anne-Marie's hand. You'll find the full amount, plus an extra hundred." He offered her a benevolent smile. "I want to donate a little something to the mission myself."

"Bless you, Mr. Donavan. Bless you." Sister Anne-Marie squeezed his hand gratefully, then carefully tucked the envelope away beneath her robe. "If you will be so kind as to provide me with a piece of paper, I will write you a bill of sale."

The bartender searched around and eventually came up with a label torn from a whiskey bottle.

"And a pencil?"

A piece of charcoal was located, and Sister Anne-Marie quickly wrote out the bill of sale on the back of the label, signing her name in bold letters.

"And now, gentlemen, if you will excuse us, we must gather our men and be on our way."

"Of course, Sister."

A.J. and the men watched as the three sisters glided across the room, the hems of their black habits disappearing out the door with a whisper.

Breathing a sigh of relief, the men went back to the card game as A.J. stepped up to the bar.

"Well, Mr. Donavan, looks like you got yourself a real fine deal," the bartender congratulated as he filled A.J.'s glass.

"Yes, sir," A.J. tucked the bill of sale away in his pocket, right proud of himself. It wasn't often a man could fall into a herd of prime longhorns and come out smelling like a rose. "Hate to take advantage of the little women that way, but you saw what happened. It was all their idea."

The two men chortled.

"Yeah, it was their idea, all right." The bartender chuckled. "Two dollars a head. Mister, you just stole those cattle."

"Yes, sir." A.J. leaned back, grinning. "I surely did."

The McDougal sisters stepped out of the bar, turning in unison down the planked walkway.

"Shoot! I thought we'd see some whores," Amelia complained as they hurried along.

"Really, Amelia," Anne-Marie chided as they walked faster. "You can think of the dumbest things."

"What's dumb about wanting to see a whore? I've never been in a bar before, and from everything I've heard, that's where they—"

"Will you just dry up!"

"Will you stop being so bossy!"

"Will you both stop bickering!" Abigail snapped. "We're not in the clear yet."

Amelia decided to let it pass. Anne-Marie was in one of her dictatorial moods today. "How much do you think we made, Abby?"

"I don't know—the envelope looks pretty heavy. How much do you think, Anne-Marie?"

"It's simple enough to figure out. Two thousand four hundred and eighty-six dollars times two."

The sisters hurried along, their expressions studious as they multiplied beneath their breath.

"Four thousand nine hundred and seventy-two dollars!" Amelia squealed, and Abigail elbowed her into silence.

"Five thousand and seventy-two dollars," Anne-Marie corrected. "You forgot to add Mr. Donavan's generous hundred-dollar donation."

The sisters solemnly returned the sign of the cross to two passing men as they cut across the street.

Disappearing around the corner of the mercantile, they emerged a moment later on horseback.

"Wasn't it lucky we happened to be walking by the bar and overheard Mr. Donavan asking about those cows?" Amelia gloated.

"How many times do I have to tell you, Amelia. Nothing just 'happens' with us," Anne-Marie said serenely. "Because our cause is worthy, we are given certain opportunities we wouldn't otherwise encounter."

The sisters turned to look at the bar, then back at one another. Their eyes met, and they snickered.

"Men. How stupid can they get?" Abby mocked. She didn't have much respect for men, and A.J. Donavan had once again proven what a dimwitted gender they were. No doubt about it; they were just plain stupid.

"Evidently pretty dense." Amelia sighed. "Wonder who does own those cows?"

Shrugging, Anne-Marie tightened the reins around her gloved hand. "Who cares? What I can tell you is who doesn't own the cattle."

The sisters looked at one another, and grinning, they crowed in unison, "A.J. Donavan!"

Kicking their horses into a swift trot, the McDougal sisters rode out of town, considerably happier and a whopping $5,072.00 richer than when they had ridden in an hour ago.

Chapter 1

Five miles from Nacogdoches, Texas:
March, 1865

Some people said they had it coming; others said it was a shame they hadn't gotten it sooner.

A March wind savagely whipped the jail wagon along the dusty road as three young women dressed in nuns' habits clung desperately to the bars, eyes clamped shut, praying for deliverance.

The driver, slumped over the front of the wagon, could do little to console the screaming women, considering he had a Comanche arrow sticking through his back.

War whoops filled the air as four young braves chased the wagon, their black hair whipping wildly about their bronzed faces as they rode hard to overtake their prey.

"What do they want?" Amelia shouted, her voice nearly drowned out by the sound of thundering hooves.

Anne-Marie, eyes closed, gripped the beads of her rosary until her knuckles were white. "Hail, Mary, full of grace," she murmured, "the Lord is with thee—"

"They want the horses!" Abigail's heart pounded like the heathens' own war drums as the savages continued to gain on them.

"Tell them they can have them!"

"I hardly think they're listening, Amelia!"

"Holy Mother, Mother of God, pray for us sinners now at the hour of our death—"

Oh, this is so typical, Abigail thought cynically. *Anne-Marie prays while Amelia falls apart at the slightest sign of adversity. Of course, this could turn out to be more than a slight turn of misfortune*, she conceded as her eyes darted back to the braves. But she wasn't worried. Lady Luck had always seen the McDougal sisters through the worst of times, and she wasn't likely to fail them now.

"If you'd listened to me and let Amy handle it," Anne-Marie put the blame where it belonged, "we wouldn't be in this pickle! I told you we shouldn't have tried to trick Ramsey McQuade!"

"How was I to know he had us figured out?" Abby shouted. "He was ripe for the kill. Posing as a wealthy Negress had been brilliant—Amy could *never* have pulled it off!"

Amelia's eyebrows shot up. "And *you* did? Ramsey knew exactly what you were up to. Just because you think men are stupid, doesn't mean they all are. If you ask me—"

"No one did, Amelia!"

"Ramsey McQuade looked brilliant standing by the sheriff on the outskirts of town when we rode out with his money," Amelia went on, determined to make her point.

Abby shot her a scathing look as the wagon lurched over a rut, pitching it into the air and Amelia to the bottom of the floor.

Clasping her hands over her face, Amelia began crying and wouldn't stop, even when Anne-Marie shot her a warning look.

When the visual reprimand had no effect, Anne-Marie diverted her litany long enough to give Amelia a swift kick with the toe of her boot.

"Good Lord, Amelia, control yourself!" Abigail snapped when Amelia bawled harder. You'd think she was the only one about to be scalped. Besides, nobody was going to be scalped. As far as Abigail was concerned, the braves could have the horses and the wagon, but if they laid one hand on her or her sisters, she'd personally see that they'd rue the day they were born!

As the jail wagon careened wildly along the road, three men, sitting on top of three separate hilltops, watched the scene playing out below them.

To the west, a dapper man riding a dark sorrel sawed back on the bridle reins as he caught sight of the spectacle.

He sat for a moment, absently removing his spectacles to wipe away the thick layer of dust coating the lenses.

The sight of four young braves in hot pursuit of a wagon was of little concern to Hershall Earl Digman. Hershall didn't go borrowing trouble, thank you. He had quite enough of his own.

And it wasn't unusual for Comanche to be stirring up trouble. With the attraction of Mexican horses drawing them south, they were raiding deeper and deeper into Texas.

Since the wagon was of no value, the young bucks were obviously in pursuit of the horses, and there was little Hershall could do, or planned to do, about it.

Flexing his sore shoulder muscles, he lifted his face

to the sun, momentarily dawdling as he soaked up the warm rays.

To the east, Morgan Kane slowed his horse to a walk. His first instinct when he spotted the wagon was to ride to the women's aid. Even from this distance, he could see the wagon driver was dead or gravely injured. The women were at the Indians' mercy, and Morgan knew that with Comanche, there would be none.

As much as he would like to help, Morgan felt his sense of duty outweighing his sense of instinct. Weather had already delayed him by several days; he didn't need another interruption.

But as the women's cries shattered the peaceful countryside, Morgan shifted uneasily in his saddle. A gentleman by nature, he wasn't happy about the situation. The wagon was whipping down the road, the horses completely out of control now.

Whores on their way to jail, he argued when an inner voice nagged at him.

No one deserves a death like those women are about to face, the voice argued back.

Damn Comanche! Between the Comanche and the war, a man wasn't safe to travel the main roads.

Lifting his arm to wipe the sweat off his face, Morgan fixed his eyes on the braves as they drew closer to the wagon.

To the north, an Indian riding a large chestnut stallion topped the rise.

Tall and notably handsome, his piercing black eyes, straight brows, high cheekbones, lean cheeks, and prominent nose bespoke his Crow heritage.

The wind whipped his jet black hair as his dark eyes studied the scene below him.

Comanche.

Kneeing his horse forward, he rode closer, his eyes focused on the wagon.

The jail wagon bounced along, tossing the McDougal sisters around like rag dolls. The Indians were so close now that Abigail could see their dark eyes and youthful grins through the dust boiling up through the floor of the wagon. The boys couldn't be more than fifteen or sixteen, she thought.

Averting her gaze, she tried to block out the sound of thundering hooves. She had heard stories of women being captured by Indians and taken to live as their wives. Never in her wildest dreams could she, Abigail Margaret McDougal, imagine being a sixteen-year-old boy's squaw. She couldn't imagine being any man's squaw, and she'd fight until there wasn't a breath left in her if one of those heathens tried to make her one!

Her face puckered with resentment. If they caught her, she would fight and fight dirty. She would pinch and spit and hit and bite, and if that didn't work, she'd kick, and she knew *where* to kick, because she had heard two men talking one day about getting kicked there, and presumably it wasn't where a man longed to get kicked.

And if that didn't work, Anne-Marie would think of something to save them—Abigail's eyes darted back to the Indian drawing even with the wagon. She had to!

Jumping astride the lead horse, the brave tried to slow the team. The animals, wild-eyed from the harried chase, ran harder.

Hershall sat up straighter, watching as the ruckus neared a rowdy climax. By *Jove*, he suddenly realized, those weren't women; those were nuns in that jail wagon!

Amelia's throat was hoarse from screaming, but they couldn't stop her. The sounds of the Indians whooping and hollering as victory drew closer would terrify a saint!

Glancing frantically over her shoulder, Abigail groaned when she saw a bend coming up in the road. That's all they needed. They would be killed for certain now!

The horses galloped around the turn, and the wagon tilted sideways. Clutching the bars, Abby bit her lip until she tasted blood as the wagon tipped up to roll precariously on two wheels.

"Pray!" Anne-Marie demanded. "Pray!"

Morgan Kane edged his horse closer to the edge of the knoll. Either his eyes were playing tricks on him, or those were nuns in that wagon, he thought. Damn. *Nuns.*

The wheels hit another pothole, and the wagon went airborne again as the horses thundered around a second bend in the road. The women screamed as they heard the right front wheel snap. Lurching to its side, the wagon skidded across the road toward a briar-infested ravine.

The Indians sent up a shout of victory as Hershall Digman spurred his horse into action. Holding on to his hat with his hand, he plunged his horse down the ravine.

Morgan Kane was already riding down the hillside as the Crow kneed his horse and sprang forward.

The wagon rolled end over end down the incline,

violently tossing the McDougal sisters around inside the small cage.

When the wagon finally came to rest on its side at the bottom of the ravine, two braves were already working to free the horses.

Blades glinted in the sunlight as the leather harness was slashed. Then, with another victorious shout, the youths mounted the two horses and rode them back up the steep incline.

Morgan Kane was riding hard as he approached, but the Indians whipped the horses into a hasty retreat. Yelping with triumph, the braves galloped off to rejoin the remainder of their raiding party, who by now were waiting a safe distance down the road.

The braves cut their ponies across the open plains, their jubilant cries ringing over the hillsides.

Dropping off his horse, Morgan ran to peer down the steep slope, certain the women had been killed.

A trail of dust marked the vehicle's lightning descent, but the wagon was nowhere in sight.

Morgan whirled, reaching for his gun at the sound of approaching hoofbeats. An Indian riding a large chestnut stallion was moving in fast.

Morgan took aim but stopped short when the Indian lifted his hand in a gesture of peace. As the horse came to a halt, the Indian slid off the animal's back and hurried to look over the side into the gulch.

A moment later, both men spun at the sound of Hershall's horse thundering toward them.

When Morgan saw that the approaching rider was having difficulty controlling his horse, he shouted at the Indian, and they both jumped out of the way as Hershall shot into the clearing.

Sawing back on the reins, the red-faced shoe salesman managed to stop his horse just short of plunging headlong over the ravine.

As the dust settled, Hershall calmly settled his bowler back on his head, then climbed awkwardly off his horse.

Shrugging his shoulders uncomfortably in the too-small jacket of his striped seersucker suit, he tipped his hat at the two men cordially. "Afternoon, gentlemen."

Morgan nodded, slowly holstering his gun.

"My, my, my, my!" Hershall, round-eyed now, scurried to gape over the rim of the gulch. Fishing a large handkerchief from his pocket, he mopped anxiously at his perspiring forehead. "A most frightful turn of events," he fretted. "Are the women . . . ?" Hershall just couldn't bring himself to voice his fears. The thought of the nuns meeting such an untimely death was simply deplorable.

The three men edged closer to the ravine, their eyes trying to locate the wagon.

"Guess there's only one way to find out." Morgan glanced over his shoulder to make sure the braves hadn't decided to come back for their horses. "We'd better make it quick."

"Oh, my, my, my, my!" The thought of those savages returning just made Hershall sick. "Why ever do you suppose nuns would be riding in a jail wagon?"

Morgan shook his head. "I couldn't say."

The Indian was already making his way along the ravine. His moccasin-covered feet slid in the rocks and loose dirt as he worked down the incline.

Hershall cupped his hand to the side of his mouth and whispered, "Does the savage speak English?"

"I don't think so." Morgan started down the ravine, following behind the Indian.

Glancing anxiously at his carpetbag full of shoe samples, Hershall reluctantly joined the two men, who were halfway down the slope.

By the time the three men reached the bottom, they could see the jail wagon laying on its side. The back door was broken open, and the three nuns lay inside in a broken heap.

Wonderful, Hershall thought, setting his hat more firmly on his head. *Now I've got to bury three nuns.*

Morgan solemnly made the sign of the cross, then strode to the broken wreckage. "We better get them buried."

"Oh, my, my, my, my." Hershall thought he might faint. "I'm developing a simply pounding headache from it all."

Shoving the broken door aside, the Indian ran his dark eyes over the crumpled heap of women. His fingers touched the side of Anne-Marie's wrist, feeling for a pulse.

Stirring, Anne-Marie opened her eyelids to encounter a pair of coal black eyes.

Bolting upright, she screamed, and the Indian, Morgan, and Hershall jumped as if they'd been shot.

Realizing that the good sister thought that the Crow was part of the band who had been chasing the wagon, Morgan attempted to calm her. "It's all right, Sister. You're safe now."

Bewildered, Anne-Marie stared back at the assortment of strange men. She couldn't recall ever seeing such a mixed bag of masculinity.

She looked from the tall man with incredibly broad shoulders, to the dapper dandy in a puckered seersucker suit, whose main concern at the moment seemed to be preventing his hat from blowing off, to the splendid-looking savage whose dark eyes caused her to have the giddiest feeling when he centered his gaze upon her.

Amelia and Abigail were slowly coming around. Groaning, Abby tried to untangle her limbs from Amelia's. "Sweet Mother of God, every bone in my body's broken!"

"*Sister* Abigail."

Abby winced at the sound of Anne-Marie's voice, groaning again.

"Your habit, Sister. It's askew."

Abby quelled the urge to shout back that her bowels were askew, let alone her habit! Pushing herself upright, she shook Amy, gradually becoming aware of the three men staring through the bars at her.

Great day in the morning! Hershall was nearly felled by the nuns' loveliness. He had never seen three more beautiful women!

"Oh, dear Lord," Amy muttered, rolling to her back, glassy-eyed.

"Sister"—Abby punched her warningly—"are you hurt?"

"Are you crazy—I just had the shi—"

Abigail swiftly elbowed her again, quelling Amelia's obscene retort.

Amelia looked up. Upon seeing the men gaping at her, she pasted a serene smile on her lips and hastily made the sign of the cross. "Why, yes, Sister. I believe I've survived the fall quite nicely."

"God has smiled again," Anne-Marie said. "We must thank Him for His graciousness."

"Are you ladies all right?" Morgan asked, still finding it hard to believe that they had survived the fall with few serious injuries.

Amy grunted, trying to sort her arms and legs from Abby's. Both women groaned as pain shot through their lower limbs.

"Sister, would you kindly get *off* me?"

"Certainly, Sister, if you will kindly get your foot out of my *pocket.*"

"Well, nothing seems to be amiss," Anne-Marie assured the men brightly as she hastily straightened her veil.

Hershall bolted forward to assist Sister Abigail from the wagon. Removing his bowler, he placed the hat over his heart, bowing from the waist down. "Hershall E. Digman, at your service, ma'am."

Eyeing him sourly, Abby slid out of the wagon before he could help her. But Hershall insisted on leading her to the nearest rock. Sitting her down, he wrung his hands with despair when he noticed the beginnings of a dark bruise forming on her temple.

"You are most fortunate," he fussed, "most fortunate, my dear lady, that you weren't killed."

Pushing back the sleeve of her habit, Abby examined her skinned elbow. Was he serious? Fortunate? She didn't feel "fortunate." She had just eaten ten pounds of dust and nearly been scalped. If she got much luckier, she wouldn't live to tell about it.

Anne-Marie swayed with sudden light-headedness, and the Indian quietly stepped forward to assist her.

"Thank you," she managed. She got out of the wagon, her hand resting lightly on his bronzed forearm, an arm of such impressive width that it made her hand appear tiny.

His somber gaze met hers, and Anne-Marie felt the oddest quirk in the pit of her stomach.

Shaken, she quickly severed the electrifying contact and stepped aside as Morgan reached to help Amelia down.

As Amy reached for Morgan's hand, she caught the look in Anne-Marie's eyes, silently urging her to maintain her best veneer of "sisterly" decorum. Well, Anne-

Marie didn't have to worry about that! Amy knew how to act her part as well as or better than her sisters.

Lifting her chin, she reached for Morgan's hand, but *drat it*, the heel of her shoe caught in the hem of her habit, and she pitched face first out of the wagon.

Averting her eyes, Anne-Marie listened to the confusion as Amy stumbled out of the wagon, knocking Morgan to the ground, then landing squarely on top of him.

"Oh, my!" Amelia gasped, attempting to regain what little composure she could under the circumstances. Scrambling to her feet, she tried to help Morgan up. "I'm ever so sorry, Mr. . . . ?"

"Morgan Kane," Morgan supplied, momentarily dazed by the impact.

The Indian suddenly lifted his hand to command silence. Nodding toward the road, his eyes mutely warned of impending trouble.

Panic seized the small group as they listened to the sound of approaching horses.

"The remainder of the raiding party," Morgan guessed.

"Oh, my, my, my!"

"We better be on our way, gentlemen."

"Oh, yes, I think that would be most prudent of us," Hershall agreed. "Most prudent."

Pushing his glasses up on the bridge of his nose, Hershall extended the crook of his arm to Abigail.

Surveying it glumly, Abby knew she had little choice but to let the simpleton help her.

Morgan took Amelia's hand and began pulling her toward the incline. "We don't have much time. If you can't make it up the hill, I'll carry you."

"I can make it," Amelia assured him, still so humiliated by her clumsiness that she could die.

"Wait," Anne-Marie murmured, closing her eyes as dizziness nearly overcame her again. The Indian paused, supporting her weight until the light-headedness passed.

Morgan and Amelia were already scrambling up the hillside. Amelia's feet slid in the loose dirt, but Morgan's hands boosted her onward. She turned, offering him an affronted glare. "Sorry, Sister—we have to keep moving." He meant no disrespect to the sister, but he wasn't thrilled about the prospect of his hair hanging from a Comanche's lodge pole tomorrow morning, either.

The Indian and Anne-Marie systematically made their way up the incline. When she occasionally lost her footing, the Crow's hand was there to steady her.

Hershall attempted to take Abby's hand, but she repeatedly pushed his efforts aside. If she'd ever seen a worthless man, this was it. A dapper dandy, with his hair slicked down and his spectacles sliding down the bridge of his nose.

Scrambling up the incline, she glanced over her shoulder, concerned about Amelia, who seemed disoriented. Of course, she thought, with Amy, one could never be certain. Amy was in a perpetual daze most of the time.

Abby felt her feet slipping in the loose dirt, but Hershall's hand chivalrously shot out to support her backside. She irritably swatted it aside and muttered, *"Pervert."*

Pervert? Well! Jerking his waistcoat back into place, Hershall made up his mind right then and there that it would be a cold day in Hades before he'd offer her *his* assistance again!

As the six scrambled over the gully, they spotted the dust of the returning Comanche raiding party.

"They're moving in fast," Morgan warned.

"We're going to have to make a run for it," Hershall shouted.

Whirling, he raced for his horse, leaving Sister Abigail standing, hands on her hips, glaring after him.

The Indian bolted onto the stallion, pulling Anne-Marie on behind him.

Morgan caught Amy around the waist and lifted her into the saddle. Springing up behind her, he turned to the others. "We're going to have to split up!"

The Indian nodded, trying to control his prancing stallion.

Hershall's horse was sidestepping nervously as he attempted to mount. Abby glanced anxiously at the approaching cloud of dust, then back to Hershall's bumbling attempts to get on the horse.

When it became clear that they were going to be scalped if he didn't get his foot in the stirrup soon, she smothered a curse and irritably marched over and hoisted him into the saddle with her shoulder.

"Why, thank you, my dear—"

"Just shut up, Hershall!"

Planting her foot atop his, she gathered her skirt around her thighs, grasped the tail of his coat, and hefted herself up behind him, forcing Hershall to grab frantically for the saddle horn to keep them both from being hurtled to the ground.

Giving the horse a sound whack across the rump, Abby sent it bolting into a full gallop as Hershall held on tightly to his hat.

"Abigail! Amelia! Remember Church Rock!" Anne-Marie shouted as the Indian turned his chestnut stallion and rode off in a northerly direction.

Amelia was too busy hanging on to Morgan's waist to answer.

Gripping tightly to Hershall's flying coattails, Abby

gritted her teeth as the horse loped off to the south in a bone-jarring gait.

Why? She lifted her face to appeal to a higher source. *Why, with three choices, do I have to get stuck with Hershall E. Digman!*

Chapter 2

Once Hershall had his horse going in a straight line, he kicked it into a full gallop. Clinging tightly to his coattail, Abby prayed that he was a better horseman than he looked.

"Can't you go faster?" she shouted.

"I'm going as fast as I can, Sister!"

"Do you want me to take the reins?"

"I do not!"

Hershall fought the nun's black veil away from his face as he raced the horse across an open field, heading for a stand of timber. Once, the material blinded him to the point that he thought for certain he was going to ram the horse headlong into a tree.

Once they reached the woods, Hershall wove the horse in and out of the trees at a heart-stopping pace in an attempt to lose the zealous young bucks riding close on their heels.

"I don't know what all the fuss is about!" Abby could barely make herself heard above the crashing of thicket and flying hooves. "They're only young boys!"

"Who know how to use a knife as well as their fathers!" Hershall blustered as he spurred the horse faster.

It was close to an hour before Hershall allowed the horse to slacken its pace. By now Abby was certain that her spine was driven straight through the top of her head, but at least the young braves had grown tired of the chase and had turned away.

"Do you think we've lost them?"

"I certainly hope so." Hershall reached for his handkerchief to mop his forehead.

"Can we stop for a moment?" Abby viewed the particles of twigs and leaves stuck to the lenses of his glasses with contempt. *Pitiful.*

"Not yet. It isn't safe."

"Where are we going? And what about the other sisters—will we try to catch up with them?"

"That would be impossible. We'll ride until I feel it's safe to stop, then we'll discuss what we shall do about your situation."

Abby noticed that although he'd modified the horse's pace, he continued to ride at a brisk gait. He occasionally glanced over his shoulder to make certain they weren't being followed. When he saw no sign of the Indians, he seemed to breathe easier.

As the day progressed, the sun slid in and out of innocent-looking clouds. Late in the afternoon, the mild breeze they'd enjoyed all day took on a sudden chill. Abby huddled closer to Hershall's back, trying to protect herself from the rising wind.

It was finally sinking into her that the McDougal sisters were at the mercy of three strangers, and the realization was frightening. She had never been apart from Amelia and Anne-Marie—not ever. And this odd assortment of men who'd rescued them from certain death—who were they? Where had they come from?

For the moment she felt reasonably safe. Hershall Digman didn't appear to present a threat to her, but what about Amelia? Amelia was with—what did he say his name was? Martin Lane? Morgan Spain? Events had happened so swiftly, she couldn't remember.

And poor Anne-Marie. Her fate lay in the hands of an uncivilized heathen! She shuddered as she recalled the savage's dark, foreboding eyes. He looked like the devil himself.

"Are you cold?"

Startled, Abby realized that she had forgotten where she was for a moment. "Yes, a little."

Hershall reached into the saddlebag, removed a heavy coat, and handed it to her. "Put this on."

"Don't you need it?" The thin suit coat he was wearing furnished little protection from the sudden drop in temperature.

"I'll put on an extra shirt when we make camp."

She could see that he was only being benevolent. He had to be as cold as she was, but if he was silly enough to offer her the coat, she'd gladly wear it. "I hope that's soon," she warned him.

"I think it prudent we ride until nightfall."

"Wonderful," Abby murmured, determined to maintain her disguise. If Hershall were to discover that she wasn't a nun, he might not be so eager to help. And as bad as she hated to admit it, she knew she'd need his help to see her safely back to Church Rock Cemetery.

They rode for over another hour before Hershall finally thought it safe to make camp. Studying the darkening sky, the lines around his eyes deepened. The lowering clouds had nearly obscured the sun now.

"Looks like snow might be moving in."

Pushing aside the end of her veil, Abby studied the churning clouds. The day had dawned beautifully, but she couldn't argue that the weather looked as if it was about to change.

"What should we do?"

"We'll make camp soon."

They started off again as the sun disappeared behind another low-hanging cloud.

"Where were you and the sisters going when the Indians attacked the wagon?" Hershall asked as the horse trotted down the road.

"To jai—Sister Jane's," she amended.

"Sister Jane's?"

"Yes, she teaches a small—yes, a small school," Abby decided. "Sister Jane is ill. She sent word that she needed help, so that's where we were going." She smiled, more confident with her tale. "To help Sister Jane."

Hershall turned to look over his shoulder, meeting her gaze evenly. "Is Sister Jane gravely ill?"

"She has smallpox."

Hershall visibly recoiled.

"Oh, you needn't worry. We haven't been around Sister yet, but they say she looks wretched." Leaning closer, she lowered her voice, sensing that Hershall was a bit squeamish about the subject. "Big, ugly, runny sores, oozing with puss—"

Hershall paled, turning the collar of his suit up closer to ward off a sudden chill.

"A terrible death, they say. Simply terrible. Have you ever met anyone with smallpox, Mr. Digman?"

Hershall shook his head.

"Perhaps you'd like to meet Sister Jane?"

Hershall shook his head again, kicking the horse to a faster gait. The sister, though holy, talked too much.

The horse had the worst gait Abby had ever endured. It was like riding on a wagon full of rocks, and Hershall didn't help matters. He was a terrible horseman.

"Please," she finally gritted through clenched teeth, "could you either slow down or speed up?"

Hershall temporarily allowed the horse to drop back into a smoother gait. Shifting her weight more evenly in the saddle, Abby adjusted her habit to a more dignified angle.

"Sister, why were you traveling in a jail wagon?"

Abby noticed that he seemed to have a one-track mind. "It was the only conveyance available—is there a town nearby?" she asked, hoping to change the subject.

"I'm not certain." Actually, Hershall didn't know where he was at the moment. He had known, prior to rescuing the sister, but now he would have to get out his map and study it again.

"I hope there is." A frown creased the sister's forehead. "I must send word to the mission—"

"What mission might that be, Sister?"

"It is but a small, insignificant mission near the Mexican border."

"The Mexican border?" Hershall frowned. "That's a considerable way from here."

"Yes, our work takes us on many long journeys. The sisters and I have vowed if we are ever parted, we shall return to a cemetery near there to be reunited."

"Why the cemetery?"

"The cemetery is of special significance to us." She didn't elaborate further.

"Well, as soon as I find a stage road, you'll be on your way," he promised.

"Mr. Digman, I was rather expecting you to escort me there."

"To the border?"

"I know it would be a small bother, but—"

"No, ma'am. I'm sorry, I can't take you to the border. But I will see you safely on the stage," Hershall promised.

"What are you doing that's so important that you can't take me there?" Abby returned in a snappish rush.

Surprised by the sharp edge in the nun's voice, Hershall turned to look over his shoulder at her.

"I mean," Abby amended her tone sweetly, "what do you do for a living, Mr. Digman?"

"I sell shoes."

She smiled. "Oh, how nice." *She might have known.*

Glancing at the sky, Hershall saw a spring storm was definitely about to descend upon them. If the clouds held as much snow as they promised, it would be unpleasant.

At any rate, he had to make camp soon. Had he been alone, he would've continued riding through the night, but the sister couldn't be expected to endure the weather.

It was another twenty minutes before he found a small clearing that looked promising.

"This seems like an acceptable place to camp for the night," he announced.

Thank God. Abby breathed, relieved, as she slid

stiffly off the horse. If she'd had to stay in that saddle another five minutes, she would have *screamed*.

The wind was steadily picking up, whipping the trees and bushes nearly to the ground. Hershall held on to his hat with one hand while he secured the horse to a nearby tree.

"Well," he said, rubbing his hands together as he hurried back, "some hot coffee should help chase the chill. I'll get a fire started, rig some sort of shelter, and then see what I can scare up for supper."

"May I help?" she asked, more from a feeling of obligation than real interest.

"Oh, no, no, no. You just make yourself comfortable." She watched as he scurried away to put on an extra shirt before he began setting up camp.

Tucking her hands in under her armpits, Abby paced, pausing occasionally to try to stamp feeling back into her feet.

When Hershall returned, he was carrying a bedroll and a few cooking utensils. "Just have a seat, Sister," he yelled above the howling wind. "This will only take a minute."

"No, thank you. I'll just stand if you don't mind." *If the simpleton doesn't hurry, we're both going to freeze to death!*

Clasping her wrists beneath the sleeves of her habit, she paced faster.

Although she tried not to, her eyes kept going back to Hershall's suit. The fabric was thin and totally inadequate for blizzard attire. The linen seersucker was a most unattractive brown stripe that puckered at the seams.

The trousers—they were too short, but it didn't matter, because they matched the sleeves, which were too short, too.

And that ridiculous bowler he was so afraid the wind was going to snatch away. The silly-looking hat hid most of his hair, but that was all right, too, because he had it slicked down with some sort of greasy pomade. He was a mess.

She had to admit his square jaw made him seem a tad more attractive than she'd first thought, but the spectacles ruined the one concession. They kept sliding down his nose, and he kept shoving them back up with his forefinger until she wanted to rap him across the knuckles and tell him to stop it!

"Are you comfortable, Sister?"

"Just fine, Mr. Digman!"

"It won't be long now," he promised, and her smile encouraged him to take all the time he needed.

Unrolling a piece of heavy canvas, Hershall shook out the wrinkles. A sudden gust of wind caught the canvas and snatched it out of his hands. The material winged off, landing a few feet away in the clearing.

As he ran to get it, the wind caught his hat and sent it skipping across the ground.

Forgetting the canvas, he scrambled after the bowler, chasing the hat around the small clearing, darting to and fro, to and fro, as the wind repeatedly caught it and sent it soaring out of his reach.

Abby sat on a rock, watching him dart in and out, chasing the canvas, then his hat, then the canvas, then his hat.

Absolutely pathetic.

The canvas soared in her direction, and her left leg snaked out, trapping the material securely beneath her foot.

Hershall, still in pursuit of the hat, scrambled down a slight ravine and disappeared momentarily. Abby assumed that he thought they could sleep in the hat to-night, since he had lost interest in the tent.

When he emerged from the gully, realizing what he'd done, he looked ready to burst into tears. "Oh, my goodness! I've lost the tent!"

"I have the tent, Mr. Digman."

"Oh, you do?" His face brightened. "Wonderful!"

She kept her foot firmly planted on her one means of survival as Hershall scrambled up the ravine and ran over to her.

Lifting her foot, he smiled as he dutifully removed the piece of canvas. "Oh, dear me, dear me!" he crowed. "We would have been in a fine pickle if we had lost our tent."

We had lost our tent?

"Indeed we would have, Mr. Digman."

Scurrying over to a sturdy-looking bush, Hershall draped the canvas over a low-hanging limb. "I'll have us set up in no time at all," he called brightly.

"Take your time, Mr. Digman." Which she knew he undoubtedly would.

Twenty minutes later, he'd managed to get all four corners staked to the ground.

"There now. You sit inside where it's warmer, and I'll build a fire."

"I could help—" she began, blinded by visions of a wayfaring stranger finding them frozen stiff as a board by the time *he* had a fire started.

"No, no, I wouldn't hear of it. I'll have a roaring fire going in no time at all. Then we'll both feel better." He edged her toward the opening of the small lean-to. "Go on now, it's cold out here."

Abby reluctantly crawled into the lean-to, wishing to high heaven he would let her help. She had a hunch that she was more adept at starting fires than he was.

Dropping the flap back into place, Hershall scurried off again.

Twenty minutes later Abby lifted the piece of canvas, watching as Hershall hurried about the campsite, still gathering fallen limbs and bits of twigs for the fire.

"Better lay some rocks in a small circle to contain the fire, Mr. Digman," she called out helpfully.

"Thank you, Sister!"

A moment later she yelled again. "I'm really quite efficient at starting fires—I could help, Mr. Digman!"

"You're much too kind, Sister. Just stay where you are."

Huddling deeper into the fleece lining of Hershall's coat, Abby tried to think of something warm. The image of Amelia and Anne-Marie surfaced in her mind, and she felt better. They'd only been apart for a few hours, but she missed them already.

Easing the flap aside, she peeked out again. She knew it. Hershall was kneeling beside a circle of rocks, wasting matches.

Time after time the wind blew out the match, but he patiently removed another from the box and struck it.

After repeated failures to produce even a tiny spark, Abby was ready to scream. Glancing down at her lap, she found her fists balled together tightly. Her fingers *itched* to burst out of the tent and snatch the stupid match out of his hands. She'd have had the fire lit thirty minutes ago!

By the time Hershall managed to coax a tiny spark, she had nearly bitten her tongue in two trying to keep quiet.

She watched as he bent over the thin thread of

smoke, blowing, then carefully feeding leaves into the flame, blowing, adding a few shavings more, blowing—

Puff . . . puff.

The flame struggled to grow brighter as he hurriedly fed it more small twigs, then larger branches.

Just when he thought he had it whipped, a sudden gust of wind snuffed the feeble flame, and he resignedly reached for the box of matches again.

She couldn't stand it any longer. She didn't know how many matches he had left, but it probably wasn't enough.

Bowling out of the tent, she marched toward him, set on taking the matches away from him.

Hershall, unaware of the sister's approach, was doubled over the flame, carefully fanning the smouldering embers.

"Mr. Digman!"

Bolting upright, Hershall's spectacles plunged to the bridge of his nose. "Yes?"

"Please . . ." she blurted helplessly. "I'm really quite good at starting fires—"

"Nonsense, Sister." He smiled, pointing to the thin wisp of smoke just starting to curl from the pile of sticks. "As you see, I already have one started."

A blazing hell! she seethed.

Motioning her to the tent, he went back to the business at hand.

Rolling her eyes with disgust, Abby checked her foot just short of booting him face first into the fire. There he was, hunkered over a pile of twigs and leaves, his too-short pants revealing his hairy ankles above the tops of his shoes, while she sat inside that miserable excuse for a tent, *freezing*.

As the fire caught, Hershall got slowly to his feet. The branches popped and were crackling noisily now, sending a plume of white smoke into the air.

Unaware that Sister had not heeded his suggestion to return to the tent, he arched his back and stretched lazily.

Striding by him, Abby threw her hip against his backside, hard.

Before Hershall could catch himself, he pitched forward. "God Almighty!" he burst out, barely managing to catch himself before plunging headlong into the fire.

"Oh, my goodness!" Abby exclaimed, her hands covering her mouth in horror. "Did I *bump* you?"

Hershall took on something awful, jumping up and down, slapping wildly at his smouldering pants legs.

"I'm so sorry," Abby cried, trying to look properly repentant.

"Just look at my spats!"

Abby looked. They were all sooty.

"Oh, I'm ever so sorry! I was so eager to warm myself by this nice, toasty fire that I was reckless."

She bowed her head remorsefully. "I shall say twenty extra Hail Marys tonight and ask God to forgive me for my carelessness."

She was sure she'd heard Hershall Digman swear, and, as if to add insult to injury, the wind snatched his bowler again and sent it skipping across the small clearing into a nearby brier patch.

"Oh, dear, your hat, Mr. Digman. Let me go after it."

Hershall bit back the urge to throttle her. "Please don't bother, Sister. Just tell me where it is," he spit out.

Turning, Abby pointed to the hat, ensnared in the thickest part of the brier patch. "Right over there."

Jerking his waistcoat back into place, he turned on his heel and stalked into the brier patch.

"Hurry back," Sister called.

Or don't. By now, she couldn't care less.

Chapter 3

A cold rain was starting to fall, and the temperature was dropping at an alarming rate. The smell of coffee bubbling on the fire was the only concession to abject misery as darkness encompassed the campsite.

"I apologize for the meager fare." Hershall crawled inside the tent, half-frozen. He lit a candle and stuck it into the ground. "We'll have something hot to drink soon. I'm afraid chickory is all I can offer, but it'll help wash down the cold biscuits."

"I'm sure the fare will be adequate," Sister returned staunchly.

"Perhaps in the morning I'll shoot a rabbit, so you'll have a hot meal."

Abby had to admit a hot meal would be nice, but at the moment she wouldn't turn down cold biscuits. She tried to remember the last time she'd eaten. Sometime yesterday, she thought. The jailers had set three bowls of something that resembled gruel inside the dank cell. The meal was as cold and merciless as the jailers, and Abby hadn't been able to make herself eat. Anne-Marie

39

warned her that she had to eat enough to keep her strength up, but Abby had flung her bowl across the cell, vowing to starve first.

Since death now appeared a more imminent possibility, she gratefully accepted the cup of coffee that Hershall handed her.

Sipping the scalding brew warily, she allowed the comforting heat to penetrate her fingertips.

"Careful, Sister, you'll burn yourself."

"I would consider it a blessing, Mr. Digman."

Hershall laid two biscuits and a strip of jerky on a cloth and handed it to her. Scooting to the opposite side, he began to eat his meal.

Before he had finished one biscuit, Abby polished off both of hers and was eyeing his hungrily. The bread was hard and dry, and she felt like she had swallowed a ball of cotton, but she was grateful to be eating at all.

Biting off a piece of jerky, Hershall chewed it thoughtfully as he studied the nun. A smile quirked the corners of his mouth as he watched her pick up the strip of jerky and examine it.

Biting into the leathery fare, she frowned. Biting harder, she managed to tear off a small hunk, then proceeded to chew it hungrily.

"Is the meat tender enough for you, Sister?"

"Oh, yes. Just fine, thank you." She wallowed the jerky around in her mouth for several minutes before gagging it down.

Hershall had to admit that if the sisters he'd known as a boy had been half as attractive as Sister Abigail, he'd have taken more interest in school.

His teachers had been old, pudding-faced disciplinarians, with hair growing on their upper lips, and all of them had been handy with a ruler across his knuckles. But Sister Abigail, Hershall mused, there was something different about Sister Abigail. She didn't say a prayer before her meal.

But she did have a charming oval face, a mouth that begged to be kissed, and the most beautiful eyes Hershall had ever seen. When the wind flattened her habit against her nubile curves—well, though Hershall didn't look, a man would have to be blind not to notice the ripe fullness of her breasts and the—

Hershall suddenly pitched forward, choking on his blasphemous thoughts.

Sister absently reached over and patted him on the back. "There, there Mr. Digman. Perhaps you should take smaller bites."

"Yes." Hershall tried to clear his watering eyes. "Thank you, Sister. I will."

Later, when they'd finished, Hershall came to his knees and began to neatly rearrange the blanket he was sitting on.

Abby watched him fuss, mentally shaking her head in amazement. He was so persnickety she wondered how he'd made his way in this rough country, especially with a war going on.

The rain was coming down harder, driven by a howling wind that threatened to collapse the small lean-to.

"I'm sorry I can't offer better facilities, but I didn't expect to spend the night on the trail," Hershall apologized. When the blanket was free of any sign of wrinkle, he sat down again.

Removing his spectacles, he polished them with a white cloth he had extracted from his saddlebag. "This part of Texas usually has very moderate weather this time of year," he remarked. "But I suppose in March you can expect most anything."

"Yes, I suppose that's true." *I wonder how old he*

is? Late twenties? Early thirties? It was hard for her to judge.

"Have you served in the war, Mr. Digman?"

His eyes briefly refused to meet hers. "For a short interlude, but I was wounded in a most—well . . ." He colored, and she could see he found the subject most distressing. "They thought it best I return to my family."

Good Lord. He's a eunuch, too. "I'm so sorry."

"Oh, don't you fret. The wound healed quite adequately."

She sipped her coffee thoughtfully, wondering about that. "Where did you say you were going, Mr. Digman?"

"Louisiana," Hershall said.

"To see family?"

"Oh, no. My work takes me there."

"Are you married?"

His face flushed painfully. "Oh, my, no."

"What a pity. A fine-looking gentleman such as yourself?"

His face grew redder. "I know, I know, but to be frank, Sister, I've never had much luck with the female persuasion," he confessed.

"Nooo," she scoffed.

"Oh, I know what you're thinking. Many a woman would consider herself blessed to have a man such as myself, but," his sigh was wistful, "my work keeps me busy. It isn't the war injury—you understand, but my work that prohibits my taking a wife." He peered at her intently. "You *do* understand?"

Oh, completely. "Yes, I'm sure that's true."

Hooking the rims of his glasses over his ears, he observed her innocently. "Of course, having taken a vow of chastity, you don't have to worry about such things."

"What 'things' are those, Mr. Digman?"

"Taking a husband."

She smiled. "No."

"Having taken the vow of obedience and poverty, your needs are simple."

She nodded subserviently, aware that a woman's needs would have to be simple with a man like Hershall.

"Who do you sell your shoes to, Mr. Digman?"

"The army," Hershall stated. "An army marches on its feet, does it not?"

"Yes, but times are hard. I've heard that some Confederate units are in such bad shape they barely have shoes at all." Abby knew little about the war. She'd heard talk, but since she didn't know anyone involved in the fighting, current affairs were of little concern to her.

"There are some who are able to afford my wares," Hershall assured.

Abby set her cup beside the candle as Hershall dug into the saddlebag for his map. Lowering it closer to the flame, he studied it.

"What direction are we traveling?" she asked casually.

"Northeast."

"And we will come to a town soon?"

"We should."

"It is imperative that I leave as soon as possible," she reminded him. "Sister Amelia and Sister Anne-Marie will be sick with worry if I fail to meet them at the cemetery within a few days. They'll think something bad has happened to me."

"Now, now, Sister, you needn't be concerned." Hershall folded the map and put it back in the saddlebag.

"It will also take a few days for the sisters to reach the cemetery."

"Mr. Digman," Abby lay her hand on his arm, "isn't there some way I can persuade you to escort me to Mercy Flats?"

"Mercy Flats?"

"That's where the cemetery is located—the cemetery where I'm to meet the other sisters."

"I'm sorry. That would be impossible. I must be in Shreveport by the end of the month."

"But this is a mission of the Lord. Surely you can spare time to serve the Lord," she coaxed.

"Ordinarily I could, Sister, but it's important that I conduct this sale. We can't have the South marching barefoot, can we?"

"From what I hear, the South has been marching barefoot for some time!"

His brows lifted. "Are you a northern sympathizer, Sister?"

Turning away, she jerked the blanket tighter around her neck. "As a servant of the Lord, I take no sides. It was merely a comment. God loves everyone."

"Even you?"

She turned back. "What?"

"I said," he tipped his hat graciously, "evenin' to you."

"Are you going somewhere?"

"Well, it is late, and we do have a long ride ahead of us tomorrow."

"I suppose. . . . But my relatives have no 'side,' " she said, wanting to clarify her earlier statement.

"Unfortunately," Hershall returned calmly, "it appears that in war we are forced to take sides."

"My family hasn't."

"And why is that, Sister?"

"Well, because—because my family were immigrants," Abby lied. "My grandparents were sent here from France."

"France?"

"Yes. France. Immediately following Napoleon's defeat in the Russian campaign."

"The devil, you say."

She looked at him sternly. "I do not speak of the devil."

"Of course. Forgive my slip of the tongue."

"It's quite true, you know. My roots are in France."

"Why were your grandparents sent to America?"

"When Napoleon was defeated, my grandparents were in grave danger, so my great-grandfather sent them to America so they would be safe."

"And your parents?"

"They died when I was very young, leaving the nuns at the mission to care for me and my two sisters."

"The mission is an orphanage?"

"Not any longer. Sister Agnes and Sister Lucille are very old now, and they can no longer care for children. They dedicate themselves to prayer and to providing food and shelter to the less fortunate."

"I noticed the strong resemblance between you and the nuns you're traveling with. Is it possible the three of you are blood sisters?"

Tears suddenly welled in Abby's eyes, and her resolve weakened. She couldn't see that it would hurt if he knew that Amelia and Anne-Marie were her real sisters, and it might even make her feel less lonely to confess it. "Yes. This is the first time we've ever been apart."

Aware he'd touched a nerve, Hershall apologized. "I'm sorry. This must be difficult for you."

She leaned forward, her eyes meeting his pleadingly.

"Please, Mr. Digman, won't you reconsider? It would only take a few days to escort me back to—"

Hershall turned a deaf ear, preparing to retire for the night. "It's getting late, Sister. It's time we turned in."

Well fine! she seethed. Let him be that way. She didn't need his help. She'd get back to the cemetery on her own. She should have known better than to ask a man for help in the first place!

"You may have the extra blanket," he offered, because he undoubtedly knew he was being such an ass.

She glanced around the tightly confined area. "Where will you sleep?"

"Due to the nasty weather, we'll have to share quarters." When he saw her look of distress, he added, "The Lord will understand."

"Of course, Mr. Digman. If you would be so kind as to allow me a moment of privacy—my devotions, you understand."

"Of course." Hershall obediently crawled to the tent opening. "I'll wait outside."

"Thank you. You are ever so kind."

Crawling outside, Hershall stood, turning his collar up, then made a mad dash to the shelter of a large tree. Sleet was falling in a peppery sheet now.

When he was gone, Abby yawned, stretching out lazily on the blanket. *Simpleton*, she thought as she closed her eyes. *Why couldn't I have been rescued by someone with half a brain?*

Outside, Hershall paced back and forth beneath the tree, stamping his feet and rubbing his hands together as he watched the worsening weather. His eyes darted periodically to the tent for any sign that Sister's devotions were complete, but he found none.

He just hoped she would pray quickly. His suit was already soaked, and his feet felt like two blocks of ice.

Inside the tent, Abby rolled to her side lethargically. She didn't care if Hershall Digman's feet froze to the ground. It would serve him right for refusing to take her back to the cemetery.

When an hour passed and the sister still hadn't called, Hershall was fit to be tied. How *long* could one woman pray? he agonized, blowing on his hands to try and restore feeling.

Swearing, he struck off in the direction of the tent just as Sister Abigail finally sang out, "You can come in now, Mr. Digman!"

Gritting his teeth, Hershall muffled a curse against the fates that had set him on that rise when a jail wagon full of nuns needed help.

Throwing back the flap of the tent, Hershall entered the shelter like a bull moose in heat. His seersucker suit was soaked through. Snow was piled in the brim of his bowler hat, and ice formed a ring around the perimeter of his spectacles rendering him legally blind.

Rolling to her back, Abby yawned, adjusting her blanket primly. Their earlier conversation rang in her ears. I can't take you to Mercy Flats, Sister. I have to sell shoes. Well, Mr. Digman, if that's how it's going to be, look out. Abigail McDougal can match you ounce for stubborn ounce. "Is it getting worse out there, Mr. Digman?"

Hershall could not bring himself to answer with a civil tongue. His knees were knocking together so hard that he was barely able to wrap himself in the one blanket he hadn't given her.

"My, my. You look half-frozen," she chided.

Blowing out the candle, Hershall resolved to hold his temper.

"Good night, Mr. Digman." Sister's words were lost in a yawn. "I'm ever so grateful you gave me the extra blanket. I'm so warm and cozy, and I'm sure I'll have a wonderful sleep. In my prayers, I told the Good Lord how grateful I am.''

Hershall clamped his teeth shut to stop them from rattling out of his head.

Abby hitched the blanket up closer. Oh, how she would love to be around in the morning to see the look on his face when he discovered the good sister had stolen his horse and left him on foot.

He'd be sorry he had refused to help her!

Before the hour was past, she heard soft snores coming from his side of the tent. Easing out of the blanket, she pushed aside the tent flap and peered outside.

Drats. Snow was falling slow and steady now. That would make traveling difficult, if not impossible.

Rooster spit, she thought irritably. *I can't find my way in a blinding snowstorm! The horse would leave a trail a blind man could follow.*

Resigned she'd have to wait until better weather to make her escape, she crawled back to the blanket, determined to make the best of a rotten turn of luck.

Chapter 4

"Sister Abigail! Better come and get this meat before it burns," Hershall called out as he rustled around the fire the next morning.

Dumping a fistful of chickory into the pot of boiling water, he tested the game roasting on the fire for tenderness. "Yoo hoo, are you awake, Sister?"

Lifting her head, Abby squinted impatiently. *Ye gad.* It was barely light enough to see her hand in front of her face. What fool was yapping this early in the morning?

"Hurry, hurry, hurry," Hershall sang out brightly.

Rolling back onto her back, she winced as she recognized the fool's voice: Hershall Digman.

"Come, come, come, now, Sister." Hershall clapped his hands briskly. " 'Tis a new day!"

" 'Tis a new day," she mimicked.

When Sister failed to respond, Hershall walked over and tapped on the flap of the tent. "Time to get up, Sister."

Jerking upright, Abby irritably checked her veil to make sure her hair was properly concealed. Anne-Marie and Amelia knew to leave her alone for at least an hour after she got up; *Hershall Digman* obviously didn't.

Yanking the flap aside, she wrapped the blanket around her shoulders and dragged herself outside. The biting winds snatched her breath away as she stood up, pulling the blanket around her chin more tightly.

Gingerly picking her way to the camp fire, she muttered under her breath as her shoes sank above her ankles into the two feet of snow that had fallen during the night.

Hershall glanced up, a big smile lighting his face. "Good morning, Sister! I trust you slept well?"

"As if I were in Eden," she said crossly. Lifting her hands to the fire, she eyed the three plump birds roasting on the spit. "You get up this early every morning?"

"Oh, my, yes! Can't sleep your life away! Coffee?"

"No, thank you."

"Oh, but you must have something. We have a long ride ahead of us."

"I don't eat first thing in the morning."

"Oh, but you should. You'll be hungry within an hour." He poured her a cup of coffee and wedged it between her hands with a curt order, "Drink it."

Turning away quickly, he stifled a sneeze.

"Catching a sniffle, Mr. Digman?"

"It would appear so." It would be short of a miracle if he didn't come down with a roaring case of consumption, thanks to her.

Seating herself on a rock, Abby held the hot coffee between her hands, trying to keep her eyes open.

"Drink your coffee, Sister. We'll have meat shortly."

She wished he would leave her alone. Her stomach rolled at the thought of eating a greasy old bird at this hour of the morning.

"Drink your coffee, Sister. It's getting cold."

Eat, Sister. Drink, Sister!

Bringing the cup to her mouth, she took a sip to shut him up. The strong chickory seared its way down her throat.

Choking, she leaned forward, spitting the bitter liquid on the ground. "Good God—ness sakes!" she blurted.

Hershall turned. "Is something amiss, Sister?"

"The coffee," she strangled out, "is too strong."

Hershall turned back to the fire. "Gets the blood pumping, doesn't it?" He stifled another sneeze.

Setting her cup aside, Abby huddled deeper into the blanket as she watched him turn the spit. He wasn't a tall man; in fact, she'd bet he wasn't three inches taller than she was. When they talked, he addressed her almost at eye level.

Beneath the seersucker suit, his shoulders were broad, and his waist surprisingly trim. In fact, he appeared to be quite well proportioned for a shoe salesman. His hands were wide and strong, and his arms—poking from those ridiculous sleeves—appeared tan and masculine.

Hitching herself closer to the fire, she took another sip of the coffee. It was so awful it had a certain fascination about it. "Why is it so cold? My feet are freezing."

"Weather's unpredictable," he conceded. Removing the spit from the fire, he extended the birds to her.

She viewed the meat, trying to keep from gagging. "I'm not hungry."

After removing one of the birds, he handed it to her. "Eat."

Flipping the hot bird from hand to hand, she reminded herself that they were on the trail, not in a dining room, so he could be excused for his appalling lack of social graces. "Can't I have a plate?"

"You don't need a plate to eat this." Breaking one of the birds apart, he bit into the savory meat, showing her. "Better stop juggling the meat and eat it, Sister. We may not be lucky enough to have such succulent fare tonight."

Clearing a small area of snow off the rock, she laid the meat beside her. "I'm hoping we'll reach a town today."

"Well, there's no harm in hoping."

Picking gingerly at the bird, she tried to pull one of its scrawny legs apart. "It's raw," she complained.

"Perhaps you'd prefer mine."

She gave him a cranky look. "After you've eaten off it?"

"Then perhaps the third one would be more to your taste." He got up and handed the bird to her.

Picking through the second piece of meat skeptically, she shook her head. "No, this one's raw, too."

"Then perhaps," he said, trying to retain his good humor, "you would like a piece of jerky."

"Well . . ." She looked at her half-raw bird, then at his nice, plump, brown one that looked for the world to her as if it were cooked to perfection. "Maybe I *will* try yours."

"I've already taken a bite of it," he reminded her.

"Well," she snapped. "Can't I just eat the half you haven't slobbered on?"

"Fine." He handed her his bird and took hers. He'd learned a long time ago not to argue with a woman. "And just so you'll know, I don't happen to 'slobber' on my food, Sister." His smile was charitable, but just barely. "Just so you'll know for future reference."

Shrugging, she bit into the meat. It wasn't bad, not as done as it looked, but not as raw as the one he was stuck with.

They finished eating, and Hershall began to break camp.

"Are we leaving now?"

"Yes, ma'am."

"But it's so cold—can't we stay a few more hours until it warms up a little?"

"I thought you were in a hurry to reach the next town."

"I am, but it's too cold. Couldn't we wait until it warms up a little?"

Of the three sisters, why did he have to get stuck with the whiner? Hershall agonized. "Perhaps instead of complaining, you should pray for sunshine, Sister."

Perhaps I should pray that you'll disappear, she thought, but held her tongue.

When camp was broken, Hershall hurried over to the small mirror he'd hung on the tree. He set the tall bowler hat with its petersham hatband and sassy little curled brim upon his head and fussed with it, turning it this way, then that, trying to get it adjusted just so.

Abby had an urge to rush over, jerk that hat off his head, and with both hands ruffle his greased-back hair until it stood on end.

Turning from the mirror, Hershall balanced one foot on a log and brushed at his ash-coated white spats. "You must ready yourself, so we can be on our way, Sister."

She eyed him sourly. He must be kidding. "At this hour of the morning, I'm as ready as I get, Mr. Digman."

He straightened, his eyes running over the rumpled blanket she clutched to her throat, her wrinkled habit, and matted veil.

"And a vision of radiance you are. Do you plan to wear the blanket as we ride?" he asked.

She clutched the blanket around her more possessively. "Yes."

"Then shall we be on our way?"

She noticed his eyes sometimes turned an uncommon shade of gray when he looked at her. An icy hue, actually, which seemed strange in such a little nothing of a man. It was almost as if the Lord had made Hershall Digman, then stood back to survey his creation with a critical eye and decided to be a little kinder by adding just a faint touch of smoke to make his eyes quite attractive.

When they were ready to leave, Hershall helped Sister into the saddle, then removed the map from the saddlebag.

Kneeling beside the horse, he smoothed the map out on his thigh to study it. As near as he could tell, the closest way station was a full day and a half away.

A day and a half.

Thirty-six more hours—*long* hours with the nun. Penance enough for any sinner.

Swinging into the saddle, he picked up the reins, anxious to be on his way.

"I still don't know why we can't stay here," she complained. "At least until the sun—"

That darn Hershall nearly caused her to swallow her tongue as he kicked the horse and galloped out of camp like the devil himself was on their heels!

By the time the sun did peek out from the clouds later that morning, Hershall was ready to hand Sister Abigail to the first Comanche war party he ran into.

Was it his fault the horse had an uneven gait? The mare's gallop had never bothered him.

Did he *ask* her to doze off and nearly kill herself when she *fell* off the horse? He had not.

Was he in control of the weather? No, he wasn't God. If he were, he'd have struck her dead hours ago.

"Really, Mr. Digman, wouldn't it be better to take a more traveled road?" Abby ducked as another low-hanging limb slapped her in the face. She could swear he was riding under the low branches on purpose!

Hershall pretended he didn't hear her as he pushed the horse toward a thick grove of trees.

"Mr. Digman! Do you have any idea where you're going?" she demanded a few minutes later as they turned down a narrow trail that wound through the woods.

"Sister, would you please leave the guiding to me?"

"No! Not if it means you're going to get us lost."

"We are not lost."

"Then where are we?"

Hershall's back stiffened with resentment. "In the woods," he informed her sullenly.

"I can see we're 'in the woods'! What woods? Why can't we just take the main road?"

"Texas nearly has martial law. No one travels without a pass."

"We don't have a pass?"

"Do you have one?"

He realized his tone was bordering on irreverence, but he was sick and tired of her questioning his judgment!

"Of course not. I'm a nun!"

"I don't recall a clause excluding nuns," he managed to say through clenched teeth.

"Well, there should be. We do, after all, travel on missions of mercy."

"Mercy," he muttered.

"What?"

"Nothing."

"Wait a minute. My veil is caught again."

Hershall halted the horse for the tenth time that morning and waited for her to unhook her veil from a thorny limb.

"Look at that. A hole in my veil. Sister Jane won't be happy about this, let me tell you. She's very meticulous about how her sisters look." Abby grabbed for his waist as the horse set off again in a bone-jarring gait.

By noon Hershall was pushing the horse hard, ignoring Sister's constant muttering about the bushes that grabbed at her habit, the limbs that persisted in trying to pluck her veil from her head, the roughness of the horse's gait, the cold, the wind, the snow. She was hungry; she needed a private moment; she needed another private moment; the list rambled on until Hershall couldn't take it any longer.

At noon he found a small clearing, and they stopped to eat.

Wedging her piece of jerky into the corner of her mouth, Sister paced agitatedly back and forth, ranting on and on about life's miseries, as if Hershall didn't have a few of his own.

Striding back and forth, hand on hip, she vent her frustrations on the shoe salesman, blaming him for everything short of being personally responsible for starting the war.

Hershall calmly sat beneath a tree, trying to block out the sound of her shrill, belittling voice.

A watery sun broke through the clouds midafternoon. Though it was barely above freezing, the rays began to melt the snow from the tree branches.

"Oh, not again!" Sister groaned dramatically as yet another icy drip slid off a tree limb and splattered on her forehead.

Wadding up a corner of her veil, she swiped it away, heaving another disgruntled sigh as she grabbed for his waist again.

"Whoooee!" Hershall's voice shot up three octaves higher as her hand missed his waist and accidentally landed between his legs.

She corrected the mistake immediately, but the incident clearly left Hershall shaken.

"Is there something wrong, Mr. Digman?"

"No, nothing." She was so innocent about men that she was unaware of where her hand had landed, Hershall thought, relieved that they both were spared the ordeal of her embarrassed apologies.

By late midafternoon, Hershall's jaw was permanently clenched. He'd never met a woman who could think of so many things to gripe about. You'd think she was used to the best of circumstances—a comfortable coach, a soft bed, meals served—instead of the Spartan lifestyle he knew nuns chose when they entered the convent.

"Oh, not again!" she muttered for the hundredth time.

"What's wrong now?"

"What's *wrong*?"

Hershall realized his mistake immediately. She was off again, her berating voice ricocheting throughout the forest, bemoaning the fact that she was soaked to the skin and frozen to the saddle. Hershall resolutely whipped the horse faster, determined to make it through the day.

Around four o'clock, he decided he couldn't go on. He'd planned to ride until dark, but she had his nerves humming like a telegraph wire.

"Why are we stopping?"

"We're going to make camp."

"Praise the Lord," Abby said, breathing, sliding off the horse the moment it stopped, eyeing the mare distastefully. The darn thing wasn't worth stealing, but she knew it was her only hope of escape tonight.

Hershall went about setting up camp, oblivious to her concerns.

Abby watched, smirking. He'd made no secret about not being happy with her today, but she wasn't going to lose any sleep over that. She bet he'd be really upset if he knew that she had deliberately let her hand slip today just to provoke a reaction from him.

He was so dense!

Actually, he hadn't felt as wimpy as he looked, and when she'd touched him where she knew she shouldn't, he had jumped as if he had been shot between the eyes with a double-barreled shotgun.

He might be an insipid little shoe salesman, but he had responded appropriately enough to a woman's touch.

She'd have to allow him that.

Chapter 5

"I'm building the fire now, Sister."

"That's good, Mr. Digman."

"Just sit right there on that log and rest yourself," he called.

"I'm sitting, Mr. Digman," she called back.

Striding to a nearby log, Abby sat down to watch Hershall cut cedar branches to lay inside the tent. *Let him get his feet wet*, she thought. *He has extra shoes.*

It only took a minute before he had her shaking her head and mumbling under her breath. It was amazing how he could turn the simplest task into a full-blown disaster. There he was hacking at the limbs, repeatedly knocking his bowler off into the snow.

She groaned, diverting her eyes when his persistent bumbling caused a whole section of snow to collapse down the collar of his jacket.

He spent five minutes prancing around, trying to flip snow out of his shirt. A full ten minutes was wasted before he was composed enough to get back to work.

Tossing the piece of canvas over a low-hanging

branch, he grabbed for the support rope. He frowned when he noticed the big knot that he'd jerked into the rope in his haste to break camp that morning.

He lifted the end of the rope and peered at the snarled hitch, then began trying to loosen it. Squinting over the bridge of his spectacles, he picked and worked, and worked and picked, his teeth worrying his tongue as it lolled his lower lip. The scowl on his face deepened as the pesky knot, in spite of all he did, refused to budge.

Clamping his teeth firmly atop his lower lip, he grasped the knot with both hands and began twisting and pulling, determined to loosen the coil.

Losing patience, he yanked it, jerked it, then in complete disgust pitched it aside and tramped back to the fire to warm his hands.

"Having trouble, Mr. Digman?"

"No, Sister. I thought since it'll be dark soon, I'd better hunt for game. I'll tinker with the tent later."

Glancing up at the sky, she frowned. "Looks to me like it's going to snow again. Don't you think you should put the tent up first?"

"I can only do one thing at a time," Hershall said shortly.

"I can help—"

"No!"

My, my, Hershall's getting downright testy, she realized, but decided to let it pass. He was impossible to argue with. Besides, he was pigheaded and unreasonable, so why waste her breath?

"You get started on your evening devotions," he told her as he reached for his gun. He wasn't about to spend another hour stranded beneath a tree, freezing his tail off while she prayed. "I'll scare up a rabbit."

She thought he would scare most anything but refrained from telling him so. Stepping closer to the fire, she watched him load the gun, then fade unceremoniously into the strand of timber encircling the small clearing.

Something big with fluttery wings darted overhead, shattering the wintry stillness. Abby glanced uneasily over her shoulder, wondering how long it would take him to shoot a rabbit. If his fire-building or tent-erecting skills were any measure, it wouldn't be soon.

Huddling closer to the fire, she waited for the encroaching darkness. She didn't like the dark, but she wasn't about to admit that to Hershall. Only Amelia and Anne-Marie knew about her phobia. She'd tried to overcome her fears, but she'd had little success. When evening shadows deepened, a strange feeling gripped her insides, a feeling much like the one she'd had when she, Amelia, and Anne-Marie had climbed into Father Luis's green apple orchard and eaten their fill.

For days the McDougal sisters were forced to keep the mission outhouse within close running distance.

Father Luis had assigned the sisters a novena for their foolishness, but it hadn't bothered Abby. Since she'd spent the better part of the first four days sitting in the outhouse anyway, she'd had plenty of time to say a litany of prayers.

Lifting her hands to the fire, she let the heat penetrate her fingers. It would be warmer tomorrow, she promised herself. And tomorrow, she would be on her way back to Mercy Flats. The thought of seeing Anne-Marie and Amelia made her feel better, even though it was starting to snow again. The wind caught a spray of red embers and blew them away. They skipped across the snow, forming a rosy pattern until they died.

Rubbing her upper arms, she repressed a shiver. It was suddenly so quiet and lonely in the clearing. The dripping of the melting snow seemed louder, and something mysterious rustled in the shadows.

When a log in the fire snapped, she jumped, her heart lodging in her throat as she peered into the underbrush. It was only a small animal, she assured herself, but the knot in her throat grew more pronounced.

She suddenly wondered what Amelia and Anne-Marie were doing. Were they as lonely and frightened tonight as she was?

Well, she was almost certain Amy was frightened. Amy was afraid of everything. Anne-Marie was good at taking care of herself, but Amy needed all the help she could get. It used to annoy Abby that she had to watch out for Amy, but right now, she missed her so much that she wouldn't mind it at all.

The tall, dark-haired man who had snatched up Amy and ridden off with her looked like the sort of man who could take care of himself. Her gaze searched the stand of timber. The very opposite of Hershall E. Digman.

But poor Anne-Marie. She'd been rescued by that—well, that Indian. Chewing her lower lip thoughtfully, her gaze returned to the fire, angry when hot tears burned behind her eyes. An Indian! What if he was one of the savages who had chased the jail wagon? What if he had been the leader? What if right at this very moment—

No, she wouldn't allow herself to think such an unpleasant thought. Anne-Marie was just fine, and so was Amy.

Snuggling deeper in the blanket, she stirred the fire, thinking about her family. The McDougal sisters were born barely a year apart, sired by Hamish "Irish" McDougal, a redheaded, fiery-tempered Irishman known for his beguiling tongue and his talent for holding his liquor. Irish was a man who could charm the bark off a tree if it suited him but found it impossible to hold a job because of his quick temper.

Mary Catherine McCurdy, the sisters' mother and Irish's soft-spoken wife, was, the girls had been told, as sweet and gentle as Irish was boisterous and gregarious. Mary Catherine had a lot of dreams. One was that her three daughters would be educated by the sisters at the mission, which had suddenly become reality when Irish and Mary Catherine had died in a smallpox epidemic that had swept Mercy Flats when Amelia was two, Abigail three, and Anne-Marie four.

Because they had nowhere else to go, Irish and Mary Catherine's daughters were taken to the mission orphanage to be raised by the gentle sisters.

Abby smiled as she remembered growing up at the orphanage. She had to give the sisters credit; they'd tried. When they'd discovered the girls were a fright when teamed together, they'd tried separating them. But the sisters had raised such a ruckus that there was nothing to do but put them back together. Then together they had been worse than a plague. What one hadn't thought of, the other two had. Even as young girls they'd shown a talent for trickery. To fill time they'd learned to "imagine." They'd formulated stories that won them cookies from the cook, pesos from strangers, and they'd been most creative in finding ways to avoid evening prayers.

The games had started innocently. Because the sisters had been kind enough to take them in as orphans, the girls had decided that the order would never want for anything. And they'd kept that vow. In the years since, half of everything they'd gained from their endeavors had gone to support the mission.

Assuming that their gifts of money had been acquired

honestly, the sisters were overjoyed whenever they received monetary gifts from the McDougals.

As long as the nuns chose to believe that the three girls were earning that money forthrightly, the McDougals could agree not to tell them otherwise. It was, after all, not a very big lie, and it wasn't really hurting anyone—except whatever victim they had chosen to deceive—and they had always taken great pains to make sure that their prey could afford to take a small loss.

At times it bothered Amelia to use the nun's habit as a disguise, but Abby never gave it much thought. The masquerade, after all, was only a lark, and they meant the sisterhood no disrespect.

Feeding more sticks into the fire, Abby glanced toward the woods, wondering what was taking Hershall so long. Where was that man? It was getting darker by the moment, and he was still wandering around looking for something to shoot.

There wasn't a sound, except for the tiny scurrying of wildlife and water dripping from the barren tree branches. Shouldn't she have heard the gun go off by now? Did he even know which end of the gun to point? She should have gone herself. The meat would be hanging over the fire, all plump and brown by now.

She sighed. *Honestly.*

"Uneasy about something, Sister?"

Abby started, nearly swallowing her tongue at the sound of Hershall's voice. Glancing over her shoulder, she discovered he was standing right behind her.

Straightening, she glared at him. "Where did you come from?"

Lifting two plump rabbits, he smiled. "Hunting."

"I didn't hear the gun go off."

"Oh, my, my. I never shoot the furry little creatures," he chided.

She stared back at him crossly. "What do you do? Run them down and club them to death?" Even he couldn't be that stupid.

"No, but I do provide a merciful death," he assured her as he carried the rabbits to the stream to clean them.

"A merciful death?" She shook her head. Absolutely pitiful. "How long will it take to cook them? I'm starving."

"You should have eaten your breakfast."

She frowned, hardly able to miss the thinly veiled mockery.

You should have eaten your breakfast, she mimicked, lifting her hands to the fire again. *And you should blow it out your ear, Mr. Digman.*

The smell of rabbit sizzling over the fire filled the air as Hershall once again turned to the job of erecting the tent.

Abby watched as he patiently worked the stubborn knot, wondering how a man as inept as he had survived in the wilderness. She could have gotten the knot free in minutes! But the more he worried with it, the tighter it got.

Stoically fixing her eyes elsewhere, she vowed that he wasn't going to upset her again. Anne-Marie was right about her; once she lost her temper, she wasn't responsible for what she said. Besides, losing her temper would only hurt her cause, not enhance it. If she allowed her anger to boil over, he would surely catch on to the fact that she was only posing as a nun, and the knowledge that she'd tricked him could anger him so that he might refuse to help her at all. No, it was better to sit here and keep quiet and just wish she could wring his neck like a Sunday chicken.

But her eyes refused to cooperate. In spite of all she did, they drifted back to Hershall.

His spectacles kept sliding down the ridge of his nose, and he'd pause, patiently shoving them back up with his forefinger. As he bent closer, his front teeth worried his lower lip as he plucked at the knot.

Give him a few more minutes. He'll get it, she allowed charitably. Yet even with her tolerance, he managed, if anything, to make the knot tighter.

He'll get it, she told herself, fixing her eyes firmly on the roasting rabbits.

But ten minutes later he was still bent over the knot, picking, picking, his tongue resting on his lower lip anxiously.

He'll get it!

Pick, pick, pick, pick, pick, pick, pick.

Give him time. He's not exactly a bolt of lightning, you know.

Pick, pick.

Just a few more minu—no, dammit! She'd had all she could stand! He was never going to get that knot out; he *wasn't* going to get the tent up before Christmas; and she was not going to sleep in the open, simply because of his sheer idiocy!

Springing from the log, she screamed. Her sudden high-pitched shriek sent Hershall reeling backward.

She was marching toward him with a murderous look in her eye. "Shitfire, Hershall! Can't you even undo a simple knot?"

Hershall struggled to right himself, fighting to adjust his spectacles that had landed lopsided on the bridge of his nose, blinding him.

"Give me that rope!" She snatched the knot from his hands, her eyes daring him to challenge her.

Stunned, he meekly handed it to her.

"Honestly!" Whipping the skirt of her habit over her shoulder, she dug into the pocket of the trousers she wore beneath and fished out a small knife. Flicking the blade open with her thumbnail, she slashed through the knot, tossing the piece of frayed rope into the fire.

Swiftly tying a new knot, she handed the rope back to Hershall, who by now was gaping back at her, slack-jawed.

"There! Now rig the damn tent!"

She turned and stalked away, leaving a round-eyed Hershall staring after her.

Chapter 6

For a moment, Hershall sat paralyzed with the rope resting limply on his lap. Slowly but surely, the significance of her behavior sank in on him. Why, the little conniver! She was no more a nun than he was a priest!

Marching back to the fire, Abby jerked off the dark veil and pushed her fingers through her hair to loosen it. *Well, now you've done it,* she thought, but she didn't care. She couldn't stand it another minute!

A hand suddenly clamped on her shoulder. "Hold it a minute, Sister." Turning her around, Hershall faced her. There wasn't the slightest sign of chivalry in his eyes now. "What is going on here?"

"Why, nothing, Mr. Digman," she stammered lamely. "It is positively inexcusable the way I've acted. I'll go into the woods and seek privacy, so that I may reflect on my sinful—"

His grip on her shoulders tightened painfully. "*What* is going on?" he repeated tightly. His eyes raked over her coldly, coming to rest on the lustrous cloud of dark hair that swung free to her waist.

"Going on? Why I—please, Mr. Digman, you're hurting me—" She couldn't believe the strength he'd suddenly developed. Twisting free from his grasp, she drew herself up defensively. "Just leave me alone!"

"You're not a nun," he jeered.

She shrugged, trying to bluff her way out of it. "You don't know that for certain."

"You're *masquerading* as a nun!" Hershall was staggered by her audacity. "Are you even a Catholic?"

"Yes, I'm a Catholic," she spat back, as if it were any of *his* business!

"And your sisters? They're also posing as nuns?"

Her smile was as glacial as his tone. "Yes."

"For what purpose?"

"So that we can travel safely."

"Travel where, safely? Why would three sisters posing as Catholic nuns want to roam through the countryside with a war going on?" he demanded indignantly.

Oh, this is going to really lay him low, she thought, but she didn't care. If he wanted to be so nosy, why not? "Because we 'roam' the countryside bilking strangers out of money," she mimicked.

"Ohhh." His hand shot to his heart as if he were about to faint. Heaving a sigh of disgust, she grabbed his arm and steered him to a nearby log. All she needed was for him to die on her.

Lowering him to the log, she removed his handkerchief from his pocket and dipped it into a puddle of melting snow. "Don't look so stricken. It happens, you know."

"But that's utter blasphemy," he accused as she began to wipe his forehead with the wet cloth in an attempt to bring the color back to his face.

"Every cent of the money we take goes to the mission," she consoled. "If it wasn't for our work, the mission couldn't survive. The sisters are all so old they can barely keep the place open, even with our financial contributions.''

"Contributions!" Hershall was clearly appalled by her euphemistic rationalization.

"Now, now, settle down, Mr. Digman.'' She dipped the cloth into the puddle again, then brought it back to wipe his face.

He lifted his eyes to her reproachfully. "Do the sisters know how you acquire the money?''

"Heavens, no. They think we earn it honestly.''

"Ohhhh.'' His face contorted with pain as his hand went back to his heart feebly.

Eyeing him warily, she waited until a hint of color began to return to his features.

"Are you going to be all right?''

Pushing her hand aside, he glared back at her sullenly. "I will be *fine*, thank you.''

She would have preferred to have preserved her disguise, but since he knew that she wasn't a nun, she could shed the habit. Bending forward, she caught the hem of the skirt and yanked it up and over her head.

The castigating look Hershall gave her was too much. In a fit of pique, she wadded up the material and threw it at him. The bundle hit him in the face, nearly knocking him off the log.

Grabbing for support, he righted himself, stunned by the transformation that he was witnessing. A magnificent-looking young woman stood before him, wearing close-fitting brown twill trousers and a snug shirt that betrayed a body a man only dreamed about.

While Abigail McDougal had been lovely before, she was stunning now. Hershall couldn't take his eyes off her. His gaze dropped to her slim, wild beauty, fantasizing about the havoc she could cast upon a man.

Coming to his feet, Hershall's eyes locked with hers. "Who are you?"

"Abigail McDougal." Abby bent to comb the tangles out of her hair with her fingers.

"You were in that jail wagon because you'd been caught in one of your swindles," he accused.

Straightening, Abby met his gaze at eye level. "Really, Mr. Digman. What do you think?"

"But posing as nuns!" The sheer sacrilegious nerve of her actions still rendered him speechless.

"That's right, and now that you know who I really am, you have to take me back to Mercy Flats."

His hand shot to his forehead indignantly. "I most assuredly do *not*. If I refused to take you back when I assumed you were a nun, I certainly won't take you back now that I'm aware you're an imposter!"

"Oh, big deal."

He folded his arms and stared at her.

Mimicking his actions, she folded hers and stared back. "It seems we've reached an impasse, Mr. Digman."

"*I* am going to Shreveport."

Lifting her brows, she repeated, "And I'm going to get to Mercy Flats."

"Then I suggest you better get started."

"I don't have a horse."

They were standing nose to nose now, their features flushed with anger.

"Perhaps you should have thought of that before you had your temper tantrum, *Sister*!"

"Perhaps I did, Mr. Digman!" Her eyes were flat, hard, and filled with contempt as the underlying meaning of her words sank in on him.

"You leave my horse alone," he warned in a harsh undertone.

"I haven't touched your horse, but I will if you don't take me back to Mercy Flats."

Hershall straightened, drawing a deep, fortifying breath. In all of his thirty-one years, he had never had the misfortune to meet such a woman. Jerking the sleeves of his jacket back down into place, he struggled to control his anger. The very idea of her posing as a nun and milking innocent victims out of money and thinking she could get away with it infuriated him. What was this world coming to? "Under no circumstances will I take you to Mercy Flats," he said coldly.

"All right, then give me the money, and I'll take the old stage."

"Absolutely not."

"But you have to! You can't just leave me out here alone!"

His left brow quirked with rancor. "Oh, really? Just watch me."

Abby panicked. He couldn't leave her out here alone! He couldn't do that, no matter how rotten he was. "Why you're—you're an ass!"

"Ha! *I'm* an ass? I'm not the one—" He broke off, waving his hands, helplessly at a loss for the proper term for her. "I'm not the one defiling the cloth!"

"Defiling the cloth!" She raised her hand to slap him, but he blocked the reflex in midair.

His eyes narrowed menacingly. "I wouldn't do that if I were you." His eyes locked with hers, and Abby detected a threat she hadn't seen before. Hershall no longer appeared so meek.

"You take me to Mercy Flats," she demanded.

"When hell freezes over," he calmly returned.

A sob tore at her throat. "Please, I'm sorry I lied to you. . . . But I didn't ask you to rescue me. All I want to do is get back to my sisters—" she pleaded brokenly.

Anne-Marie and Amelia would be waiting at the cemetery for her. He just couldn't leave her out here alone—in the dark. Her heart beat wildly. For the first time in her life, she was frightened—really frightened.

"That's not my problem. The horse is mine, and I'm going to Shreveport."

"Your shoes can wait! I can't."

"You aren't my concern. Selling shoes is."

"You wouldn't leave me out here alone."

"Oh, wouldn't I?"

"I could be killed, or worse." She would beg if she must.

"No."

"Please." She would grovel, she didn't care.

"No."

"You're making me mad."

Turning a deaf ear, he walked back to the fire. "I'll be leaving early, Miss McDougal. I'll try not to disturb you."

"Ohhh!" She picked up a rock and threw it at him.

After ducking, he straightened his bowler. "You should do something about that temper. It doesn't become you."

She picked up a bigger rock and flung it at him. "I don't even know where I am!"

"Oh, you seem like an enterprising enough young woman. I'm sure it won't take you long to find out a detail that small."

"You're hateful!"

"You are, too."

She watched as he walked away, her stomach rolling with fear. Now what would she do?

"I won't put up with this," she called to his retreating form. Her foot defiantly shot out to kick the habit to one side.

Calmly removing one of the rabbits from the spit, he ignored her.

She grabbed up the habit and ran to the fire. Before he could stop her, she flung it into the flames.

"There," she said smugly as the black fabric went up in smoke. "Now you'll have to take me. I don't have a disguise anymore, so I can't travel alone."

Pouring a cup of coffee, he handed it to her dispassionately. "You'd better sit down and rest, Miss McDougal. You've got a long walk ahead of you."

She snatched the coffee from his hand and slammed the tin cup down on a nearby rock.

Hershall sat down and began to eat, unmoved by her tantrum.

"Then give me money for the stage fare."

He laughed.

She strode around the fire, jerked his glasses off, threw them down on the ground, and stomped on them.

His mouth dropped open as he stared at the mangled debris. One earpiece lay to one side, while the other stuck straight up in the air.

"Well—dammit!" he sputtered. Coffee spilled down the front of his trousers as he heatedly sprang to his feet. Mad or not, she had no call to stomp on his glasses!

Whirling, Abby marched off as Hershall snatched up the spectacles, anxiously examining the mangled rims. He couldn't believe she'd do such a thing!

After digging the dirt off the lenses, he irritably settled the spectacles back on his nose, trying to adjust the cracks to where he could see around them.

Since it was dark, Abby didn't wander far. She carried her cup of coffee to a nearby rock and sat broodingly, watching him fuss with his old glasses. She was glad that she had broken them. She hoped he couldn't find his butt with both hands; it served him right.

Drawing a deep breath, she tried to calm herself. Now what was she going to do? Since she'd broken his glasses, he'd never help her.

"I've changed my mind, Miss McDougal. I *am* going to take you to the nearest town, and once we're there, I am going to alert the sheriff to your little games."

She looked up to find Hershall, his glasses askew, in his too-small jacket, his too-short pants, and with a self-righteous expression, glaring down at her.

Her fingers gripped the cup of coffee, and in one quick gesture, she flung its contents at his face.

Spinning on his heel, he stalked back to the fire with coffee dripping off his shattered lenses.

His threats didn't intimidate her, and he wasn't taking her *anywhere*, she vowed. Because by morning, she'd be gone.

Chapter 7

She was going to steal his horse.

Hershall wasn't dumb.

She was waiting for the right moment, then she'd steal the horse and leave him afoot—or at least that's what she thought.

But Hershall thought otherwise.

She wasn't about to pull anything funny on him.

Huddling on her side of the tent, listening to the wind whip the canvas flap, Abby plotted. Once Hershall was asleep, she'd creep out of the tent and take his horse. There had to be a town someplace nearby. When she found it, she'd think of a way to get enough money for a ticket for the stage. She'd be back in Mercy Flats before Hershall could tell anybody what she'd done.

Her plan was so simple she almost laughed. Hershall E. Digman didn't know what he was up against if he thought he could get the best of Abigail McDougal.

She lay for a long time listening to the wind howl through the tree branches. It seemed a long time before she heard Hershall's breathing grow regular, but finally it did. She was tempted to move quickly, but she bided her time, waiting until she was sure he was sound asleep. It'd be just like him to try to outsmart her.

Close to an hour passed before she quietly sat up, carefully easing the blanket aside.

Scooting a couple of inches, she glanced over her shoulder, listening to see if his breathing had altered. When it appeared that it hadn't, she scooted faster.

Easing the flap aside, she got to her knees and was about to crawl out when a hand suddenly clamped around her calf.

"Surely it isn't morning yet, Miss McDougal."

Blast his rotten hide! "I, uh, need to make a trip into the bushes," she murmured.

"What?"

"Need-to-make-a-trip-to-the-bushes," she repeated nervously.

"I'll go with you."

"No!"

"Miss McDougal, I couldn't let you go out there alone and unprotected."

"I'll hurry."

She pushed the flap aside, but the hand tightened its grip on her calf. "I'll go with you," Hershall repeated dryly. "There could be coyotes running around, and we wouldn't want you getting hurt, now would we?"

"It's really not necessary—" *Think fast, Abby.* "I, uh, don't feel very well. It must have been that under-cooked rabbit—" Inventing a gag, she clapped her hand over her mouth and tried to look deathly ill.

"Your stomach's upset?"

She nodded. "And . . . the other." She pointed to her stomach, rocking back and forth as if she were ex-periencing stabbing pains. "Please, Mr. Digman. I'm not lying. My stomach hurts something awful."

"I wouldn't think of letting you suffer, but I will go with you."

Burying her face in her hands, she wept. Softly at first, then becoming more exuberant as hot tears rolled from the corners of her eyes. Rocking back and forth, she cradled her stomach, her wails growing more pronounced.

"Your theatrics are noteworthy, but you're wasting them on me. If you leave this tent, I go with you," he told her, flatly unimpressed by her caterwauling.

"I would rather *die* than have you watch me," she said, sobbing.

"I can arrange that, too."

"In all my life, I've never—ever used the bushes with anyone watching me."

"I won't watch you."

She cried harder. "You'll still hear me."

Swearing, he sat up and jerked the blanket off his legs. "If I let you go alone, you're not to get fifteen feet away from this tent, do you understand me?"

"If I stay that close, you'll still *hear* me," she wailed.

"Twenty feet, not a foot more." He was beginning to hate this woman.

She hurriedly scrambled out of the tent on her hands and knees.

"You'd better be back in a few minutes," he called.

As soon as the flap dropped back into place, Hershall reached for his shoes. He didn't trust her as far as he could throw her.

Before he could get his left shoe on, he heard the sound of hooves breaking through the underbrush.

"Dammit!" Bolting out of the tent, he saw her on the horse, bearing down on him with a murderous intent in her eyes.

Jumping backward, he stumbled and pitched for-

ward. Grabbing the tent for support, he swore again as
the canvas gave way and he collapsed amid a flurry of
strangled profanities.

Rolling to his feet, he angrily shoved the spectacles
back into place, shouting after her, ''Bring that horse
back here!''

Abby's jeering laughter seared his dignity as the horse
streaked by him and galloped out of camp.

He stood for a minute, listening to the sound of fading hoofbeats. If it wasn't for his saddlebags, he could
let her go and hope a rattlesnake got her, but damn her
worthless hide, she was smart enough to realize she
couldn't survive without the jerky.

Breaking camp, he fashioned a backpack with the
canvas and rope, then picking up his shoe satchel, he
struck off on foot, determined to hunt her down and
shoot her like he would a rabid dog.

Abby raced along the snowy road, kicking the horse
into a faster gallop. A spiritless moon lit the pathway
as beast and rider sprinted along the winding road.
Pushing the horse harder, she hoped to put as much
distance as possible between Hershall and herself. He
wasn't a threat on foot, but he had shown a peculiar
assertiveness tonight that warned her not to take any
unnecessary chances.

The moon slid behind a cloud, forcing her to slow
the horse's gait. Riding more slowly now, she prayed
that the moon would come out again. At times, she
could barely see her hand in front of her face.

The horse clopped noisily along the dirt road, the
sound of her hooves echoing eerily in the darkness.
Forcing back the lump of fear suddenly crowding her
throat, Abby assured herself that she had done the right

thing. It would be light before long; there was nothing out here to harm her, if she didn't stop.

Her hands gripped the horse's mane tighter.

She was a good horsewoman, and the horse was sure-footed. It could outrun a wild animal—if it wasn't too big, and if it was absolutely necessary.

It suddenly seemed so *dark*. And she was out here alone—in the dark.

An owl hooted, and she pressed closer to the horse's neck. Maybe she should have waited until sunup to make her escape.

This is a fine time to think about that, Abigail. Anne-Marie's censuring voice echoed back to her. *You should have waited until daylight.*

The horse carried her swiftly through the fallen snow. Abby prayed they'd come to an intersecting road, so that she could get her bearings. If the moon came out soon, she'd have nothing to worry about, but the night was as black as ink. She could barely make out the lay of the land, much less decipher north from south.

By the time she'd ridden over an hour, she was hopelessly confused. She didn't have the slightest idea in what direction she was traveling.

She reined the horse into a clearing and stopped to consider her options. If she was going north, then all she had to do was veer to the left and she'd be headed back to Mercy Flats. But if she'd gotten turned around and was riding south, then she would undoubtedly run into Hershall trying to make his way to the nearest town. Nudging the horse's flanks, she started off again with uncertainty still plaguing her.

Dawn was streaking the sky when she spotted a stream ahead. She slid off the horse and allowed him to drink while she stretched her cramped muscles.

When she was able to feel her limbs again, she knelt

beside the stream and cupped her hands to drink of the cold, sweet water.

Her stomach growled, reminding her that she had eaten little in the past twenty-four hours. She dreaded the thought of more jerky, but it was better than going hungry.

While the horse drank, she rummaged through the saddlebags, wishing she hadn't been so impulsive and burned her habit. Traveling alone would be easier with the disguise.

She would need to be careful now to avoid others who might be on the road. Besides soldiers, there were any number of miscreants who might accost her, and she had no weapon to defend herself. She'd begged Anne-Marie to let her carry a gun hidden in her boot, but her sister had refused, saying that she was worried that Abby would shoot herself—or worse.

After removing the jerky, Abigail unwrapped the paper and stared at the leathery meat, wondering if she could bring herself to eat it. She tore off a strip and stuffed it into her mouth, then dug deeper into the saddlebags. Hershall's map was in there. If she could understand it, she could figure out where she was.

She couldn't believe the collection of junk that man carried. The contents of his saddlebags were worse than an old maid's dresser. There was a jar of pomade, a shoe catalog, a knife, a pair of dark glasses, an extra pair of white spats, a comb, and a mirror. But no map.

Moving to the opposite side of the horse, she dug into the other bag and unearthed a man's shirt. Laughing, she imagined Hershall's consternation at losing his shirt to a woman. She tossed it into the bushes.

As she was about to close the bag, her hand brushed an object she couldn't readily identify. Frowning, she dug deeper, pulling out a small brown leather packet.

Curious, she untied the string around the fat folder. The packet was stuffed tight as a tick with some kind of papers.

Unfolding them, she hoped they were maps of the territory. She experienced a keen sense of disappointment a moment later when she saw they weren't maps at all; they were just a bunch of writing that didn't appear at first to make a lick of sense.

Wondering why Hershall had kept them, she sat down on the creek bank, squinting in the dim light, to study them further.

The first sheets were copies of messages from General Ulysses S. Grant. One paper was dated April 2, 1864, and addressed to General Butler. Her eyes skimmed the page quickly. Apparently, Grant had been given a commission to organize the Northern armies, which, until this date, had operated independently. From what Abby could ascertain, Grant was now busily creating a unified effort against the Confederate army.

His message to Butler was, in effect, to take all the forces at his command that could be spared and move to the south side of the James River. Her eyes widened. Richmond would be his objective.

Her eyes moved to the second page, where there was another like message, this one addressed to Sherman on April fourth. Grant wrote:

It is my design, if the enemy keep quiet and allow me to take the initiative in the spring campaign, to work all the parts of the army together and somewhat toward a common center. . . .

She read on, realizing that Sherman was being told to move against Johnston's army, to break it up, to get as far into the enemy territory as possible, to inflict all the damage he could against the resources of the Confederacy.

Her hand lifted to cover her heart as she read on. The third sheet was a copy of a message which directed General Meade to stick to General Robert E. Lee.

Wherever Lee goes, there you will go also.

The fourth sheet was a directive to General J. Kirby Smith, commander of the trans-Mississippi department of the Confederacy. The message warned General Smith that General Banks and his Union troops were marching from the east to take Shreveport. Smith was directed to immediately gather all forces to repel the attack.

Stunned, Abby let the pages flutter to the ground as she stared into the water. What was Hershall, a shoe salesman, doing with—

The answer suddenly hit her.

Hershall E. Digman wasn't a sappy shoe salesman! He was a Confederate spy—posing as a sappy shoe salesman!

Springing to her feet, her eyes narrowed with fury. Damn his worthless hide! He'd lied to her. *Lied* to her! She couldn't believe it. She began to pace back and forth, driven by rage. Hershall hadn't been avoiding the roads because he was stupid, or because he didn't have a pass. He'd taken the hard way because he was afraid of being discovered by Union soldiers!

Why, the worthless toad! He'd been so indignant about her posing as a nun, while all along he was nothing but a lying, low-down, conniving—sneak!

She paced more furiously. How dare he pull such a stunt on her? How dare he!

Furious now, Abby snatched up the sheets of paper and shoved them back into the leather packet.

Swinging back on the horse, she kicked it hard, sending it off in a full gallop.

As the sun came up, Hershall walked down the road, shifting the saddle from his left shoulder to the right one. His shoes were rubbing a blister on his heel, and the bowler kept falling off. He knew he should throw the damn thing away, but he wouldn't.

But when he got his hands on Abigail McDougal, there wouldn't be enough left of her for the buzzards to fight over.

The sun's warmth melted the small skiffs of snow littering the ditches. He flinched as his ankles sank into another muddy rut. When he found that woman he . . . Glancing up, he heard the sound of hoofbeats approaching.

Darting swiftly into the bushes, he listened as the hoofbeats grew closer. The riders appeared to be a large group. All he needed was to get caught by a patrol, he thought cynically.

Crouching behind the row of heavy thicket, he watched as a company of Confederate cavalry came down the road at a fast clip. From the lather ringing their horses' necks and the number of wounded in the saddle, it was obvious that the men had been involved in recent battle.

As the lead horse drew close enough for Hershall to get a good look at the rider, his face broke into a relieved grin. Parting the thicket, he stepped out into the center of the road, waving the company to a halt.

The lead rider reached for his pistol as Hershall called out to him, "Captain Broder, sir!" He executed a mock bow.

Frowning, Les Broder slowed his horse, astonishment overcoming his drawn features. "Drake?"

"In the flesh."

Swinging off his horse, Les grasped his old friend's hand. "Barrett Drake! Good God, man, what are you doing dressed like some damned tinker!"

Flashing him a tired grin, Barrett clasped his friend on the back, relieved to see a familiar face. "That's what I am, Les—for all practical purposes." He glanced at the soldiers, who were so exhausted that they seized the interruption to doze for a moment in their saddles.

"A tinker on foot?"

"Well, that's a different story. One I don't have time to go into right now."

Grinning, the captain shook his head as he surveyed Barrett's rumpled seersucker suit. "You look like hell."

"I feel like hell," Barrett acknowledged. The two men clasped each other's shoulders affectionately.

"It's good to see you." Les had aged ten years since Barrett had last seen him a year ago. But the war had a way of doing that to a man.

"We just fought one mother of a battle." Les's smile faded as he turned to assess what was left of his company. "I hate this damned war."

Barrett glanced at the row of riders. "Could you spare an old friend a horse?"

Les's eyes moved to the back of the company, where fifteen riderless horses followed, the fallen soldiers' gear still tied to their backs. "Take your pick," he offered in a voice that suddenly sounded very tired.

Drawing Barrett aside, Les asked quietly, "What's going on? The last I heard you were with Smith in Texas."

"I'm still with Smith," Barrett admitted. "I'm doing a little work on the side—" He left unspoken the fact that he was carrying messages for the Confederacy, but Les picked up on the connotation.

"I thought they left that up to civilians."

"Not this time."

Les's eyes darkened. "You're taking a risk, aren't you?"

Barrett shrugged. "Someone has to."

"Things are moving quickly," Les admitted. "What do you think?"

"I don't know." Barrett hated to admit what he thought was going to happen. The South was losing the war. "You know Grant's received his commission from Lincoln."

Les frowned. "Where we've been you don't hear much news."

"Lincoln has told Grant to organize all the Union armies. From what I hear," Barrett paused, unable to say all that he knew, "Meade still commands the Army of the Potomac, but Sherman is heading up affairs in the West. Johnston's in trouble, and maybe Smith. If the North can open a way between the Atlantic coast and Mobile, they'll divide the Confederacy north from south, like the conquest of the Mississippi has parted it east and west. If that happens, the Confederacy is in serious trouble, Les."

Drawing a deep breath, Les lifted his face to the sun. He couldn't get the stench of war out of his nostrils. "I wish it was over. I wish I was back in Atlanta," he said, his voice growing softer, his drawl more pronounced. "I wish I was on the veranda at home sippin' a tall glass of tea, with a splash of bourbon, a breeze comin' in off the river. I wish Kathleen was by my side—God, I miss her." There were times, if he thought hard enough, that he could remember the way she smelled and the feel of her lying next to him. "Sometimes I think back to the days before all this started, and I think about how innocent we all were. I thought

I'd never leave Georgia, thought I'd just inherit my papa's place and farm it, grow tobacco and cotton, and be happy.'' His smile was sadder but wiser. ''I was a damn fool, wasn't I?''

''Every man has his dreams, Les.''

''Last I heard, the farm had been burned down. Daddy's gone. Momma's gone to live with her sister in Atlanta. When I hear the ignorant things people say about the war, about it all being over slavery, I want to shout that it isn't. It isn't that at all. Remember when we were back at the Academy, when war was just rumor? Remember how patriotic we were, how blind we were? Why, we believed it was going to be over in just a matter of months. Now it's gone on for years, and there don't seem to be no letup in sight.''

''Hold on a little longer,'' Barrett encouraged softly. ''Just a little longer. We're not in it because of the matter of slavery. We're in this because the South should be able to govern itself, the way we always have.''

''The Northerners don't know anything about us. Why should they tell us what we can and can't do? We're not traitors. We love our homes and our land, just like they do. And we're not politicians lining our pockets with war profits. We want the freedom we're due. And because we're willing to fight, we're losing everything we've got. It doesn't make sense.'' Les viewed the ruins of his company, his eyes sick with regret. ''It just doesn't make sense.''

''No, but we have to hope it will someday.''

Lifting his hand, Les motioned to a young corporal. ''Jackson! Bring that bay over here.''

A moment later, Barrett had a horse again. ''Can't thank you enough, Les. Hope I can repay the favor someday.''

Lifting his eyes, Les said wearily, "You know how to stop a war?"

"No."

Walking back to his horse, the captain swung into his saddle. "Me neither." He shifted to look back over his shoulder at the fourteen riderless horses. "But I wish I did."

Chapter 8

Brittlefork: pop. 86

Abby viewed the weather-beaten marker with a sigh of relief. Brittlefork was a town near the Texas-Louisiana border, if that man on the road had told her right.

Kneeing the horse forward, she entered the small town. Like most east Texas towns, weather-beaten storefronts lined the main street. The livery stood at the edge of town, surrounded by corrals. There was the usual mercantile, dress and millinery shop, interspersed with the dry goods store, a boarding house, an eating establishment, a hotel, a barber shop, and the inevitable saloons. The saloon keeper of The Gold Nugget was outside this morning, sweeping the sidewalk as Abby rode past, smiling.

The door of the livery stable creaked as the owner shoved it aside. Slowing the horse, Abby waited until the owner glanced up at her.

"Mornin'," he said, nodding to her.

"Good morning."

Sliding off the horse, Abby followed him into the shed's cool interior. Swain Hollister was a scant little man with a trim white beard and twinkling blue eyes. His stooped stance belied the quickness of his step, making it hard to tell his age.

"Does the stage come through Brittlefork?"

"Yessum. Every Thursday around noon. Or afternoon. Depending on what the soldiers do. Sometimes they take the horses right off the stage, did you know that—" He reached for a pitchfork, momentarily distracted. "Sorry, didn't catch your name, little lady."

"Betsy Ross," she lied, remembering hearing something about a woman making a flag or something.

Turning, Swain tipped his hat congenially. "Pleasure, Miss Ross. I guess you be wantin' to take the stage?"

"Yes. Has it encountered any trouble this week?"

"Haven't heard a thing, ma'am—oh, it'll break a wheel occasionally. Never can be sure about that kind of thing," he conceded. "But it'll be through here sometime or other, you can plan on that."

"What's today?"

Swain paused, scratching his head. "Well, now. Must be Thursday, I reckon."

Thursday. Abby's eyes closed in relief. Good. With a little luck the stage would be here in a few hours. "Thank you."

"You're new in town, aren't you?"

"Kind of."

Swain eyed her saddleless bay, wondering why she would be riding bareback. "Want to stable your horse?"

"No, I want to sell her to you."

The man frowned, eyeing the horse. It looked to him like the animal had been rode hard and put away wet. "Well, now, don't reckon I'm in the market for a horse today, missy."

"I'll sell her real cheap."

Swain walked slowly around the horse, scratching the top of his head. "Looks a might ribby to me—I'd have to put a lot of hay in her to get her back in shape." He shook his head regretfully. "I'm afraid I'd insult you on what I could offer."

"You won't insult me," she promised. She hated the horse.

Swain thought about it again. He'd like to help her out, but the animal was worthless. "No, I'm sorry. With money as scarce as hen's teeth, I can't be wasting what little I got, but I will stable her for you for say, a quarter?"

She didn't have a nickel. "No, thank you. I'll just tie her around back in the shade if you can spare a piece of rope."

Swain smiled. She was a right pretty female, even if she was dressed like a man. "You gonna leave her there long?" Swain didn't know where she was off to, but she must not plan on staying long if she planned to leave the horse tied to a tree.

"No, not long." Since she had no money, she couldn't pay to board the horse, but she figured when she didn't come back, the livery man would be forced to feed and water the animal.

"Help yourself." Swain motioned toward a pile of rope lying on the floor. "Water trough is in back."

"Thank you."

Once the mare had drunk her fill of water, Abby

led her around the building and tied her in the shade of a large tree.

Digging through the saddlebags, she took out the leather folder and removed the messages. She glanced around to make sure no one was watching her, then she folded the papers and slid them down the front of her shirt. Fishing back into the bags, she removed the pair of dark glasses and stuck them into her pocket.

As she came around the corner of the building, she saw that the livery owner was preoccupied with a customer now. The two men were bent over, examining a horse's hoof.

Quickly stepping inside the livery door, she waited a moment for her eyes to adjust to the dim interior. She could hear Swain and the customer talking as she moved deeper into the shadows.

A moment later, she heard the horse trot away and Swain enter the livery again. Whistling off-key, he moved up and down the hallway, mucking stalls and pouring grain into bins.

With practiced ease, Abby's eyes took stock of the livery. A plan was slowly forming in her mind that would allow her to buy a stage ticket, but she would need specific articles for the ruse. She quickly located the blanket that was thrown across the end stall and a battered hat hanging from a peg beside the grain bin.

As Swain bent to inspect a worrisome nick on a horse's leg, she quietly stepped from the shadows and gathered the blanket and hat, then snatched two nice red apples from the peck sitting on the floor as she tiptoed out the doorway.

Hurrying behind the building, she shook out the musty blanket and headed toward the alley. She gave a quick look over her shoulder, then ducked around the corner, tucking her hair beneath the stolen hat as she approached the back of the café.

Easing the screen open, she looked inside. The cook had his hands shoved into a pan of hot soapy water, washing dishes. He seemed oblivious to the world as Abby's hand crept between the screen and door frame and snatched one of the tin cups he'd just washed.

Continuing on down the alley, she stopped at the mercantile next. The store was open, and she was relieved to see two women inside, discussing the merits of the bolts of new fabric that had just arrived. The owner shuffled in and out the back door, carrying in supplies as he complained to his wife about the dad-burned cat trying to trip him.

Tossing aside her apple core, Abby stepped inside, pretending to study the saddles at the back of the store. When she was certain that the two women were immersed in gossip and that the owner was distracted by the cat, an oak cane joined the tin cup beneath her blanket.

Casually sauntering out the door, she darted back down the alley. Only when she'd distanced herself three stores away from the mercantile did she dare to release the breath she'd been holding.

It was midmorning when Barrett rode into Brittle-fork. Leaving his horse at the livery, he headed straight for the sheriff's office.

The town was busy for the middle of the week. Since the war had begun, both it and the blockade had brought about an economic revolution in Texas. The exportation and importation of goods had nearly ceased. Limited trading could be done through Mexico and by blockade runners, but still goods were precious and hard to come by.

The absence of most able-bodied men had thrown the burden of providing the necessities of life upon the women. Having been raised in a household where ladies were protected from the rigors of daily life, Barrett was disturbed by the sight of women chopping cotton and working in the fields. The war had changed everything, and he hated it.

It wasn't an uncommon sight to see women trying to sell the extra produce from their gardens or butchering to put up their own meat. Some had been known to sell their cattle, chicken, and hogs to the Confederate army themselves.

Barrett spotted the sheriff's office at the end of the street and walked faster. A child darted out, and in Barrett's attempt to sidestep a young mother and her two small children, he nearly stumbled over a blind beggar who was sitting next to the jail entrance.

After steadying himself and then the mother, Barrett tipped his hat to the young woman pleasantly.

"And a good morning to you, ma'am."

The woman nodded, hurrying her children along the walkway.

Barrett started into the sheriff's office when the beggar's cane shot out to block his entrance. "Alms, alms for the blind."

He fished a coin from his pocket and tossed it into the beggar's tin cup.

"Thank you. God bless you," the beggar intoned.

The sheriff turned at the sound of the door opening, and his gaze measured the shoe salesman quizzically. "Yes, sir. What can I do for you?"

"Hershall E. Digman, at your service." Barrett bent

from the waist, extending his hand in greeting. "I have a bit of a problem that I hope you might help me with."

The sheriff's eyes ran over the man, noting the seersucker suit and the spiffy bowler perched atop his head. "I'll try. You're new in town, aren't you?"

"Passing through." Hershall smiled, extending his hand again.

The two men shook hands.

"What seems to be the problem?"

Barrett turned a wooden chair toward the desk, then lightly dusted it with his handkerchief. "Well, you see, Sheriff, I sell shoes. And while on my way to Shreveport," he paused to sit down before continuing, "I happened into an odd situation."

"And what might that be, Mr. Digman?"

"Well," Hershall leaned forward, lowering his voice, "I felt the need for . . . well, for feminine companionship. . . . " His serious blue eyes met the sheriff's, clearly seeking his counterpart's understanding.

"And?"

"And all was going well—you understand, swimmingly well—but when the encounter was over . . ." Hershall cleared his throat in obvious embarrassment. "Well, apparently the woman wasn't satisfied with the price that we had agreed upon, so she stole my horse."

The sheriff frowned. "Stole your horse?"

"That's right. Stole my horse. Now the horse isn't my main concern. I can purchase another horse, but the woman ran off with my saddlebags, which contain personal possessions I don't intend to lose."

"So you want me to find the woman?"

"That's right. I wish to press charges."

The sheriff's brows lifted. "What charges?"

"Horse theft."

"You said the horse didn't matter."

"It doesn't, but my saddlebags do. They were a gift from my mother, who is now," Hershall removed his hat in respect, "deceased, God rest her soul."

"Well, now, Mr. Digman." The sheriff stood up, considering Hershall's request. There were a whole lot of things he'd rather be doing than chasing a soiled dove. "Well, I can see where that'd upset a man, but don't you think maybe you're jumping the gun a bit?"

"Jumping the gun?"

"Yes, you know what they say: 'Hell hath no fury like a woman scorned.' "

"The devil wouldn't lay hands on her, plus, the woman *stole* my horse," Hershall returned curtly. "I believe there's a law against horse theft."

"True, but I'm willing to bet once she cools down, she'll realize the gravity of her rash decision and turn your horse loose. When she does, someone will find it and bring it into town. You leave me your name and address, and I'll see that the saddlebags are eventually returned to you."

Well, wouldn't that be just dandy! Barrett seethed. If she turned the horse loose and it wandered around with the saddlebags containing the messages, there was no telling who'd read them.

The worst that could happen would be that she'd already found the messages and read them, then turned the damned horse loose. There was no doubt in his mind that if she knew that he wasn't Hershall Digman but actually Captain Barrett Drake, she'd break her neck blabbing it to the wrong people.

Time was running out. His only hope, though it was slight, was that she was somewhere nearby, and that the sheriff would be able to find her, and soon. As it was, he'd have to ride hard to reach Shreveport in time to warn Smith that Banks was approaching with a large force of Union soldiers.

Walking over to the stove, the sheriff poured a cup of coffee. "Coffee, Mr. Digman?"

"No, thank you. I just want my saddlebags."

"Won't do no good to get yourself worked into a lather. Me and my boys will do what we can to help you." The sheriff took a sip of coffee and flinched at the taste.

"There's one other thing you should know about this woman, Sheriff. She's a con artist. She and her sisters have been posing as nuns to bilk unsuspecting men out of their money."

The sheriff's brows lifted in surprise. "Nuns, you say?"

Hershall nodded. "Nuns."

"That's low," the sheriff conceded.

"I have reason to believe that she may be near Brittlefork, and if she is, she's going to pick your town like a banjo. Mark my words."

"The devil, you say."

Hershall nodded gravely.

"And you say you think she's headed in this direction?"

"I think she'll try to take the stage out of here. She's anxious to reunite with her sisters in Texas. When do you expect the stage to arrive?"

"Around noon today, if it gets here."

"Good. Mark my word, she'll show up."

"What'd you plan to do in the meantime?"

"I'll keep an eye out for the stage if you'll organize a posse. It is imperative," Hershall couldn't stress the point enough, "that my saddlebags be found and returned to me expeditiously."

"Well, I'll do what I can, but I can't promise anything. There's a lot of territory out there a woman can hide in if she takes a notion."

"Yes, and this one's wily," Hershall said. *Mean and wily,* he added silently.

The sheriff stood up and walked to the gun cabinet. "I'll get a couple of men together, and we'll scout the area. What's the woman look like?"

"Pretty, dark hair, eyes an unusual shade of green."

"Height?"

"Five two or five three." Hershall wasn't positive. All he knew for sure was that she could look him straight in the eye when she was lying to him. A direct descendant of Napoleon. *Ha!* And he'd bought it! "I'll be at the hotel if you need me."

"What do you want me to do with her if I do find her?"

Hershall was tempted to say show no mercy, hang her, but he restrained himself. "Seeing her behind bars will be sufficient."

As Barrett left the office, he nearly tripped over the beggar, who was sitting directly in front of the doorway now.

"A penny for the beggar?"

Hershall peered sanctimoniously at the pauper over the rim of his spectacles. "You're blocking the doorway."

"Alms for the less fortunate?"

"I've already given you a coin."

The beggar lowered his head and tapped his cane beseechingly.

Dropping a second coin in the beggar's cup, Barrett

stepped around the pathetic soul and set off with a jaunty step in search of a hot bath and a few hours of sleep.

Chapter 9

Six hours had passed, and still no sign of Abigail McDougal. Around four that afternoon, Barrett decided to join the search. The sheriff, while appearing cooperative, had failed in his efforts to find the woman.

He stepped out of the hotel and tipped his hat at a passing lady, smiling at her glance of dismissal. As Hershall Digman, women overlooked him, which was the purpose of the disguise, though sometimes his male ego was stung by their abrupt dismissals. He was, after all, a man, and when he encountered a lovely woman he liked to see her smile back.

Continuing down the sidewalk, he worked to loosen his shirt collar. A lazy heat blanketed the town, making the suit that much more miserable. He'd give everything he owned to be back in uniform. The collar was choking him, and the undersized jacket was nothing short of murder.

There was no sight of the stage yet. He'd watched from the window of the hotel room, but as yet, the Wells and Fargo was as elusive as Miss McDougal.

As he crossed the street, it occurred to him that Abby might not have come into Brittlefork. She could have become confused and ridden in the wrong direction, or she could have simply outsmarted him and ridden until she came to a way station. If she chose that route, then it was possible that she would turn the horse loose with the saddlebags intact. Cold fear gripped him. The only thing worse than her discovering the papers would be for her to turn the horse loose for anyone to find his things. Damn! The woman gave him indigestion!

The sheriff looked up as Barrett entered the stuffy office.

"Howdy."

"Just wanted to see if you'd heard anything about the woman."

"Nope."

"Are you looking?"

"Yep."

"Do you have a posse working on it?"

"Yep."

"Have they seen anything of her?"

"Nope."

"Since you aren't having much luck, I thought I might join the search."

After getting slowly to his feet, the sheriff walked over to the stove, carrying his coffee cup. "Don't much like anyone interfering in my duties, Mr. Digman."

"I don't plan to interfere in your duties, Sheriff. I'm merely offering my assistance."

The sheriff's stubborn stance made it clear that he didn't want any help. "You're gonna have to give me and the boys more time. You're in too big of a hurry."

"I have shoes to sell; I need to be on my way."

"Then be on your way." The sheriff walked back to the desk and sat down. "I told you, you leave me your name and address, and I'll see that you get your bags if they show up.''

Annoyed, Barrett turned, about to leave, when the sheriff's voice stopped him. ''I wouldn't be doin' anything foolish, Mr. Digman. Here in Brittlefork, I'm the law, and I don't take lightly to a man disputin' that. You give me time, I'll find your horse.''

Barrett left the office a moment later, undaunted. The sheriff's thinly veiled threats didn't bother him. If Abigail McDougal was still in the area, he'd find her. He strode to the opposite side of the street and entered the livery stable. Swain came out of one of the stalls, smiling. ''Can I help you?''

''Do you have a carriage I might lease? I thought it was such a pleasant day that I'd take a ride into the countryside.''

''Sure do. A nice little one with brass fixtures. Got a nice black to pull it.''

''That should do nicely.''

''It'll be a fine rig for a pleasant ride. How long would you be needin' it?''

''Until dark, I'd imagine.''

''Sure thing. Take me a few minutes to harness 'er up.''

Barrett waited while the old man harnessed the rig. Leaning against a hitching rail, he studied the main street of Brittlefork, watching each female who walked by for signs of that vile woman in disguise.

''Here she is.''

Barrett paid him, then climbed into the rig. The old man had been right. It was a handsome outfit. It would have been perfect for an afternoon's drive, if that was what he'd intended.

Giving a whistle, he drove the rig down Main Street,

stopping at the café long enough to purchase a jar of lemonade.

Continuing on his way, he nodded amiably at passersby, nodding to the ladies who were hanging over the rail of the veranda above the bar.

"Hi sweetie," one particularly well-endowed redhead called.

Hershall tipped his hat graciously.

"Stop by and buy little ole Lola a drink tonight, darlin'!" a blonde's lilting voice invited as the carriage rolled past.

The sheriff had moved himself from behind his desk to the shade in front of the office. He sat with his chair leaned back against the wall, balanced on the back two legs, his feet propped up on the hitching rail.

Barrett nodded curtly as he passed.

For the remainder of the afternoon, Barrett drove the buggy up and down various roads and trails leading out of Brittlefork, looking for any sign of Abby. But he saw no one.

Hot and discouraged, he stopped toward dusk beneath a big shade tree and drank lemonade. His time was running out. If he didn't locate her soon, he had no other choice but to ride on, hoping he could remember enough about the contents of the messages to assist Smith.

The darker it grew, the more desperate he became. He widened his search, but each time he came up empty-handed. Several times he stopped and tied the horse to a tree to investigate the heavily wooded areas, searching caves, approaching several empty cabins, hoping to discover signs that she might have spent the night. But when it became so dark that he could no longer see, he knew she had defeated him.

The night was as black as pitch as he started back to

Brittlefork. He let the horse set his own pace while his mind reviewed the odd set of events that had taken place since he'd first seen the jail wagon with its strange cargo. A new, more disturbing thought occurred to him. What if the little fool had gotten herself killed? The Mc-Dougal sisters were a brave lot when together, but alone Abby would be prey to a lonely soldier who had been without the comforts of a woman for too long. He didn't know why he found the thought disagreeable, but he suddenly did.

By the time he returned the rig to the livery it was late, and he was hungry. He walked to the café, located a table, and ordered. As he drank a cup of coffee, he found himself listening to the talk surrounding him.

The café was busy tonight, filled with locals and travelers. Some were upset that the stage had been delayed. Others were laughing and commenting that the stage was late because it was so worn out that the driver's seat had come loose from the main body. Unfortunately, the driver had been on the seat at the time. His agility had just barely saved him from falling and being dragged to death behind a running team. Rumor had it, the stage would be delayed another day until a new seat could be constructed.

Barrett's attention was suddenly caught by a conversation between two men sitting at a table directly behind him.

"I don't think the South can last much longer, not after the whippin' they been takin' lately." The man lowered his voice. "You heard what happened in Sherman's raid a few weeks ago."

"I've heard the talk. Some say it'll be over before long, but talk's cheap, Will, just like blood, real cheap."

"I know, but they say Sherman's been whippin' it on those Yankees lately."

"Like I say, talk's cheap. There seems to be no end to the suffering. I seen enough war to last me a lifetime, and just because people say the South can't hold out much longer, don't make it so."

"Well, at least Lincoln's boy is servin' now."

Barrett knew that Robert Todd Lincoln, oldest son of the president, had divided his time between Harvard University and the nation's capitol and had never felt the impact of the 1863 Conscription Act. Young Robert had long been the target of widespread gossip and criticism for not serving his country, especially when Illinois was conspicuously eager to fill its quota of young, able-bodied men.

"Yeah," the man said, laughing mirthlessly. "He's servin' as official escort to commanders and notables, including his father. That's not quite the same as having your boy on the firing line, now is it?"

Barrett thought of Lincoln's political maneuvering. Whether it had been a patriotic gesture or a bid to stifle the growing criticism of his family, it was still unclear. The fact was he'd hired a substitute for himself in September of 1864. A young man by the name of John S. Staples had been willing to hire out to fight in the chief executive's place, so in October John had been escorted to the White House, where he'd shaken hands with Lincoln, and Lincoln had then been presented a framed official notice certifying that he had "put in a representative recruit." Later, the president had found out that the cost of his substitute was $750, an unusually high figure.

"No, but I hear his mother, Mary, couldn't bear the thought of losing the boy. You know the president and his wife lost their son Eddie when he was only six, then eleven-year-old Willie three years ago.''

Barrett had heard the rumors that Mrs. Lincoln had been so inconsolable after Willie's death that she'd taken to her bed for days whenever anyone had made mention of Robert entering the war.

Finally, in an act of desperation, Lincoln had penned a letter to Grant, a man whom he had made general-in-chief, asking if it would be possible ''without embarrassment to you or detriment to the service, to arrange for Robert Todd Lincoln to go into your military family with some nominal rank.''

Grant had complied with his president's wishes and had suggested that Robert, who had no military training or experience, should enter the army with the rank of captain, with the anticipation that he would be made an assistant adjutant general on the headquarters' staff.

''I know all about the president's troubles.'' The voice retained its affability, but there was a change of tone. ''Me and my Martha have already lost two boys, and a third is still fighting, so I find it hard to sympathize with Mary Todd Lincoln, especially since many of us feel this is her husband's war in the first place. What mother wants to lose her son?''

''None.'' The other man agreed. ''Not one mother, Will.''

Signaling for his check, Barrett finished the last of his coffee, then paid his bill, disturbed by the men's conversation and Abby's strange disappearance.

He stepped outside, absently drawing a cheroot from the inside pocket of his suit coat. Cupping the match against the slight breeze that had sprung up, he lit the cheroot, drawing deeply on the smoke as he mentally prepared himself for the worst. The way things looked, the sheriff wasn't going to find her—

His thoughts were interrupted as he felt a light tap on his shoulder. Turning, he found a young Quaker woman looking at him.

"Yes, ma'am?" His eyes suddenly narrowed when he recognized the intruder. "You!"

"Don't 'you' me, you filthy beast!"

His head snapped back and forth as she slapped him crisply across the cheeks with the leather folder. "How dare you lie to me! You conniving, no good, sneaky, low-down, lying, miserable excuse of a man!"

"*Me*, a liar?" Barrett hissed, glancing up and down the street to see if she was drawing attention. "That's like the pot calling the kettle black, isn't it, Sister McDougal?"

"Shut up!" She smacked him across the cheeks again. "Just shut up!"

"Quit slapping me with that pouch!"

"*Shut up!*" She whacked him again, hard.

Grabbing her wrists, Barrett pulled her into the alley for a final showdown. If she wanted war, she was going to get it!

Chapter 10

"You hit me with that pouch one more time—" Barrett grabbed for the leather, but she hit him again.

"Where have you been?"

"Wouldn't you like to know!"

Twisting free of his grasp, Abby glared back at him, rubbing her wrists. "You brute!"

Barrett stared at her plain gray dress, shawl, and matching bonnet with disgust. "What are you doing dressed like that? Have you no shame?" The drab attire was lightened by a sheer cap worn under her bonnet and a sheer white scarf folded about the throat.

"None," Abby spit back. "How did you think I was going to travel? Because of you, I burned my habit!"

He had never met a woman—or a man for that matter—with more heretical audacity! There appeared to be no limit to how far this woman would go to serve her own purpose. "First Catholic, now Quaker. If God doesn't strike you dead, I'll eat my hat."

"Which, by the way, would be doing us all a favor," she allowed as she eyed the silly bowler. She then snatched his spectacles off and peered through them, nodding her head irritably. "Just what I thought. These are nothing but clear glass!" Just another one of the props he'd used to defraud the innocent!

He snatched his glasses and put them back on, then leveled his gaze upon her accusingly. "You are, without a doubt, the most irritating woman I've ever met!"

"Well, well, well," she sneered, glad that she'd upset him. "Does my dress offend you? As you said, isn't that a little like the pot calling the kettle black? You're traipsing around the country posing as a shoe salesman, when in fact you're a *spy* for the Confederate Army!" She whacked him across the shoulders with the pouch.

Grabbing her hand, he stilled her attempts to flog him again. "What I am is none of your business!"

"You're a spy!"

"Keep your voice down." Barrett anxiously glanced at the entrance to the alley. "You'll have us both in jail! Give me those papers."

He tried to snatch the pouch out of her hand, but she held them over her head, out of his reach.

"Never."

"You'll give them to me, or I'll break your neck," he warned in the most ominous voice she'd ever heard him use.

"Just try it, and I'll kick you where you don't want to be kicked." Holding the packet behind her, she backed up against the building and planted her feet firmly.

"Give them to me." Barrett repeated.

"No. You're a miserable, lying fiend. You call me a thief, but you're a bigger one."

Their eyes locked obstinately.

"Give me those papers, Abigail."

"No." Those papers were going to make him take her to Mercy Flats, and he wasn't getting them!

"Keep your voice down."

"Why? Don't you want everyone to know who you are?" She raised her voice. "Don't you want everyone to know *who you really are, Mr. Digman?*"

Barrett grabbed for the packet, but Abby shoved his hand away. "Help, oh, someone please help me!" she yelled, planning to cause the biggest stink this town had ever witnessed.

Clamping his hand over her mouth, Barrett swore at her as they began to struggle. Abby stomped on his foot in an attempt to get him to free her mouth, but he only tightened his grasp on her arm as he tried to wrestle the pouch away from her.

"Let me go!"

"Give me that pouch!"

"I'll die first!"

"Don't tempt me," he grunted.

They scuffled, finally falling to the ground as they became locked in a stubborn duel. Screaming, she fought him, but he had suddenly developed the strength of Goliath. He had the leather packet almost in his fingers when she wriggled from beneath him.

Swearing, he caught her arm and jerked her back.

"See how you like this!" she grunted.

He quickly sidestepped her trouncing knee and flipped her around so that her back was to him. Trying to hold her was like trying to hold a sackful of furious cats. Legs and arms were going in all directions, nails scratching, feet clawing. He barely escaped the ferocity of her teeth on the back of his wrist as he fought to control her. When his hand brushed against her breast, she froze. The funniest feeling came over her. It was almost a pleasant diversion.

She suddenly screeched with fury and hurled herself at him, hating him for making her feel that way. Catching the full brunt of her weight, Barrett toppled to the ground, taking her with him. "Give up, McDougal. I'm gettin' those damn papers!"

"Never, never, never, never!"

The couple rolled around on the ground, unaware of the two men who'd come out of the saloon, heading down the alley now.

"Get off me!" she shouted.

"Not until you give me those papers."

"Get your finger out of my *eye*!"

"Get your foot out of my throat!"

As they rolled to their sides, both spotted the men at the same time, and Barrett's hand quickly prevented Abby from calling out.

"Don't you dare," he warned in her ear.

His head exploded in stars as she threw him a right hook, catching him in the nose. Blood spurted, and his hand came up to stem the flow as she belted him again.

"Help! Help me!" she screamed as she scrambled to her feet and started to run.

Barrett grabbed for her, snagging the hem of her skirt as her screams grew more frantic. "Help! Oh, please, someone help me!"

"Here now! What's going on here?" The sound of feet thundering down the alley drew closer as Barrett groaned and rolled to his side. How in the hell was he ever going to explain why a shoe salesman was wrestling with a Quaker woman?

"Oh, please, help me, sirs!" Abby cried. "This man is a beastly lunatic!"

Dragging a handkerchief from his pocket, Barrett brought it to his bleeding nose. He closed his eyes, waiting for the inquisition to begin.

"What's goin' on here? What do you think you're doin', mister?" The bigger of the two men grabbed Barrett by the scruff of his neck and roughly jerked him to his feet.

"Uh, just a little disagreement, gentlemen." Barrett forced a wheezy laugh, trying to make light of the incriminating circumstances. "Nothing serious, I can assure you. Her father doesn't approve of me, but I told her I wasn't thinking of marrying her father—"

He could hear Abby feigning a faint behind him.

The second man quickly stepped over to support her wilting frame. "Oh, thank thee, kind sir . . . it was so horrifying. . . . "

"Are you all right, ma'am?"

"I think so. I cannot thank thee enough for saving me."

"She is lying through her teeth," Barrett said tightly. "She—"

Before he could protest, a man had grabbed his arms and slammed him against the wall, cracking his skull.

As he tried to shake his head to clear the threat of unconsciousness, Barrett found himself flat on the ground with a knee planted firmly in the middle of his chest.

"Listen—she's *lying*. I can explain."

When his vision cleared, he found himself looking down the barrel of a Colt .44 pistol. He could hear the other man soothing Abby, who was standing with her hands folded and her eyes downcast.

"Are you sure you're all right, ma'am?"

"I—I think so."

"It's dangerous for a woman to be out after dark without a man's protection," he chided kindly.

"My mother is most ill, sir, and she needed medicine so badly that I ventured out on my own. But I had no idea that a man like this," she cast a jaded look in Barrett's direction, "was allowed to roam the streets at will." She dusted the dirt from her shirt, sniveling.

"Now, now. Don't cry. You're safe now."

"Oh, thank thee, sir." She smiled brightly. "Thou hast been most kind."

"What do you want us to do with this piece of dung, ma'am?" The man quickly realized his slip of the tongue. "Pardon my language, ma'am. That just slipped out."

"Now just a minute—" Barrett tried to lift his head, but it was smashed back to the ground with the leather sole of a boot.

Abby kept her head down, but her glance at Barrett was explicitly pointed. He stared back at her coldly as she calmly hid the leather pouch in the folds of her skirt. "Though my life is simple and I believe in peaceful ways, I cannot, in my heart, permit this man to roam freely where he might harm others." Her eyes hardened. "Take the miserable brute to jail."

Barrett caught his breath as his captor lifted the boot from his face, but immediately his breath was mashed back out of him as he was jerked to his feet and slammed against the wall of the building again.

"We'll make sure he remembers to leave gentle folk alone," one of the men declared. "He won't be bothering a woman again."

"Oh, I thank thee, sir, for coming to my rescue and for thy kindness. I will pray for thee."

Stepping closer to Barrett, her eyes locked with his. "And I will pray for thee, too. Thou needs it," she added sweetly.

"I'm going to hunt you down like a snake," Barrett growled. "And when I do, you're going to regret the day you ever met me, Abigail McDougal."

Turning back to her rescuers, Abby mobilized two fat tears to roll down her cheeks. "He speaks unkindly again."

The last Abby saw of Barrett were his feet skimming along the dirt as the two men dragged him from the alley toward the sheriff's office.

"Have a nice day, fool," she muttered, then turned and struck off for the hotel. She'd collected enough money as a beggar to treat herself. And now that Hershall E. Digman, or whoever he was, was out of her hair, she planned to take full advantage of her good fortune.

When she entered the hotel lobby, she met the clerk's curious look with the sweetest smile she had.

"I'd like a nice room, please. A front one, if possible. And could thee arrange to have hot water for a bath brought to my room by six tomorrow morning?"

"Certainly, ma'am." He turned the register around toward her. "Just sign here."

Abby smiled, accepting the pen. "Lovely day, was it not?"

"Yes, it's been right pleasant."

Bringing the pen to her chin, she thought for a moment, then in a flourishing hand wrote Prudence Penn.

She handed the pen back to the clerk and waited for the key.

The clerk read her signature and scratched his head. "Penn, huh?"

"Yes. My father is a direct descendant of William Penn, the first man to establish a religious colony in Pennsylvania in 1682."

"Is that a fact?" The clerk looked adequately impressed. "That Penn, huh? That's real interestin'." If that didn't beat all. It wasn't every day that the hotel had such a notable guest.

Reaching for the key, Abby warned him firmly, "Please, thou must treat me as thou would any other."

The clerk watched her walk away, smiling fondly. He had to hand it to them Quakers. They were real humble people, all right. Real humble.

Chapter 11

"Digman! Roust yourself."

Barrett sat up, swinging his legs off the cot. The sheriff stood outside the cell, looking through the bars at him.

The key slid into the lock, and a moment later the cell doors swung open. "Ten dollars and you can go."

"Ten dollars!" The fine seemed excessive to Barrett, even if it was for assaulting a Quaker woman.

"Any man who'd abuse a woman, and a God-fearin' Quaker woman at that, is lower than a rat's ass in my opinion. But I can't hold you longer than twelve hours," the sheriff conceded, "or I would."

Wincing, Barrett reached for his suit jacket, trying to disregard his splitting headache.

"Men in Brittlefork don't pick on defenseless women," the sheriff went on, "or aren't you aware of that, Mr. Digman?"

"I know—"

"I don't want to hear it."

Barrett walked out of the cell, pulling on his coat.

"Them Quakers are peace-lovin' people, or don't you know that?"

"I do know—"

"I don't want to hear it!"

Barrett realized that it was useless to argue with him. He'd tried for over five hours to convince him that the "Quaker" woman was the one who'd stolen his horse, but the sheriff had just stared at him, positive that he'd gone loco.

In short, Abigail McDougal had him right where she wanted him: in one hell of a mess.

"That fine is highway robbery," Barrett grumbled as he followed the sheriff to his desk. Bending forward, he tried to brush the wrinkles out of his seersucker trousers. "The whole incident is a misunderstanding—"

"I don't want to hear it."

The sheriff unlocked the safe as Barrett stepped to the mirror to adjust his bowler. The sheriff watched from the corner of his eye, thinking the big sissy should be ashamed of himself.

Handing Barrett his personal belongings, the sheriff started in on him again. "Why a man would want to hurt a woman just don't make any sense. Wrestling her to the ground like she was some big old man or something. We just don't act that way here in Brittlefork, Digman."

"I understand, but I'm trying to tell you that she's the woman—"

"I don't want to hear it! Now I want you out of town by noon, you understand?"

"Perfectly." Counting out ten coins, Barrett paid the fine. "I still think this assessment is highway robbery."

"I could hang you, if that'd suit you better."

Coming out of the jail a moment later, Barrett

glanced up and down the street. With his luck, the damned woman had disappeared again.

Well, she could run as long and as hard as she liked, but when he found her—and he would, if it took him the rest of his life—she was as good as dead.

Because of her, his credibility in Brittlefork was ruined. By noon everyone in town would have heard how Hershall Digman, the shoe salesman from Des Moines, had attacked a young Quaker woman and wrestled her to the ground "like a big old man or something." No one was going to believe that she had lied about his attacking her. It was hard enough for him to believe.

Not a man in town would be willing to help him now. In fact, he considered himself damned lucky that he hadn't been ridden out of town on a rail.

He leaned against a post, reaching into his pocket for a smoke. Yessir, she had him in one fine mess. She'd stolen his horse; so now he was trying to spy for the South while riding a horse clearly marked with an army brand. The only clothes he had were the ones on his back, and for him to continue to pose as a shoe salesman in Brittlefork would be about as worthless as teats on a stallion.

He'd spent his last dollar on the fine, and here it was seven o'clock in the morning, and he didn't have the slightest idea where to go. And to top it off, the McDougal woman still had his papers.

It was hard to believe how simple his life had been a short forty-eight hours ago.

He glanced up, match in hand, as the door to the jail opened. The sheriff walked out, carrying his rifle.

"Thought I told you to move on, Digman."

"I'm going. I just—"

"I don't want to hear it." The sheriff raised the gun and began firing at Barrett's feet as he sprang off the porch and started through the center of town in a dead run.

Dodging bullets, Barrett danced his way to the city limits, vowing that he would get even with Abigail McDougal if it killed him!

Coming awake slowly, Abby stretched herself, thoroughly enjoying the luxury of having slept between clean sheets for the first time in weeks.

Outside her window, birds were chirping and the sun was shining brightly. It was going to be a glorious day!

Languidly stretching again, she listened to the sounds of Brittlefork coming to life as a balmy breeze stirred the lacy curtain at the window. The mouth-watering aroma of bacon frying came to her as the scent drifted tantalizingly through the open window.

Rolling lazily onto her side, she laughed as she remembered the look on Hershall's face when he'd been hauled off to jail last night. If he was the best the South had going for it, no wonder it was losing the war. Her mind wandered, and she idly wondered if his name really was Hershall Digman or if he'd lied about that, too.

A tap sounded at the door, and she groaned sluggishly. "Who is it?"

A woman's voice answered. "The maid, with your bath, ma'am."

"Just a minute." She pulled herself out of bed, wrapped the blanket around herself, and padded barefoot to the door. Opening the door just a crack, she found the maid with two large buckets of steaming water sitting on the floor beside her.

"Hot water for your bath, ma'am."

"Yes, come in."

Abby opened the door wider and waited as two young boys carried in a copper tub and set it in the middle of the floor. For the next several minutes the boys worked to fill the tub with the buckets of steaming water.

As they left the room, the maid turned back to Abby and curtsied. "If you be needin' anything more, just pull the cord above your bed."

"Thank you. Have you any word about the stage?"

"No, ma'am, nothing at all."

"You will notify me when it arrives?"

The young girl curtsied again. "Yes, ma'am."

A moment later the door closed, and Abby ran to the tub. Closing her eyes, she sighed in ecstasy as her fingers dipped into the warm water. A real bath. She could hardly wait to sink into the mound of steaming bubbles.

An hour later she was still leisurely soaping herself, humming beneath her breath. It could be hours or days before the stage arrived, so she felt no pressing need to hurry. Ducking her head beneath the water, she rinsed the last of the soap out of her hair. She had nearly forgotten how good it felt to be so wondrously clean.

As she toweled dry, she said a prayer of gratitude. The citizens of Brittlefork had been uncommonly generous to the "blind beggar" sitting in front of the sheriff's office. She snickered. Even Hershall had been most kind. Before she'd known it, she'd had enough coins to pay for a stage ticket, a few necessities at the mercantile, board and bath, and enough left over to buy herself the delicious ham and egg breakfast she was about to enjoy.

If, by any stroke of luck, the stage came through today, she'd hop on it and get well away from any threat of Hershall E. Digman by tonight. Besides, he might stay in jail for weeks. She hoped so. Smiling, she dusted herself lavishly with the scented powder she'd purchased by her financial windfall. In a few days, she'd be back in Mercy Flats, and all this unpleasantness would be behind her.

She reached for her new hairbrush and absently drew it through the thick, wet tangles in her hair. Her eyes fell upon the plain gray dress lying on the floor where she'd peeled out of it last night. She'd just bet that the lady who owned the garment would be surprised to find it missing from her wash line this morning.

The dress was a little big for her, but it didn't matter. She was used to making do. Anne-Marie had always counted that as one of her sister's strong points—making do. But she did wish that the dress was clean. If the stage failed to come by noon, she'd have it washed and ironed, so it wouldn't feel so stiff and sticky over her new muslin undergarments, which she had also purchased with her tidy little profit.

The door to her room was suddenly kicked open.

She whirled, the brush clattering to the floor. Giving a gasp of astonishment, she shrieked as she recognized the intruder. "Hershall Digman! You get out of here!"

Barrett leveled his finger at her, his eyes pulsating with outrage. "I am going to murder you," he said succinctly. So succinctly that her heart began to pump like a steam locomotive.

Gathering the towel tighter to her bare breasts, she started easing backward toward the bed. Hershall didn't look like himself this morning. His nostrils were flaring, and his eyes were glazed like they belonged to a wild animal.

"I am going to personally strangle you with my bare hands," he snarled. "I'm going to string you up by your heels and slit your gullet like a Christmas turkey."

"You wouldn't dare." *He wouldn't dare—would he? He doesn't even have a gun—does he?* Her face drained, leaving two red spots on her ivory cheeks.

"My dear lady, where you're concerned, I will dare *anything*," he lashed out. He'd had to run out of town like a damned hare to escape with his life, and she was going to pay for his humiliation. Oh, she was going to pay.

Abby noticed the clothes that he was wearing and snorted with contempt. Now *he* was dressed like a Quaker. How dare he copy her disguise!

"Where did you get those clothes?" she snapped.

"Stole them off a clothesline."

"You thief."

"Ha!"

Abby was puzzled. This was Hershall all right, yet there was something different about him this morning. The silly little bowler was gone, and so was the seersucker suit. He was no longer wearing the wire spectacles, and the spats had been replaced by plain, but highly polished, brown boots.

Shock and anger lit her eyes as she stared at his drab, collarless suit and broad-brimmed hat. Though he was only a few inches taller than she, the new Hershall exuded a confidence that the old Hershall could never have pulled off. The soft, well-defined lips that were smiling back at her in a twisted snarl were downright attractive.

She had thought she'd detected something different about him while she'd been masquerading as the beggar in front of the sheriff's office yesterday, but until this moment she hadn't tried to fathom the change. Now it hit her. It was his commanding air and his wicked good looks. His shoulders were broad, his hips slim, and the play of muscles rippling through his thighs quickened her pulse until she felt positively silly. And his hair. She was speechless as she stared at the soft brown waves that fell to his shirt collar. Hershall had transformed himself into a devilishly handsome man.

Coming to her senses, Abby sprang forward, hoping to slam the door in his face, but Barrett's newfound forceful personality was no match for her.

Shoving her aside, he stepped into the room, his eyes brazenly taking in her nearly naked state. His pulse suddenly accelerated, and a jolt of desire hit him. It had been months since he'd been with a woman. His eyes skimmed her slim wild beauty, and he wondered if the events of the past few hours had sent him over the edge. He suddenly wanted her. Wanted her—the way a man wants a woman, not the way a half-crazed animal would want to strangle a she-devil! His eyes refused to leave her ripe, young body. Drops of water dotted her breasts, arousing in him the craziest urge to reach out and disperse the bubbles with his fingertips.

Lifting her chin a notch, she met his gaze defiantly. "Get out of here before I scream."

"Scream all you want." He closed the door and turned the key in the lock. "You try to punish me again," his eyes arrogantly roamed over her, deliberately singling out the provocative swell of her breasts, "and this time I guarantee, lady, I'll deserve it."

For the first time since she'd met him, he frightened her. She had never considered him dangerous, but now she wasn't so sure. He had a hungry look in his eyes, one that warned of another elementary power, yet to be released.

She drew a quick deep breath and started to scream, but he clamped his hand over her mouth. "I'm warning you. You make one sound, and I'm not responsible for what I'll do."

When a man had to crawl back into town on his damned belly, it put him in a bad mood.

"Get out!" Her words were muffled, but he understood her meaning.

"Not this time, sweetheart."

They began to struggle, falling back onto the bed, as Abby fought to free herself from his hold.

"You're not getting away this time, McDougal." Barrett threw his leg across hers, pinning her to the mattress. "Where are those *papers*?"

"Muummmmph!"

"I want those papers!"

She tore his hand away from her mouth and spat in his face.

"Damn it!" He wiped the spittle away, incensed.

"How dare you use that kind of language in my presence!" She slapped him hard, then clawed her nails down the length of his cleanly shaven face before he trapped her wrists.

"Let me go!"

"You're not going anywhere until I have those papers." His grip tightened until she was writhing with pain. "Where are they?"

"I won't tell you!"

"You will, or I'll break your pretty little neck."

"I'll call for the sheriff, and he'll throw you in jail again!"

He toughened the grip on her arm, ignoring her threats. "That only works once. Now give me the papers before I hurt you."

"You're already hurting me!"

"I'll hurt you worse," he threatened.

"All right," she finally grunted. "I'll get you the stupid papers, then I don't want to ever see you again!"

"It will be my pleasure—oh, no you don't," he quickly blocked her effort to roll from beneath him. "I'm not that stupid. Tell me where the papers are, and I'll get them."

"No. I'll get them. They're not in the room."

"Then forget it. The minute I turn you loose, you'll run out on me again. I'll get them." He wouldn't trust her to walk across the room, let alone leave it.

It was clearly a standoff. Abby knew that if she told him where the papers were, he could easily take her money and stage ticket, and then she would be detained another whole day trying to regain financial solvency.

Her lips firmed with stubbornness. "You're *not* going to get them," she said.

"You will either give me those papers, or I'm going to march your little fanny straight over to the sheriff's office and convince him, at gunpoint, if necessary, that if he'll wire San Antonio, he'll find out that your real name is Abigail McDougal, and that you and your sisters are wanted for running con games."

"He wouldn't believe you."

"Somebody's bound to remember three beautiful nuns. What do you think, Abigail?"

Drawing his hand through her hair, he jerked her head off the pillow. His mouth was only inches from hers now, and she felt her strength draining. She'd never been this close to a man before. She'd like to pretend that she hated the way he made her feel, but she couldn't. She almost welcomed the havoc he was wreaking inside her body.

"Go ahead, and I'll tell the sheriff that you're a Confederate spy. You'll be shot before sundown." Though she'd never personally witnessed a man's execution, she would stick around to watch this one.

Forcing himself to be civil, Barrett checked his anger. They were getting nowhere. He'd try reasoning with her. He figured if that didn't work, then he would shoot her. At this point, he'd cherish the latter but settle for a compromise.

"All right. Look, I have to get those papers to

Shreveport by the end of the week. I know you don't
give a damn whether the North or the South wins this
war, but it matters to me, and to thousands of men who
are right this minute giving their lives for something
that you and your sisters take for granted—freedom.
Freedom, lady, to go and do and be what you want.
Not everyone has it.''

The logic in his tone and the grave set of his features
reaffirmed how important the papers were to him. He
wasn't just angry that she had outsmarted him; he was
actually desperate to get those papers back. She wasn't
immune to his logic, nor was she immune to the horrors
of war. She'd seen women sobbing when their men had
marched off to fight, and she'd heard babies crying for
their fathers. War was ugly, but she hadn't started it,
and there wasn't anything she could do to stop it.

''I don't like the war any more than you do. And I
would give you your old papers, but they're my ticket
back to Mercy Flats.''

He snorted. ''How are those papers going to get you
back to Mercy Flats? You didn't know they existed until
twenty-four hours ago.''

''Oh, but I do now, don't I? And if I refuse to give
them to you, then you'll have to take me back to Mercy
Flats.'' Abby didn't like being on her own. The world
was a whole lot bigger—and darker—than she'd realized. And she wasn't accustomed to traveling without
her sisters; so until she could get back to Amelia and
Anne-Marie, Hershall would have to do. She didn't like
him, but he was a man, and he could get her back to
the cemetery safely.

''Abby,'' Barrett argued wearily, ''I can't take you to
Mercy Flats. I work for a man who has thousands of
men under his command. Those men are facing imminent death, unless I get those papers to Smith by the

end of the week. It doesn't matter that he's a Confederate commander. It would be the same if he were a Union soldier. Getting those papers to Shreveport could make the difference in getting this war over. And I don't know a person—North or South—who doesn't want that to happen.''

"I can't give you the papers.''

Barrett closed his eyes. "Why not?''

"Because if I give you the papers, you'll leave me here.''

"I won't leave you here. I told you I'd see that you get back to your sisters, and I will.''

"I don't believe you." How could she? He was mad enough to string her up by her heels—like a turkey, he'd said—so if she gave him the papers, that would be the last she'd see of him. After all, he'd lied about being a shoe salesman; why should she believe he would suddenly keep his word about taking her back to Mercy Flats?

"Damn it, woman!" Barrett exploded. "Can't you get it through your head? I don't have the time to take you anywhere! I've wasted too much time with you as it is.''

"See! It's exactly as I thought. You'd be nice to me until you got those papers, then you'd be gone!''

"Give me those papers!''

"No.''

Scrambling from beneath him, she rolled off the bed. Marching to the other side of the room, she began pulling on her clothes.

"Where's my horse?''

"I won't tell you.''

He swore again, but she ignored him. "The way I see it, we're stuck with each other, Mr. Digman, until we can figure out a way to get rid of each other.''

Barrett buried his face in the pillow in frustration. Drawing a breath of resignation he finally lifted his head and yielded quietly, "All right."

Abby frowned, waiting for him to go on. When he didn't, she prompted hesitantly. "All right, what?"

"All right, we're stuck with each other. Since I'm going to Shreveport, come hell or high water, and since you refuse to give me the papers, it looks like you're going with me."

"Only if you agree to take me to Mercy Flats once the papers have been delivered." Abby didn't like this arrangement, but he left her little recourse. It was obvious that he was as mean and stubborn as she.

"All right, but as God is my witness, I'm agreeing to this only because of my duty to my country."

"Sure, sure," Abby muttered, disgruntled. She understood that; he didn't have to rub it in. "But the papers stay with me until we reach Shreveport."

"That isn't—"

"It's that way, or not at all."

"All right. You keep the papers—but make damn sure that no one else sees them."

"We'll travel as man and wife," Abby decided. "No one will be likely to ask a Quaker couple to show a pass."

"We'd better hope they don't."

Abby hurriedly began stuffing personal articles into her newly purchased reticule.

"We'll need money," Barrett said.

"I have money."

Sitting up on the side of the bed, he looked at her. "How did you get money?"

She turned, smiling. "I earned it. Oh, by the way, Digman. Don't get any funny ideas about us posing as man and wife. If you so much as look at me crooked—"

"Good Lord. I'd sooner bed a porcupine, if that's what you're getting at."

She wrapped her hair into a coil at the base of her neck and jabbed a pin through it. "The feeling is mutual. Oh, one more thing, is your name really Hershall Digman?" Lord, she hoped not.

Standing, Barrett bowed to her mockingly. "Captain Barrett Drake of the United States Confederate Army."

"Well, Captain Drake," Abby jerked the strings on her bonnet snugly, "you'd better keep your hands to yourself if you want to live to make major."

He stared back at her dispassionately. "And you're to do the same, Miss McDougal."

Well, honestly, Abby seethed as she followed him out the doorway, does his bloated male ego think she'd actually *want* someone like him?

Chapter 12

The train clattered monotonously along the tracks as Abby squirmed again, trying to get comfortable.

"Sit still," Barrett chastised from the corner of his mouth, when she seemed intent on disturbing everyone sitting around them.

The train was crowded this morning. The only place Abby and Barrett could find to sit was next to a heavy-set woman by the name of Wanila Knob, who talked a mile a minute.

Elmer Beemocker sat opposite them. Elmer sold women's undergarments. The drummer seemed determined to discuss in great detail the merits of the variety of corsets he sold.

Wanila, who could have used a corset, was traveling to meet her husband, who had been injured during a battle and was hospitalized in Louisiana. She had talked incessantly about the six children she'd left at home and the injustices of the war into which her husband had been drawn, each comment accompanied by dramatic sniffs and great sighs of misery. Her mission,

Barrett and Abby were told many times, was not only to visit her husband, but to persuade his commanding officer to let him return to his family.

By the glossy sheen in Barrett's eyes, Abby could see that he was about to perish from boredom.

Squirming again, Abby switched her bottom sideways, causing Barrett to turn again, frowning. "Will you sit still?"

"I don't have any room," she complained. She glanced at Wanila's generous bulk hanging over the seat, and her lips puffed resentfully.

"Don't say it," Barrett warned.

She glared back at him, wondering how he could read minds.

"Move over," she said crossly. "It's hot enough to fry an egg in this stuffy old rail car."

"Forget it. I'm as familiar with this seat as I intend to get."

Abby gritted her teeth, trying to make the best of a bad situation. She'd wanted to ride horseback to Shreveport, but Barrett had insisted that they go by train to make up for the time she'd squandered.

She wiggled edgily, aware of the infant in the seat behind them. The child was fussy and had bawled for hours.

I don't blame you, baby, Abby thought. *I'd cry, too.* It was so hot she could hardly breathe. No one dared open a window because of the black soot and smoke belching from the engine smokestack three cars ahead. But even soot would be preferable to the smoke rolling from the cigars of the two men sitting across the aisle, deeply engrossed in a conversation about buffaloes.

Pulling a handkerchief from her purse, she fanned herself. She would give everything she owned to be able to open the two top buttons of her high-necked dress. Sweat was trickling down her sides and between her breasts, and she pressed the cloth against her throat to absorb the dampness.

"If my Darnell don't get to come home, I don't know what me and the children will do," Wanila bemoaned for what Abby was sure was the tenth time. Abby could see her studying her from the corner of her eye. "Your kind don't believe in war, do you?"

Lifting her chin, Abby dabbed the sweat from her neck. "The Friends of Society believe that war is contrary to the life and teaching of Jesus," she murmured.

"You call yourselves 'Friends of Society'? Why is that? I thought you was Quakers."

"Quaker is but another name. We are called Friends, because that is our philosophy. We believe there is good in everyone. If thou believe in living day by day with family, neighbors, and everyone thou meet, thou art a friend, is that not correct?"

Wanila shifted, jamming Abby more solidly against Barrett. "Then why call yourselves Quakers?"

Exchanging a pained glance with Barrett, Abby continued, "The name was acquired when our founder, George Fox, was arrested and put in stocks. When the judge was about to send him to the Derby jail for six months, Friend Fox became defiant and shouted, '*Thou* should quake at the name of the Lord!' The judge roared, 'Quake! Thou, sir, are the quaker!' Then the crowd chanted, 'Quaker, Quaker.' " Abby mopped at her chin again. "So that is why we are called Quakers."

"You're makin' that up," Barrett hissed.

"I am not!" she hissed back.

Anne-Marie had made her study all religions in case it should come in handy, like right now, for instance.

The train suddenly lurched, throwing the passengers in the car violently forward.

Abby's nails clawed Barrett's leg as she grabbed on to him to keep from being thrown to the floor. Women and children screamed over the high-pitched, squealing brakes. Men cursed and demanded to know in angry voices what was going on.

The passengers' necks were whipped forward, then jerked painfully backward as the train slid to an ear-splitting, spark-shooting, screeching halt.

Silence reigned as each took stock to discover if anything was broken, then bedlam broke out. Men were cursing; children were crying as they picked themselves up off the floor; and women started babbling in confusion.

The conductor raced down the aisle toward the door, calling for everyone to remain calm.

Abby met Barrett's anxious look. Were they being stopped for inspection of their travel papers? If so, they were in trouble again.

"Oh, Lord help us! We're going to be scalped!" Wanila moaned.

Straining to see over the woman's ample bosom, Abby tried to catch a glimpse out of the window. "What is it? Indians? I can't see anything!"

The door to the rail car burst open, and two masked gunmen entered, their six-shooters leveled on the passengers.

"Everybody sit real quiet like, and nobody gets hurt," the one in front ordered.

Abby felt Barrett tense beside her.

"What do we do now?" she whispered.

"Whatever he says," Barrett acknowledged quietly. For the first time since they'd boarded, the travelers in the car fell silent.

The men were an intimidating lot. The leader's clothes were filthy, his hat pulled low over his eyes, a handkerchief covering the lower half of his face. The second one looked equally nasty, his eyes cold and menacing. Abby felt a quiver of fear on her insides, and she scooted closer to Barrett.

The men moved down the aisle, their eyes sweeping through the car, evaluating each passenger. The barrels of their guns moved over the travelers threateningly.

Pausing in front of Barrett, the leader motioned for him to step into the aisle. "You there. You and your wife step out here."

"My wife and I mean thee no harm," Barrett said.

"Git out here!"

"Now just a minute—" Abby blurted.

Barrett laid his hand warningly on her arm. "I pray thee, gentlemen, we mean thee no harm."

The barrel of the gun centered on Barrett's temple. "Git out of that seat, mister. Right now."

Barrett and Abby sprang to their feet simultaneously, crushing both of Elmer Beemocker's feet in their haste to comply.

Wide-eyed, Wanila watched, stuffing her handkerchief deeper into her mouth to keep from screaming.

Remaining calm, Barrett pulled Abby in front of him. She felt his hand resting in the middle of her back as the two men started herding them down the aisle.

"Where are the papers?" Barrett whispered.

"I have them," she whispered back.

"Well hidden?"

"You don't see them, do you?"

"Make certain they don't leave your hands," he warned.

Well, sure, Barrett, she thought irritably, *I'll fist fight both of them if they try anything.*

"Where do you think they're taking us?" she whispered.

"I have no idea."

"Don't you find this odd?"

He glanced over his shoulder at her, and Abby blushed. Of course he didn't find it normal.

She found his hand resting in the center of her back comforting as they marched toward the back of the train. A hundred thoughts raced through her mind. Who were these men? Why did they choose Barrett and her? Surely they looked like the least-threatening couple on the train. And if they did kill her, what about Anne-Marie and Amy? They would never know what happened. She blinked back welling tears. This was awful.

As they stepped out onto the platform, they saw a third masked man, waiting astride his horse and holding the reins to four others.

"You and your woman mount up," the leader told Barrett.

Abby glanced up at Barrett, and he nodded, silently urging her to comply. Lifting her skirt slightly, she made her way slowly down the steps.

Barrett boosted her into the saddle, then mounted behind. "Just stay calm, and do what they say," he said again.

The train was already moving. Abby could see Wanila's face pressed to the window, gawking at them. Abby tried to take comfort in the knowledge that once the train reached the station, at least someone would know they had been taken captive, not that it would do them any good. No one knew who they were. They'd introduced themselves as Mr. and Mrs. Levi

Howard, a Quaker couple on their way back home from visiting family in Texas.

The three men pulled their masks down as they kicked their horses into a gallop. The leader was a despicable-looking animal, lean and hungry in appearance. His brown hair was long and shaggy, his eyes black and unreadable.

The other two men were similar in appearance, and Abby wondered if they were brothers, or if they looked alike because they all were dirty and had the same belligerent manner. Everything about the men was worn and faded, but their gear was neat, and their horses showed good care. Still, their faces lent no clue as to who they were or why they'd taken her and Barrett captive, nor did it help allay her fears of what they planned to do to them.

The party rode hard for over an hour. The outlaws, one riding ahead, two behind, kept quiet. The men's grim expressions revealed nothing as they preserved a strained silence.

When Barrett would allow the horse to fall back, one of the men would move up alongside them, his dark look warning Barrett to keep pace.

During a brief rest stop, Barrett was allowed to escort Abby into the underbrush under the pretext of her needing privacy, but the men's guns remained trained on them.

"What could they possibly want with us?" Abby agonized as they disappeared into the bushes.

"I don't know, but we'll find out soon enough."

"You don't think they know who you are—"

"No."

Abby shivered.

"Abby, you have to keep those papers hidden," he

warned. Barrett would do all he could to protect her, but the situation could easily get out of hand.

Loosening the first three buttons on her dress, she removed the leather packet, then lifted her skirt and hurriedly shoved the packet behind the waistband of her muslin drawers.

"Is this safe enough?"

Barrett's features sobered. "I don't like putting you in danger like this. Give me the papers—"

"No!"

Taking her by the shoulders, he faced her, his eyes grave now. "Now listen to me closely. When we get to where they're taking us, I'll distract them long enough for you to get away. Take one of the horses and ride like hell. It shouldn't take more than a couple of days for you to reach Shreveport. Go directly to Kirby Smith—no one else. Ask around. Someone will show you where he's camped. Do you understand?"

Abby nodded, for the first time fully aware of the danger they were facing.

"Can I trust you to do this, Abby?" The gravity in his eyes once again told her how important it was that the papers reach their destination.

As she nodded, her pulse hammered in her throat. She hoped that it didn't come to that, but if it did, she'd get the papers to Smith—one way or another.

"You two. Get out here!" one of the outlaws shouted.

"Barrett." It was the first time she had called him by his given name, and strangely enough, he liked the sound of it.

"Yes?"

"If it works out the other way—you know, if you should get away and I don't, will you tell my sisters—" Abby broke off, unable to face the prospect of never seeing Amelia or Anne-Marie again. "Will you make sure my sisters know what happened to me?"

Barrett took her hand and held it for a moment. Their eyes met, and there was no animosity this time, just a mutual need to offer each other comfort. "That's not going to happen."

"I know, but if it should—"

He squeezed her hand reassuringly. "If it does, I'll personally see that your sisters know."

With a small smile, she bit her lip to keep it from quivering as they walked from behind the bushes and got back on the horse.

It was late afternoon before the riders stopped again. When Abby saw the small deserted-looking shack, she glanced at Barrett apprehensively. There wasn't a sign of life anywhere. They had ridden for hours and not seen another soul.

The leader reined in and quickly dismounted. The other two men quickly followed suit, gesturing for Barrett and Abby to do the same.

The leader bounded up the set of rickety steps, kicked the cabin door open, and entered. The two other men walked behind Barrett and Abby, nudging them up the steps and into the cabin with the barrels of their guns.

As Abby's eyes adjusted to the cabin's interior, she saw that it was little more than a pig squalor.

Inside the shack was an incredibly dingy room containing a table and chairs, a broken cabinet, and a crude fireplace fashioned against the south wall. Sitting beside the fireplace was a wooden baby crib, and Abby could see an infant sleeping there that looked to be no more than a year old.

To the left was a closed door, which Abby assumed was a bedroom.

The leader strode to the closed door and opened it a crack, peering inside the dim interior.

"Hattie Mae?"

The tenderness that suddenly lit his voice shocked Abby.

"Lute? Lute, is that you?" The woman's voice sounded very weak.

Abby glanced at Barrett, whose face remained expressionless.

"It's me, baby. I got us some help."

Lute turned, his black eyes pinning Abby. "You've gotta help my woman."

Leaning forward, Abby tried to see around him into the bedroom. "What's wrong with her?"

"She's been sickly the past few days. Been coughin' real hard. The baby's startin' to come, and it ain't time yet."

Abby's eyes moved to the child sleeping peacefully in the crib, then back to Lute quizzically.

"The new baby," Lute said shortly. "It ain't supposed to get here for another three months, but it's comin' anyways."

Abby wilted with relief. "Is that why you brought us here?" Lute, assuming that she was a Quaker, must have reasoned that she would know about these things. Her initial relief was immediately overcome by gripping fear. She couldn't tell him she wasn't a Quaker without explaining why she and Barrett were dressed as such.

She glanced at Barrett as she debated whether or not to tell on him. If she told this nasty-looking man that Barrett was a spy, then he could help her get back to Mercy Flats.

She looked at Barrett, then back to the nasty-looking man. No, it wouldn't be worth it. "Listen, I don't know anything about delivering a baby," she told him.

Lute's hand moved to his holster, and his eyes narrowed. "You're lyin'."

"No, I'm not lying," Abby promised. "I really don't know anything about delivering babies. I don't know anything about babies at all."

Lute didn't believe her. "You're a woman, ain't ya?"

"Yes, but I've never had a baby, and I've never even been around anyone who's had a baby," she assured him.

Calmly stepping behind Barrett, Lute laid the gun barrel at the base of his neck. "Your man don't have much to say, but I'd shore bet you wouldn't want to have to bury him afore you learned something, now would you, Quaker woman?"

Barrett looked at Abby helplessly as Lute pressed the gun tighter against his neck.

Meeting his distraught glance, she bowed hesitantly. "What do you want me to do?"

"I don't rightly know—that'll be for you to decide." Lute tapped the gun prophetically against Barrett's temple.

She could let him shoot Barrett. She could just stand here and let him blow Drake's head clean off. It'd pay him back for being so mean to her.

"Well, let me think." She started to pace, prolonging Barrett's agony. She could at *least* do that.

"You're wasting time, Quaker woman."

Abby racked her brain. She didn't know a thing about delivering babies, not even enough to pretend that she did.

"Abigail, you could pray for Hattie Mae," Barrett

prodded between clenched teeth, when he saw her face was a total blank.

"Yes, I could pray for Hattie Mae," she offered quickly. "I could pray real hard."

Lute nodded. "Whatever you need to do. Just so's nothing bad happens to Hattie Mae."

"Lute!"

Hattie Mae's agonized screams shattered the silence, and Lute shoved Barrett toward the doorway.

Dragging her feet, Abby entered the dim bedroom. She'd never been around babies, much less helped bring one into the world. The sisters at the mission had meticulously avoided telling her anything about "birthing babies." Lute believed that a Quaker wife would have to know something about midwifery, but since Abby wasn't a Quaker, she was as ignorant as a rock about such things. Anything could happen to Hattie Mae, and if the worst did happen, Lute would hold her responsible.

She heard Lute's ominous voice affirming her pessimism from behind her. "Just so's you don't get any funny notions, I'll keep your man with me. If anythin' happens to Hattie Mae, or th' baby—"

He didn't need to finish. Abby clearly understood what would happen. *God help us all*, she thought as she walked toward the woman writhing on the bed. If everyone was expecting her to save Hattie Mae, they were all in for a big disappointment.

"Sit." Lute gestured for Barrett to take a chair at the kitchen table. "Spook, you and Rolly might jest as well make yoreselves comfortable," he told his two friends. "This here could take awhiles."

The two men took off their hats and hung them on a peg beside the cook stove. They drew two more chairs up to the table and sat down to wait as Lute took a bottle of cheap whiskey out of the cabinet and set the bottle in the middle of the table.

Rolly reached inside his coat pocket, dug out a pack of cards, and began shuffling the deck, while Spook lit the lamp and turned up the wick.

It wasn't long before the three men were absorbed in a game of cutthroat.

Barrett kept noticing an odd-sounding thump at the front door. When the thump persisted, Lute, still sorting his hand, pushed back from the table and went to see about it.

Opening the door, he allowed a skinny, liver-colored hound to sidle into the room. The dog yawned widely, then dropped in front of the fireplace and shut its eyes.

"Hattie Mae don't like for the dog to be in the house," Spook reminded Lute.

"What Hattie Mae don't know ain't gonna hurt her," Lute mused absently. He poured three glasses of whiskey, then glanced questionably at Barrett. "Don't guess you people drink?"

Barrett shook his head.

"Didn't figure so."

Barrett's gaze focused on the door to the bedroom as the three men played a couple of hands. There was no sign of Abby, and he wondered what she was doing.

It became apparent that the men played poker together often. The cards were dispensed about as fast as the drinks from the bottle of whiskey.

"Got a run a' luck there, Rolly," Lute sat back, taking a swig from his glass as Hattie Mae's brother dragged in another pot. Tossing down the last of the liquor, he poured some more.

"Lady Luck always did like me," Rolly bragged.

"A mite too well," Spook muttered. His highest card the last two hands had been a ten.

Lute raised his brows. "You complainin'?"

"Naw, just deal the cards." Spook knew when Lute got all liquored up, he riled real easy. If it weren't for the fact Hattie was all the family he had, he wouldn't even come around.

Lute glanced toward the bedroom, where everything was quiet now. "Wonder what's going on in there?"

"Don't know. Hattie ain't screaming no more," Rolly noted optimistically.

"Yeah, noticed that."

The dog lifted his head, giving a wide, whiny yawn.

"You'd better git that dog outta here before Hattie hears it," Spook warned Lute again. "She don't like that dog."

Lute ignored him as he dealt another hand.

Rolly was on a hot streak, winning the next two consecutive hands. Lute's features grew more tense as Rolly continued to rake in the pile of money from the center of the table. Lute seemed to take the losses in stride, but his foot rhythmically twitched against the leg of the chair, making Barrett uneasy.

Barrett's eyes moved back to the bedroom door, wondering what was taking so long. Was Abby in trouble, or was she actually able to help the woman? The almost eerie silence coming from the bedroom was getting on his nerves.

The hound got to his feet and moseyed over to the table.

"Git!" Spook said sharply as the dog licked one of his boots. One thing Spook couldn't stand was an ole dog lickin' his boots. Made him sick. When the hound persisted in nosing around his feet, Spook's left boot shot out and sent him flying across the floor.

Yelping, the dog limped back to the fire, where he lay down again.

"Don't kick my dog, Spook." Reaching for the liquor bottle, Lute filled his glass again.

"He ain't your dog. He was a stray come wanderin' around Hattie Mae, and she was stupid enough to feed him."

Lute's eyes narrowed on Hattie's brother. "Don't make no give a damn how I got him, he's mine, and I don't want you a kickin' him."

Spook, having swallowed his share from the bottle, refused to be intimidated. The way he saw it, if the dog licked his boots, it was gonna get kicked, no matter who it belonged to—and it sure wasn't Lute.

"That dog don't belong to nobody."

"I feed her."

"Don't make her your'n."

"Makes her more mine than yours." To prove it, Lute called the dog back over to the table and kicked it himself.

Yelping, the dog whipped back to the fire and lay down, shooting an accusing look at both men.

"Gentlemen," Barrett began when he saw that the matter was getting out of hand. The men had had too much to drink, and they were getting abusive. "Why don't I let the dog out?"

Lute fixed his eyes belligerently on his brother-in-law. "You jest stay where you are, Quaker man. It's my dog, and if'n I want him to go outside, *I'll* take him outside."

"*Ain't your dog*," Spook insisted.

Lute's eyes turned steely. "Spook, you're aggrava-tin' me."

"Gentlemen," Barrett warned again.

"Spook, let it pass," Rolly said. "Don't matter whose damn dog it is. Deal the cards."

"No." Spook laid his cards on the table, his jaw fixed obstinately. "Ain't his dog, and I ain't a gonna say it is."

Lute sprung to his feet and grabbed the whiskey bottle, sending the cards and money scattering across the room as he broke the bottle across the table. "Now looka here! It's my dog!"

"Ain't neither!" Spook jumped up, jerking his re-volver out of his holster.

Whether he intended to shoot Lute or the dog, Bar-rett was never sure. Before he could stop the fight, Lute whipped out his gun and fired.

Barrett scrambled out of his chair and stumbled over the dog that was rushing to get out of the way. The dog yelped and ran under the table for safety.

A shot rang out, the explosion echoing throughout the cabin. Spook slumped over the table as a splash of bright red spread across his chest.

Jumping to his feet, Rolly pulled his gun to come to his friend's defense. He figured Lute had no call to shoot Spook over a dog!

A second shot rang out as Barrett dove under the table to join the dog for cover.

Lute fell to the floor, his gun still smoking in his hand. A second later, a third shot sounded, and a look of utter disbelief crossed Rolly's features as Lute's bul-let caught him clean through the heart. Dropping to his knees, Rolly pitched forward and sprawled face first on the floor.

As the guns fell silent, Barrett eased out from beneath the table. Getting slowly to his feet, he viewed the carnage, dumbfounded.

Lute, Spook, and Rolly lay on the floor, all dead as doornails.

Chapter 13

The bedroom door flew open, and Abby stood in the doorway, round-eyed. "What happened? I heard gunshots."

Barrett stared back at her, still unable to believe what had just taken place. "Well, the damn fools *shot* one another."

She stared back at him vacantly. "*Shot* one another?"

Barrett nodded, still staring at the three bodies.

"Over what?"

"Over the dog!"

Abby was finding it just as hard to believe as he was until her eyes located the three men sprawled haphazardly on the floor. "All three of them?"

"It's the craziest thing I've ever seen. One minute they were playing cards, and the next minute they jumped up and shot one another."

Wide awake now from all the commotion, a tiny head suddenly popped up in the crib. A pair of blue eyes, round with curiosity, peeked through the bars at them.

"Oh, hell," Barrett murmured. He'd forgotten all about the child!

The baby gave Barrett a toothy grin and lifted his arms, wanting to be picked up.

"Oh, hell." Barrett muttered again as the full ramifications of what had just happened sank in on him. Turning back to Abby, he asked expectantly, "Hattie Mae?"

Abby shook her head. "Dead."

"Dead?" Barrett's face turned white as a sheet. *"Dead?"*

"Not five minutes after I went into the room," Abby confessed.

"Dead?" Barrett turned, doubling with pain. Now what was he going to do? Not only did he have Abigail to worry about, but Lute and Hattie's deaths meant that they had two babies on their hands! He looked back expectantly. "The new baby?"

Abby lowered her eyes. "He didn't make it either."

"The baby's dead, too?" He doubled over again, wondering how it could get any worse.

"I've been sitting in there trying to think of a way to tell Lute." Abby's eyes moved to Lute's lifeless form sprawled next to the table. "Boy, this is really stupid, huh?"

The baby pulled himself up on the bars and began to cry. Barrett glanced at the child, then back to Abby. "What are we supposed to do about him?"

Abby hurried over to the crib and lifted the child out, trying to hush him. "There, there, baby. You must be hungry." She turned with the baby in her arms. "He must be hungry, Barrett. What do we feed him?"

The child's cries turned to screams as fat crocodile tears rolled down its rosy cheeks.

"How should I know? I don't know anything about babies!"

While Abby searched for a clean diaper, Barrett paced the small cabin. "Well, if this isn't a hell of a mess," he finally said. Now he had Abigail, an infant, and *five* people to bury. On top of that, it was still a two days' ride to Shreveport, which meant if he was going to reach Smith in time, they should be leaving right now.

"I guess we ought to bury them," Abby observed as she changed the baby's diaper.

"Barrett!" she screamed.

Barrett's heart shot to his throat. "What?"

"Look!"

He ran across the room and looked over her shoulder at the baby's bare bottom. "What?"

"It's a boy."

Muttering under his breath, he resumed pacing. Trying to organize his thoughts, he blocked out the sound of Abby's soft cooing to the baby. If he dug the graves shallow, he could cut the time in half.

The child was adorable. Abby decided he couldn't be much older than a year. He had a bright thatch of red hair and big blue eyes. Now that he'd stopped crying, he grinned a lot at her, showing off his two bottom and two upper teeth. He was about the cutest thing she'd ever seen—and the littlest. Holding out her finger, she laughed when he grasped onto it, trying to wedge it into his mouth.

"I'll see if there's a shovel around." Barrett shuffled halfheartedly to the door and paused with his hand on the knob. "It'll take me awhile to get them all buried."

"Want me to help?"

"No." Barrett's gaze focused dispiritedly on the baby. Now they couldn't travel until morning anyway. "You figure out what to do with him."

As Abby turned back to the baby, it suddenly occurred to her that both his mother and father were dead. "Oh, Barrett, what *will* we do with him?"

Shaking his head hopelessly, Barrett opened the door. He was out of answers; he had been for the past three days.

Barrett found five horses, a raw-boned cow, and a few scraggly chickens in the barn. But no shovel. After searching for over an hour he came up with a potato fork with a prong missing. It wasn't the ideal burying tool, but it was all he could find.

As he walked back to the cabin, thunder rolled in the distance. *That's wonderful,* he thought. *To top off the hellish day, it's comin' up another rain.*

It took over an hour to drag Lute, Rolly, and Spook to a small clearing behind the barn. Barrett carried Hattie and the baby, laying mother and child in a soft mound of fresh hay until their graves were ready.

At first glance, the ground behind the barn appeared to be the best place to dig. Then as Barrett rammed the prong of the potato fork into the soil and it jarred his teeth, he discovered, as with everything else lately, he'd misjudged the terrain. Where there weren't rocks, there were tree roots and the ground was as hard as clay.

He removed his coat and hat and draped them over a tree branch, then set to work. Forty minutes later he'd managed to scrape out one shallow grave.

Resting on the potato fork handle, he studied the results of his efforts. He was going to be old and gray before he got everyone buried.

Stripping out of his shirt, he wiped the sweat from his face with it, then set back to work.

As the hours passed, Abby went to the front door to open it and look out. Barrett was beside the barn, standing knee-deep in a hole. She began to feel sorry for him. It occurred to her that he hadn't asked for all this trouble, and she had to wonder how much simpler his life would be if he had ridden away that day without coming to her rescue.

She leaned against the door frame, conscious of the strange tingling that he provoked somewhere deep inside her. He'd stirred that feeling in her a lot lately, and she wasn't sure she liked it.

He'd peeled out of his shirt, and his skin glistened with sweat in the twilight. His chest was broad and muscular, covered with a dark coating of light brown hair. She watched the tight play of muscles as he swung the potato fork back and forth, and the tingling inside her grew more pronounced.

She found him attractive, more so than she'd ever suspected she could. Though their situation was anything but romantic, something about him energized her. She'd heard women giggle and talk about being drawn to a certain man, but she'd always laughed and said there wasn't a man alive that could make her feel anything but apathy. Now, standing there watching Barrett Drake work in the growing twilight, Abby was curious. What was Captain Drake, the man, really like?

Closing the door, she tiptoed over to check on the baby. He was asleep, his little bottom curled up in the air charmingly. Poor baby, she thought wistfully. Both mother and father gone.

She reached for the lantern, lit it, then carried it to the barn.

"Hi."

Grunting, Barrett hauled another good-sized rock out of the ground. "Hi."

"I fixed some corn bread. There was a pot of beans on the stove, so you can eat anytime you want." She watched as he swung the fork, digging out the shallow grave. She glanced into the barn to see that the bodies of Lute and Rolly were still waiting there to be buried. Quickly, she looked away again. "Can I help?"

"No. Better get on back to the house. It's comin' up rain."

She listened as another loud thunderclap sounded in the distance. As she turned and started back to the cabin, it occurred to her that it had rained a lot lately.

By the time Barrett had the third grave dug deep enough, the sky was black and the wind began to blow. When he was well into the next hole, he felt the first splashes of water on his back.

While his heated skin welcomed the cooling relief, he didn't relish finishing the job in a storm.

But Mother Nature wasn't concerned about Barrett Drake's comfort. Before he was finished with the fourth grave, he was drenched. It was so dark he could barely see, and rain streamed down his face and into his boots. Conditions couldn't get any more miserable.

Another hour later, Barrett, feeling totally exhausted, heaved a heavy sigh and threw the last fork full of mud into the hole. His stomach thought his throat had been cut, since he hadn't eaten since dawn.

He picked up his soggy shirt and wet coat and trudged slowly back to the cabin, oblivious of the raging thunderstorm going on around him.

Entering the cabin's warmth, he found Abby asleep on a pallet in front of the fireplace. The baby lay on his stomach beside her.

He moved to the fire to warm up. His stomach was knotted from hunger, but he was too cold and too tired to eat.

Stepping out of his wet trousers and underwear, he wrapped the thin blanket that Abby had laid out for him around his middle. He moved back to the fire to hang his wet clothes over the back of a chair to dry. He had to admit that she had done well under the circumstances. The cabin was warm; the dishes were washed; and the baby was sound asleep.

His eyes unwillingly returned to the floor, where she and the baby lay sleeping. Her hair was loose, spread out across the pallet in a silky tangle. Exhaustion shadowed her face, and she slept peacefully, her arm protectively cradling the small bundle beside her.

For one insane moment, Barrett wanted to hold her. The desire was so intense that it startled him. How long had it been since he'd wanted to hold a woman for no other reason than to just hold her?

Sinking onto the pallet, he stretched out beside Abby, staring at her in the glimmering firelight. She looked very young. Of course, she was young, Barrett realized. At least twelve years younger than he was or maybe more. And she looked very innocent. Desire, hot and unchecked, swept through him. How he would like to strip the blanket away and sample the delights her supple young body could offer a man. A smile touched the corners of his mouth as he gently reached out to touch a strand of her hair. Would she be as spirited in bed as she was out? He found the idea not only provocative but gratifying. Closing his eyes, he brought the strand to his nose, breathing its scent, knowing that if she had a protective papa, he could easily be shot for what he was thinking. She'd never been with a man; everything about her convinced him of that. Abigail McDougal was the kind of woman a man married, not the sort he took for pleasure and left by morning.

Settling the strand of her hair regretfully back on the pillow, Barrett reminded himself of that. She was young and pretty and unsettlingly innocent, and he planned to keep her that way.

He'd seek his enjoyment with a woman who expected nothing but a pleasurable encounter.

Abby was awakened sometime during the night by a whimpering sound. It took a moment for her to realize the source. Forcing her eyes open, she pulled the baby to her, tenderly stroking its soft cheek.

Barrett stirred, listening to her soothe the child. She's getting attached to the child, he thought drowsily. *That isn't good.*

A steady rain fell outside, but the thick bed of coals in the fireplace kept the room comfortable.

"Did you get everyone buried?" she murmured.

"I think so."

"Did you make Hattie's grave a little nicer?"

"Yes."

"Did you eat anything?"

"Too tired," he murmured, rolling to his side and dozing off again.

Twice more before dawn, the baby woke up and cried for his mother. Each time it took Abby longer to quiet the infant. By morning, both she and Barrett were exhausted, and the baby's crying was becoming almost constant.

Toward daylight, Barrett got up and sat at the kitchen table as Abby rocked the baby. Her hair hung limp around her face, and her shoulders were slumped with weariness. For the first time, her spirit seemed shaken.

She rocked slowly, back and forth, back and forth, patting the baby's back, blinking back tears of frustration. She didn't know what to do for the child.

"You want me to rock him?"

"I don't think he'd let you," she returned wearily.

"He's hungry, and he wants his mommy. Hattie Mae must have been nursing him."

"There are a couple of milk cows in the barn."

"I guess we'll have to fashion some sort of a bottle for him."

Barrett got up, and Abby turned her head as he got dressed.

"I'll see if I can get the cow milked."

The cow eyed Barrett balefully as he entered the barn. Bending over, Barrett ran a hand down her side. Her udder was full, but it had been many years since he'd milked a cow.

He took a bucket off a nail and scooted the stool next to the animal with the toe of his boot. He began speaking to her in reassuring tones. "All right, girl. I'll be gentle with you, if you'll be gentle with me."

The cow glanced over her shoulder, looking not at all assured that he was speaking the truth.

Tucking his head into her flank, Barrett grasped two teats and pulled.

The cow jumped, knocking the bucket aside.

Barrett scooted the stool closer, positioned the bucket again, and grasped two teats.

The cow shifted again, and Barrett followed her around the stall, determined to gain the upper hand.

Trapped against the side of the stall, the cow finally settled down. Within a few minutes, Barrett had a steady stream of milk flowing into the pail.

As he was stripping the last teat, the cow's tail suddenly whipped to one side, catching him on the cheek with the ball of cockleburs matted in the switch. His cheek stung like fire as Barrett grabbed for the bucket before it tipped over. "Soooo, Bossy," he murmured.

The cow steadied, and Barrett finished up. Relieved, he stood as the cow calmly lifted her hoof and stomped the bucket, toppling it onto its side. Half of the milk spilled out of the bucket onto the ground before Barrett managed to grab it.

"This had better be enough," Barrett told Abby as he stepped into the cabin with what was left of the bucket of milk a few minutes later. "I'm not waltzing with that damn cow again."

Abby viewed the half-bucket of milk with mild curiosity. He'd been out there an awfully long time to have come up with no more milk than that.

Setting a plate of biscuits on the table, she motioned for him to sit down. "I found a can of sorghum. It's almost turned to sugar, but it still tastes good."

Barrett sat down at the table, grateful for anything at that point.

The baby was still fussing and waving his fists in the air angrily. Abby went to work on crafting a bottle. What she came up with wasn't practical, but it worked.

She pulled the rocking chair closer to the table and put the baby on her lap. She dipped the end of a cloth into the bucket of milk. When she offered the cloth to the baby, his mouth puckered tight. Gradually, Abby coaxed his mouth open with a little pressure on his lower lip, and he managed to get a taste of the milk.

Smacking his lips, the baby hungrily sucked on the cloth.

It took almost an hour to get enough nourishment into the baby so that he was content enough to fall asleep. For the first time in hours, the cabin was blissfully quiet. Outside, the rain began to fall again, and thunder rumbled in the distance.

Barrett ate six of the twelve biscuits and drank two cups of milk as he stared through the dirty windowpane. He had exactly three days to deliver the messages. He didn't have the slightest idea how he was going to make it with a woman, and now a baby, to look after, but he had no choice. Somehow, he had to get there.

"I'll hold the baby so you can eat," he told her as he swallowed the last of his biscuit.

Abby gratefully transferred the tiny sleeping bundle into his arms.

Barrett awkwardly adjusted the baby in the crook of his arm and settled himself into the rocking chair. Gazing at the boy's shock of fiery red hair, he smiled. "Kinda cute, isn't he?"

Abby smiled as she slathered sorghum between two fat biscuits.

"Abby?"

"Yes?"

Barrett's eyes were full of concern as they met hers. "Don't get too attached to the boy."

She smiled away his concern. She didn't know where he could get an idea like that. "Don't worry, I won't."

Barrett studied the child's chubby features. "It'd be easy to do," he admitted. "Real easy."

"Don't worry, I've never even thought about babies or husbands or anything like that."

By the time she'd finished her third biscuit, Abby's eyes were so heavy she couldn't hold them open any longer.

"I've been thinking about what we should do with him," she said sleepily.

"Come up with anything?"

"He must have relatives, but I wouldn't begin to know where to find them."

"I've thought of that. The shack is so isolated."

Abby pushed her plate aside, folded her arms on the table, and rested her head atop them. She knew they had to be on their way, but she didn't have the strength. "Since we don't have time to look for any relatives, we'll have to leave the boy at a mission. If the baby does have any relatives, they'll surely try to find them. We'll leave a note here explaining what happened and what we plan to do with the baby. If we can find a Catholic mission, I'm certain that the sisters will take good care of him.'' Yawning, she glanced at Barrett to see if he was listening.

He was sound asleep in the chair, the baby lying snugly against the width of his chest.

She smiled, and her eyes drifted closed for just a moment. Barrett really wasn't so bad, she thought. ''Not bad at all,'' she murmured as visions of his bare chest danced wickedly through her mind.

The three dozed peacefully to the sound of rain pattering down on the rooftop.

Chapter 14

A clap of thunder shook the house, and the boom repeated over the hillsides.

Lifting her head sleepily, Abby opened her eyes, trying to focus them on the small windowpane. Rain was falling in torrents, and the wind was savagely battering the tops of the trees.

A flash of lightning split the sky, followed by another thunderous blast. Barrett stirred and shifted the baby's weight in an effort to restore feeling in his arm.

Abby reached over and gently shook him awake. "Barrett."

He looked up, his eyes clouded with sleep.

"We must have dozed off," she whispered. "Lute and Hattie don't have a clock, but it must be getting late."

Thunder vibrated the floor of the cabin as Barrett got up and carried the baby to the crib. The child momentarily roused and whimpered but Barrett gently patted the boy's back until he drifted to sleep.

Abby rose from the table and began to round up the

baby's articles in preparation for leaving. "I'll only be a minute. The baby will need his belongings at the orphanage."

Barrett moved to the window and looked out, his eyes grave as he viewed the worsening weather. "We can't take the child out in this storm."

Abby continued to rush around the room, packing essentials into a pillowcase she'd found. "It'll let up before long," she predicted optimistically.

But when the storm continued to rage with no end in sight, her hope began to fade. Hours later, they sat down at the table and fed the baby the last biscuit.

Abby watched Barrett from the corner of her eye, concerned about the grave set of his features. Reaching over, she lay her hand on the sleeve of his shirt. "Don't worry, it has to let up. Once it does, we'll ride hard."

"I don't know, Abby." Barrett looked at the baby, whose blue eyes stared innocently back at him as he stuffed bits of food into his mouth. "It looks like it's set in for the day."

The minutes ticked by slowly. Barrett paced the floor of the shanty, looking out the window and mentally wringing his hands as the storm raged on. The roof was leaking in a dozen places, and they'd set cups and buckets here and there to catch the drips.

By midmorning, he put on his coat and suddenly announced that he was going to scout around for any neighbors who might be able to shed light on Hattie or Lute's relatives.

Abby watched him go with a tight knot forming in the pit of her stomach. She couldn't help but wonder if he'd be back, or if he'd made a decision to ride on without her. After all, he knew enough details about the messages to alert Smith to the pending attack, even if he didn't have the papers.

He was gone over an hour. When Abby heard the horse trot up, she went weak with relief. Smiling at the baby, she said softly, "See, I told you he'd be back."

"Have any luck?" she asked brightly as he came into the cabin.

Shaking his head, he went to the fire to warm his hands. "There are no neighbors."

"Did you go far?"

"Far enough."

As night fell, Abby and Barrett sat at the kitchen table, listening to the sound of the storm. Rain lashed the windowpane, and thunder and lightning streaked across the sky with disheartening regularity.

Barrett reached for the milk bucket, his features fixed in resolve. "I'll see if I can coax more milk out that damned cow."

Abby laughed, and the lines in his face suddenly relaxed. Strangely enough, the sound of her laughter made him feel better.

She lifted her brows curiously. "What's wrong?"

"Nothing. It's good to know that you can laugh."

"I've laughed before," she said defensively.

"Yes, at me."

They smiled, and the morbid set of circumstances suddenly seemed to hold more promise.

"Well, guess I'd better get the milk." He glanced at the baby. "He'll be hungry again."

"I looked to see if Lute had a raincoat, but there isn't one in the cabin, at least not one that I can find. Maybe he had one hanging in the barn." She looked away, feeling embarrassed. "Wouldn't want you catching your death."

When Barrett returned from the barn, there wasn't a dry thread on him.

"It must not have rained on Lute," he complained as he shook the water off his hat and hung it on a peg beside the fire to dry. "Apparently, he didn't own a slicker."

They sat down to eat the last of the beans. Abby had found more cornmeal in the bin, and now a pan of cornbread was baking in the oven.

Abby felt uneasy about being in another woman's kitchen—especially when she knew where the other woman was.

There were signs of Hattie everywhere. Her bonnet was still on the peg; her shoes were in the corner by the fireplace; her hairbrush was laying beside the washstand. It was like she was still living there.

"I wish I could have done something for Hattie Mae," Abby mused as they ate.

"Was it childbirth that took her?"

"I'm not sure. Her forehead was very hot when I touched it, and she was coughing real bad."

"Did she say anything?"

Abby thought back to the last moments of Hattie's life, and she shook her head slowly. "No, she just rambled on about nothing, mostly."

Reaching for another piece of cornbread, Barrett frowned. "Lute mentioned that she'd been sick for a few days."

"I remember when we were at the orphanage, the sisters taught us to pray for healing. Sister Agnes had a weakness in the joints. They pained her something awful. The sisters told us if we'd pray for her, she would get better, but I didn't believe it would help."

A smile lit her eyes, and Barrett silently conceded that she was an exceptionally beautiful woman. Mean, but beautiful.

"But her condition did improve," she went on. "After my sisters and I had prayed about all we could, she told us that she was better, and she did seem more spry for a few days.'' She looked at him for a moment. ''Do you think prayer works?''

''I don't know. I suppose.''

''Sometimes I wonder. I mean, my mama died. And so did my papa.''

''Is that when you went to live at the orphanage?''

She nodded. ''At least the three of us were able to stay together. That was important. And the sisters were good to us.'' She smiled. ''They educated us and tried to teach us right from wrong.''

Barrett mopped up the last of the beans with a chunk of cornbread. ''Where do you suppose they went wrong?''

''What?''

He looked up, a teasing light in his eyes. ''I said, where do you suppose they went wrong?''

''Oh, you!'' She threw a dishrag at him, but Barrett noticed that this time she did it with a bit of affection.

Throughout the afternoon Barrett watched the baby while Abby rested. She'd noticed that he was still hoping for a miracle, going to the window and looking out every half hour or so. But the rain continued to fall with no letup in sight.

It was growing late when Abby stirred on her pallet in front of the fire and whispered, ''Barrett.''

''Hmm?'' He was dozing again in the rocking chair with the baby tucked in his arm.

''Barrett.''

He stirred at the sound of her voice. ''What's the matter?''

''The rain's letting up a little. Better milk the cow. The baby will be hungry again.''

Nodding, Barrett silently handed her the baby and went for another unpleasant encounter with the cow.

As he walked back to the cabin later, he stopped and sniffed the air. Lord, Drake, you're losing your grip. You're so hungry you're smelling food where there isn't any. He could have sworn he smelled chicken frying.

When he stepped inside the cabin he stopped and stared at the domestic sight before him. The baby was crawling around on the floor, while Abby bent over an iron skillet turning pieces of nicely browned chicken.

"Where did you get that?" he asked.

"Oh, I found a couple of old sittin' hens out by the barn. Since no one is going to be needing them anymore and we need a good meal, I decided to catch them and wring their necks. I used the last of the flour to coat the chicken and make a batch of biscuits."

Setting the pail of milk on the counter, Barrett relished the mouth-watering smells coming from the stove. He couldn't remember when he'd last tasted fried chicken.

"Dinner's almost ready. Better wash up."

While Barrett washed, Abby heaped mounds of fried chicken on a plate. Taking the biscuits out of the oven, she realized that this was about as close as she'd ever come to looking after a man. Actually, it wasn't so bad. It was sort of nice, actually. Maybe she wouldn't like it if she had to do it all the time, but right now she couldn't complain at all.

"I don't know when I've ever smelled anything so good," Barrett admitted as he pulled a chair up to the table.

"I didn't know I could fry chicken," Abby admitted as she set the baby on her lap.

They began to eat, sharing a compatible silence.

As Abby ate, she absently tore off small bits of chicken and fed them to the baby.

"Look, Barrett, he eats really well for his age, don't you think?"

"Does all right," Barrett admitted, "though his table manners need work." The child had thrown a piece of biscuit at Barrett twice, but other than that, he seemed pretty bright.

"That was delicious," Barrett confessed later. Pushing back from the table, he reached into his shirt pocket for a smoke. His hand suddenly paused as he remembered his manners. "Do you mind, or would you rather I go outside?"

"I don't mind." She thought it was nice of him to ask. A lot of men wouldn't have bothered.

Thunder rumbled in the distance as she stood up to clear the table. "Wonder if it will ever stop raining."

Barrett lit the cheroot and stared into the fire thoughtfully.

Abby could tell that getting the papers to General Smith was on his mind again. "If we ride hard, we can be in Shreveport by late Friday night," she said encouragingly.

He shook his head doubtfully, wary of her prediction. "Abby, if I don't get those papers there—"

"You will," she promised. "If the rain hasn't let up by morning, we'll leave anyway."

"How can we travel with a baby? It was hard enough when it was just you and me."

"The baby won't melt." Handing the child another bite of chicken, she smiled as he stuffed it in his mouth hungrily. "He's a good boy."

Good boy or not, Barrett couldn't be responsible for the child coming down with pneumonia.

Laying her fork beside her plate, Abby broached the

subject she'd been dreading the most. "You didn't hear me this morning, did you?"

"Concerning what?"

"About finding an orphanage and leaving the baby there."

"No, but it's sensible. We can't take the child with us, and we don't know if Lute or Hattie Mae had family. I rode for miles this morning, and I didn't see another cabin. I don't know what else to do."

Barrett wasn't surprised to see a wistful look cross Abby's face when she looked at the baby. He never would have thought that she was the maternal kind, but it was evident that she'd taken to the child. "I can't recall any orphanages this side of the line, but there might be something closer to Louisiana."

"I'd like it to be Catholic—if possible. The sisters were kind to me and my sisters."

The baby threw his biscuit on the floor, and Abby bent to pick it up.

Barrett stood and reached for his coat hanging on the peg. "Guess I'd better get us some water."

Abby looked up to see his eyes twinkling devilishly. A nice, gentle twinkle that brought back the little twitch in the pit of her stomach. "Would you like a bucket of water?" he asked.

"It'd be all right," she said, hardly looking up for fear he'd see the color rising to her face. No man had ever made Abigail McDougal blush, but here Barrett Drake was, offering to bring her a simple bucket of water, and she was blushing like a schoolgirl.

"The supper was so good, I might bring you two."

While he was gone, she hurriedly wiped the dishes and swept the floor. By the pile of dirt she came up with, it was evident that Hattie hadn't swept—ever. The baby played around her feet, banging a pan and a lid together.

Abby had never been around an infant, and she was fascinated by the child. Tiny fingers, tiny toes, and the tiniest hands she'd ever seen.

"You'll be taken care of," Abby promised as she picked the child up and hugged him. "Captain Drake and I will see to that."

The door to the cabin swung open, and Barrett came in dragging a galvanized washtub.

"Where did you find that?" She would have sworn by Lute and Hattie's disheveled appearance they didn't own a tub.

"In the barn loft." He dragged the tub across the floor and set it in front of the fire. "How would you like a bath?"

"A bath! That would be wonderful! Thank you!"

Thank you? Abigail McDougal telling a man, thank you?

As Barrett straightened, his eyes touched hers briefly, then quickly moved away. "I'll start bringing in the water."

Abby rinsed out the tub and put pans on the stove to heat. After making several trips, Barrett had the tub half-full, and Abby poured hot water from the stove to make it nice and warm.

"You go first. I'll wait on the porch," he said. "Want me to take the baby?"

"No, he's fine." They looked at the baby, who sat in his crib, chewing on a rag doll. "Unless you just want to hold him?"

"No, that's all right."

When the door closed behind him, Abby turned and hurried to the boxes of odds and ends stacked in the corners of the cabin to search for soap. She rummaged for over five minutes before she finally found a piece.

She stripped quickly out of her clothes and sank into the water up to her chin. Closing her eyes, she savored the feel of the steaming warmth. She knew she shouldn't dally, that Barrett was waiting to take his bath, but she couldn't remember when she'd enjoyed a tub of hot water more.

It was over fifteen minutes before she made herself climb out and towel off. Reaching for the large blanket that she'd laid across the back of a chair, she wrapped it around her body and tucked the ends snugly against her breasts.

She quickly washed out her dress and petticoats and hung them to dry on a line in front of the fire.

She moved along, aware that Barrett was standing outside, waiting. Not long ago she wouldn't have cared, but something had changed. She wasn't sure why, but she was feeling concern for him. Even though the porch roof did protect him from the rain, she'd heard him sneeze twice that day, and the last thing she wanted was for him to come down sick because of her.

After she was finished, she hurried to the front door to tell him that he could come in now. When she found that he wasn't on the porch, she closed the door and walked slowly back to the fire.

The baby was babbling to her, and she unthinkingly returned his meaningless gurgle. "He's around somewhere, don't worry."

She wasn't sure that she appreciated this sudden dependence upon him; she was beginning to feel almost as secure with Barrett Drake as she did with Amelia and Anne-Marie.

She sat down in front of the fire, combing her hair with her fingers as she exchanged gibberish with the baby. That's how Barrett found her when he returned to the cabin.

Stepping inside the room, he paused, surprised by her appearance. Her bare shoulders were shining invitingly above the blanket, and her raven hair was spilling down her back. Every thought that a man shouldn't be having about a woman ran through his mind. Especially a woman he had no intention of ever seeing again once the papers were delivered.

Yet the male in him could imagine her soft curves against him, could picture her whisperings, could hear her urging him on to the brink of insanity. It wasn't hard to fantasize about making love to a woman like Abigail McDougal. She was all heat and fire, lightning and thunder. Her passion for life would be a welcome addition to any man's bed.

With his pulse quickening, he slammed the door, causing her to look up in alarm.

"Sorry. I thought you'd be through," he apologized curtly.

"I'm finished. I called, but you didn't answer."

"I'd walked down to the barn."

She smiled at him, and more than his eyes firmed this time. "I put fresh water on the stove to boil. The baby's almost asleep, so I can sit on the porch while you have your bath."

"No need to do that. You can turn your head," he said crisply.

She obediently turned to face the fire, wondering if she'd said something to annoy him. He seemed unusually testy all of a sudden.

She absently brushed her fingers through her hair, drying it as she listened to him remove the kettles from the fire and pour water into the tub.

The sound of his clothes dropping against the floor

produced an impish grin. Bringing her fingers to her cheeks, she discovered that they were burning as the mystery of his naked body taunted her. What did a man look like when he was naked? She had never seen a man who was fully undressed; she'd never really thought about such evil things until this very moment. She hurriedly pushed the unsettling image aside, ashamed of her thoughts. Even if she did find Barrett Drake different from other men—and she wasn't saying that she did, but she wasn't saying that she didn't—the way she'd behaved since the day she'd met him had all but crushed any hope that he would ever be attracted to her. She had been wretched to him, and a man like Barrett wouldn't be apt to forget that anytime soon.

As Sister Agnes always said as she'd peered sternly over the rim of her wire glasses at her, "Abigail, you've made your bed, now you're going to have to sleep in it."

She'd never been quite certain what Sister Agnes had meant by that ominous reprimand, but she could almost bet that thinking about naked men in bathtubs would fall within her warning. Scooting closer to the fire, she fought the urge to sneak a quick peek at him over her shoulder.

"Ever had a beau, Abby?"

Startled by his voice, Abby felt the color in her cheeks deepen. She swallowed hard and fought to find her voice. "No."

"Ever want one?"

"No."

"No?"

"No."

"Why not?"

She shrugged. "I never thought I wanted one."

"Why not?"

"I have my sisters. That's enough."

"Ah, but your sisters can't take the place of a man," he needled softly.

"I don't need a man."

"How do you know? Have you ever been with a man?"

She bristled, drawing the blanket closer around her shoulders. "Maybe I have."

"And maybe you haven't." She had an air of innocence, despite the bravado she wore on her sleeve like a red flag of challenge. And Barrett sensed that Abigail McDougal would be a lot of woman for the right man. At times, he even found himself comparing her to Ramona: the flash of her smile, a turn of phrase, a certain look in her eye.

But right at this moment, there was nothing about her that reminded him of his wife. Ramona wouldn't have cared for the child; she would have expected Barrett to care for it. Ramona took; she never gave. Ramona expected; she never asked. And Ramona didn't have the sense to try to bluff her way out of a subject the way Abigail was trying to do right now.

Concerned that the conversation was becoming too intimate, Abigail started to ramble in one long breath. "I noticed the daffodils are blooming. Amelia loves daffodils. Once, when we were in Texas, a man stopped and picked her a whole bouquet, because he'd overheard her say that she thought they were pretty. Anne-Marie and I looked on with envy, because we'd never had a man do anything like that for us. The closest we'd come was when Father Juan offered to set the pickle jars on the top shelf in the root cellar for us because we weren't tall enough to reach it."

The aroma of his cigar drifted to her as she paused to catch her breath. The intimacy of their conversation had made her jittery. Her face felt suddenly hotter, and his voice, teasing her just now, caused butterflies to swarm in her stomach. She hadn't been around many men in her life, just Father Juan at the mission, and he had never affected her at all, much less in the way Barrett was doing now.

Sinking deeper into the tub, Barrett relaxed, letting the hot water rise to his chin. He studied her through a veil of blue smoke as she rattled on.

"Then there was the time when we were picking peas. There was this man who owned a neighboring farm, and late one afternoon, just out of a clear blue sky, he stopped by to bring some ears of corn to the mission and low and behold if he didn't give the ears to Amelia. Just left Sister Agnes and Sister Lucille standing there in the pea patch looking at him as if he'd clean lost his wits. Well, Amelia stopped picking right then, and she just stood there in the patch, smiling real pretty at him. He smiled back, telling her how lovely she was and how it was too hot for anyone as pretty as she was to be working in the sun. That made Anne-Marie mad, because she said later that Amelia looked awful—all sweaty, with her hair hanging down in her face and her dress dirty from kneeling in the garden. And the sun was just as hot boiling down on us as it was Amelia."

Actually, having a man around to talk to is sort of nice, Abby thought, trying to keep the conversation rolling. She would have to remember to tell Amelia and Anne-Marie that she could almost sympathize with the stories they'd heard about women falling in love with certain men. If the men were as handsome and as charming as Barrett had been today, she could almost understand their foolishness.

"Let me see, what was I talking about?" she asked.

Clamping the cheroot between his teeth, Barrett lifted his foot to scrub it. "You don't know either?"

Her shoulders lifted with indifference. "I was going to ask you if you had."

"If I had what?" He was getting used to her broken trains of thought.

"Been with many women?"

She gasped softly. Now surely she hadn't asked *that* when she'd been trying so *hard* to change the subject. She didn't care how many women he'd been with, and she wished she'd never even asked. She had a premonition that if he told her, she wouldn't like his answer.

Smiling, Barrett soaped his arms. "Little girls like you shouldn't be askin' a man a question like that."

"I'm not little," she scoffed.

"How old are you? Seventeen? Eighteen?"

"Twenty. How old are you?"

"Old enough to know better than to answer that question."

"But I bet you've been with a few."

"A few," he acknowledged.

They fell silent as a log in the fire broke, sending a shower of sparks through the grate.

"So, you think you won't ever be interested in a man," he prodded. Leaning back in the tub, he rested his head on the rim as he drew on the cheroot. "You never dream of having a husband and your own children one of these days?"

"No, I made a pact with my sisters when we were very young. We will never be apart."

"That's a pretty serious pact," he reasoned. "And you and your sisters are older now. You can say a lot of things when you're young. With three women as pretty as you and your sisters, some man is bound to come along one of these days and change one of those minds.''

Abby loosened the blanket, because it seemed to be getting awfully warm in the room. ''I'm older now, but the pact holds. We won't be separated—and certainly not by a man.''

''Well, you never know,'' he murmured. There had been a time when he'd thought he knew everything about the opposite sex; now he wasn't so sure.

''What about you?''

''What about me?''

''Do you want a wife and children of your own someday?'' She found herself holding her breath as she waited for his answer. Even if he did want a wife, he most likely wouldn't consider her, and even if he did, she wouldn't consider him. How could she ever explain something like that to Amelia and Anne-Marie?

''A wife is the last thing I want,'' he said with a finality that sounded almost gruesome.

His answer, though disillusioning, didn't surprise her. After all, no matter how alluring she suddenly found him, he was still a man.

Barrett emptied the tub, then leaned it against the porch before he came back inside. As he stepped into the room, he saw the tail of Abby's blanket disappearing into Hattie and Lute's bedroom.

She'd mentioned that she had stripped the linens and put two old blankets on the bed. She'd said it wouldn't be as nice as sleeping on fresh sheets, but it appeared that Hattie had had no more, so the blankets would have to do. They were moderately clean, and the bed would be more comfortable than sleeping on the floor.

''Why don't you take the bed. I'll sleep on the floor.

Again,'' he offered dryly as he stood at the bedroom door, watching her tunnel beneath the blanket.

The baby was, for once, sleeping like a baby.

''The bed's wide enough for two.''

Abby squeezed her eyes shut, painfully aware that the sisters would consider that a horrendous impropriety, but she didn't have the heart to make him spend another night on the floor. They had a long, hard ride ahead tomorrow, and if they were to reach Shreveport in time, they would be able to stop only when necessary. Besides, sleeping in the same bed didn't mean a thing, not if he kept to himself.

''Pardon?''

''The bed's wide enough for two,'' she repeated in a muffled voice beneath the covers.

''What would Sister Agnes think about such an arrangement?''

''Sister Agnes is charitable. Besides, I'm too tired to worry about it. What she doesn't know won't hurt her.''

''You're sure you want to work it this way?''

''Just get in bed before I change my mind.'' Rolling onto her side, she scooted closer to the wall as Barrett blew out the lamp.

The room was so dark he had to feel his way to the bed.

''Is it still raining?''

''Yes.''

''I thought so.''

It felt odd, but kind of nice, when he slid into the bed next to her. It didn't matter that they weren't married, she told herself. The good Lord knew that they'd both lie down with a skunk if it meant getting a few hours of restful sleep.

''Good night.''

''Good night.''

Barrett turned onto his side, agonizingly aware of her presence. Hattie and Lute's bed was big for a married couple, but not large enough for a man who'd been without a woman too damn long, Barrett decided, when he felt the first strong twinges of desire.

The scent of her freshly washed hair brought an ache to his groin almost as painful as the one he was having lying next to her ripe young body. The gentle movement of her shoulder as she breathed and the delicate sigh as she fell into a deeper slumber caused his blood to heat. His pulse pounded in the back of his head, and he wondered why he was putting himself through this torment. The floor would be better than this anguish.

The fire was dying low, but he felt suddenly inordinately hot as he sat up to throw off the covers.

Easing back down, he lay tensely on his side, owning up to the fact that even though she'd spared him the agony of the floor, it was still going to be a long night for him.

Drake, you're a fool. The woman is nothing but trouble. She's told the biggest pack of lies you've ever heard—from being a direct descendant from Napoleon to who knows what else, and that doesn't even include her running around the countryside posing as a nun and a Quaker and whatever else she's got it in her head to pose as!

Abby stirred, shifting to her back as she settled more comfortably on the mattress. Her arm reached across his chest, resting lightly on the patch of dark hair showing at the top of his long johns. Sighing, she drifted deeper into sleep.

Mentally groaning, he lay paralyzed, staring at her arm as if it were a rattler about to strike. She snuggled closer to his warmth, burying her head against his shoulder, fanning his face with her breath.

"Drake, you are a fool for even thinking it," he muttered as he felt beads of sweat begin to roll down the sides of his face.

A damned fool!

Chapter 15

"Shoo! Get on out of here girl!"

Barrett whacked the cow across her rump as he turned her loose the next morning. Walking by the chicken coop, he opened the door and propped it open. The last few chickens would have to fend for themselves.

Selecting two of the best horses, he saddled them, then turned the others loose. The rain had slowed to a drizzle, but the low-hanging clouds promised that it wasn't over.

Inside the shanty, Abby fed the baby by candlelight. The lantern was out of kerosene, and Abby couldn't find more. She'd washed some of Hattie's threadbare petticoats the day before and hung them to dry by the fire. While Barrett saw to the stock, she'd torn the material into makeshift diapers for the little boy. Extra blankets would be bundled behind the saddles for use at night, but even with those, the dampness and chill would make traveling uncomfortable for the child.

Packing the last of the chicken and biscuits into the pillowcase, she paced the floor, holding the baby, trying to still his fretting.

Barrett found some pieces of oil cloth in the barn and carried them back inside the cabin. He removed a knife from the saddlebags and cut holes in the cloth, then slipped one of them over Abby's head and a smaller one over the baby's.

"This should help, but by the way it looks, we're still going to get wet," he warned.

"I don't mind." She tucked the chicken and biscuits into the saddlebags, yawning. "Wonder what time it is?"

"I don't know. It's hard to tell, but I'd say it's not much past dawn."

"Well," she stripped the blanket off the bed and wrapped it snugly around the baby's head, "we're ready to go."

The look in Barrett's eyes mellowed as he watched her walk to the doorway. The last twenty-four hours had been about as bad as it could get, but he had yet to hear her complain. "Do you want the baby to ride with me?" he asked.

"I'll hold him awhile. He's cranky this morning." Smiling up at Barrett, she said lightly, "Lead the way, Captain Drake."

Huddling deeper inside the oil cloth, Abby and the baby rode on a roan behind Barrett's scarred bay. The sky was gray and overcast while the horses picked their way along the narrow trail.

As the horses rounded the barn, Abby turned, looking back over her shoulder at the five fresh graves. "Barrett, could we stop here for a moment?"

He followed her gaze and dismounted. Taking the

baby from her arms, he helped her climb down from the roan.

They stood silently at the foot of Hattie's and Lute's graves.

Water was standing on them now, making the sight even more dismal. Though she'd never known Hattie Mae, she felt an indelible bond with the woman whose child had been entrusted to her care.

She bowed her head. "Forgive them, Father, and keep them in Your care," she said in a quiet voice. "Please bless them and the son they've left behind."

A moment later, they were back on their horses and moving off in the heavy mist.

"Don't you worry, Hattie Mae," Abby called softly over her shoulder. "I'll see that your baby is taken care of."

An unexplained sadness came over her as the old shanty slowly blended into the dense underbrush. The shack was dirty, and most people would find it barely habitable, but there was something about those pitifully thin walls that had given her a sense of belonging. For the first time in her life in those few hours spent there with Barrett and the child, she'd felt like she had a real home.

During the next few hours they didn't see a sign of human life anywhere. There were no neighbors, and they passed no other travelers on the road.

The baby cried out several times, and Barrett quietly soothed him. The boy was tucked in front of Barrett now, his raincoat shielding him from the brunt of the rain. Noticing how good Barrett was with the baby, she wondered if he'd been raised in a large family.

Twice they stopped and Barrett filled a cup with milk from his canteen. While Barrett held the boy's head,

Abby tried to coax the child to drink from the cup, but he refused, twisting his head and screaming with rage. Knocking the cup away, he bawled harder, wanting his mother.

He spilled several cups of the milk, a precious commodity now that they no longer had the cow, but finally his hunger won out, and eventually he settled down and began to greedily gulp milk from the cup.

"There's no use to stop at noon," Barrett called as the horses set off again down the muddy road. "The way this rain's coming down, I'd never get a fire going."

"We can eat as we ride," she offered.

"You don't mind?"

"I don't mind. There's chicken and biscuits in the saddlebag."

By late afternoon Abby was exhausted, and the baby was squalling again. Worst of all, the milk was gone.

Kicking her horse into a trot, she moved up beside Barrett.

"We've got to find a cow."

"I know. I've been watching, but I haven't seen anything that even resembles a cow."

"Then a goat. *Anything.*" The baby's continual crying had her nerves near the breaking point.

"Are there more biscuits?"

Wearily wiping the rain out of her eyes, Abby shook her head. "No, he ate the last one hours ago."

Barrett sneezed, which startled the baby, and he screamed harder. Abby took the child from his arms and rode beside him for the next few miles. She held the baby close, trying to soothe his sobs as her eyes frantically scoured the countryside for cattle.

Growing limp from crying, the child began to nuzzle her breasts, searching for his dinner.

"Barrett, it's getting serious," she warned, sucking in her breath.

Barrett winked. "He's taking advantage of the situation."

She looked back at him quizzically.

"He's just doing what any normal man would do in his position." His grin broadened when he saw her blush.

"You should be ashamed of yourself," she scolded.

"Yeah," his eyes traveled unrepentantly over her firm young breasts, causing the color in her cheeks to deepen. "I guess I should."

But the interest in his gaze belied his words and she had to admit that a part of her was glad that he wasn't ashamed.

By dark, the child's cries had faded to pitiful whimpers. He lay against Abby's breasts, looking drained and lifeless now.

Abby's heart wrenched every time he looked up at her with those wide, questioning blue eyes.

Barrett was starting to cough, and Abby feared he was going to be sick before they found shelter for the night.

"Are you all right?" she called for at least the fifth time.

"Just a tickle in my throat," he assured her.

That's all we need, she thought as she ducked to avoid a low limb, *for one of us to get sick.*

"There's a barn up ahead," Barrett called out as thunder rumbled.

"Thank goodness," Abby murmured with heartfelt sincerity as the baby began to cry again. If there was a barn, there might be a cow.

They dismounted on the far side of the barn, and

Abby held the horses while Barrett crept around the structure to make sure it was empty. She flinched at the squeal of a protesting hinge, praying that no one had heard it.

"We're in luck."

Abby jumped at the sound of Barrett's voice as he walked up behind her. "The barn's empty, except for a cow. We'll have milk for the boy." He took the child out of her arms, then helped her off the horse.

"Is it clean?"

"The hay's fresh. We'll feed the baby, get a few hours' sleep, then be on our way before sunup."

Abby trailed Barrett into the warmth of the barn. *At least it smells clean, and it's dry,* she thought with relief.

Barrett laid the baby on the hay as Abby took off her rain gear and hung it on a nail to dry. He stripped out of his wet gear and hung it beside hers, then set to work milking the cow.

The child drank two cups of milk as fast as Barrett could fill them. Once the child's hunger was temporarily appeased, Barrett handed Abby the cup. "This is all she'll give for now."

"We'll share it." The warm milk tasted so good Abby could have gladly swallowed it all, but she made herself stop when the cup was half-empty. Handing it back to Barrett, she smiled. "That'll hold me until morning."

A strange light entered his eyes as he accepted the cup. There wasn't a dry thread on her, and water was dripping from her hair and trickling down her cheeks. The dark circles beneath her eyes gave silent testimony to her remarkable courage. She'd sipped a half cup of milk for supper and acted as if it were pot roast and gravy. "I'm sorry," he said gently. "I wish I could make this easier on you and the child."

She nodded and sunk wearily to her knees. Crawling up beside the baby, she lay her head beside his on the hay. It was so dry, so blessedly dry. "We'll be fine, we're just a little tired. Drink your milk, then come to bed. . . ." Her voice trailed off as she closed her eyes and wriggled deeper into the hay.

Thunder rolled in the distance as Barrett drank the last of the milk, then sank down on the hay beside her.

His arm instinctively drew her closer, and he smiled as he heard her sigh and snuggled closer to his warmth. Being with her was becoming a habit for him, one he wasn't sure how he was going to break.

"Your cough is getting worse," she accused drowsily. "Can't get sick . . . need you . . . ."

"I won't get sick."

The strange new family huddled together in the hay and slept.

By morning, Barrett's cough was more pronounced. Abby watched as he saddled the horses. His face was flushed, and his eyes were unusually bright.

"Maybe I should go on and you stay here with the baby until the rain lets up," she offered as she gave the baby another cup of milk.

"Stop worrying, it's just a cold," Barrett dismissed shortly. Too shortly, Abby noticed. He was cranky, and that wasn't like him.

"It doesn't sound like it's raining."

"It's not, and let's hope it stays that way."

A watery sun tried to come up just after dawn. The couple rode for over two hours before they met a traveler, who greeted the Quaker couple warmly.

"Mornin', Friend. Looks like the rain jest might be tryin' to let up for a spell."

"Would be most welcome," Barrett returned, and Abby noticed he sounded hoarse. "Perhaps thou could be of help to us, sir."

The man halted his buggy, breaking into a grin when he spied the baby. "What's that you got there? A wee little tyke?"

Abby returned his smile and lowered the blanket so the man could have a better look at the child.

"Right good-looking baby you got there. Must be real proud of him."

"Yes, he is a fine lad," Barrett agreed. "We are not familiar with this area. Is there an orphanage or a mission nearby?"

The man's brow furrowed in thought. "Orphanage?"

"The child is not ours. While on the road we happened across a woman who was delirious with fever. In spite of all we could do for the child's mother, it was the Lord's will that she pass on. We have done for the child what we could, but we cannot keep him. . . ." Barrett broke off, coughing.

Abby listened worriedly, her concern for him growing. The cough sounded much deeper.

"It would be most kind of thee, sir," she continued for Barrett, "if thou could help us."

"The tot's mama died, huh? Sad. Sad, indeed. Good thing you two happened along, though. I'm afraid there's nothin' around like an orphanage. Not much but loggin' goin' on around here, and I wouldn't leave a dog in those camps, much less a child. Wish I could help."

"Thank thee," Barrett said. "God's speed, sir."

The man touched the brim of his hat in response to Barrett's blessing, then continued down the road.

As they drew closer to Shreveport, the road became more populated. Stopping each traveler they met, they asked the person if he knew of a mission orphanage or foundling home where the child would have good care. Each person shook his head, admitting that he knew of no such place.

Toward late afternoon, a man and woman approached in a wagon. Halting their wagon, the couple nodded, listening sympathetically as Barrett explained their situation.

"Oh, the poor babe," the woman crooned, looking at the tearstained face of the little boy, who peered out sadly from the blanket Abby had wrapped around him.

"Dost thee know of a mission orphanage where we might leave the little one for safekeeping?" Abby inquired.

"Well, not close by," the woman said pensively, "but I hear tell there is one further down the road—how far, I don't know, but they say you just keep riding straight and don't take the bend in the road."

Relief flooded Abby, and she hugged the little boy closer.

Gazing up at her, he murmured, "Mama."

Stunned, her heart momentarily twisted. "Did you hear that, Barrett? He called me 'mama.' "

Barrett averted his head and coughed again.

"Caught you a chill, did you?" the man asked.

Nodding, Barrett took his handkerchief out and held it up to his mouth. His body ached, and the sun bearing down made him feel light-headed.

"Lady of Our Saints Orphanage is run by sisters,

I'm told," the man said. "Of course, with the war and all, I understand they have their hands full, but I know they wouldn't hesitate to take the child in under the circumstances. He's a fine boy, isn't he? Why don't you and your wife keep him?''

Barrett tried to speak around his coughing, but Abby settled her hand on his arm protectively. "My husband is ill, and we cannot care for the child.''

"Oh, I understand.'' The man looked at Barrett, suspicion creeping into his eyes. "I hope it isn't anything serious.''

I hope it isn't either, Abby agonized. "No, nothing serious, but we just can't keep the child.''

"Well, keep to the road, and you'll see a sign just outside Shreveport,'' the man offered. "The orphanage is off the road—I've only been by it once. You'll have to watch close. The sign is a little faded.''

"Thank you for the information. God bless thee.''

"And you,'' the couple returned. The man slapped his team across their rumps with the ends of the reins and continued on his way.

"Well, it sounds like what we're looking for,'' Barrett said.

Brushing the little boy's hair back from his face, Abby gently kissed his forehead. "Yes, it sounds exactly like what we're looking for.''

Barrett glanced back at her, concern darkening his handsome features. She was getting too fond of the baby. He knew it, but there wasn't a thing he could do to stop it.

Later that night Barrett set up the small tent and made a pallet for the boy. Milk was more plentiful now. Small farms dotted the countryside, and he had learned to skim a fence and milk a cow before Abby could count to twenty.

"One more night," Barrett said after supper that night. Wrapping a blanket around his shoulders, he squatted closer to the fire. The baby was asleep, and their little camp was peaceful. Overhead, stars dotted the evening sky. "This time tomorrow night, we should be enjoying Smith's food and hospitality."

"I wish we had some meat." Abby sipped a cup of milk, not wanting to think about the time when they reached General Smith's camp. She realized that the messages they were carrying were important and that delivering them in time could determine the outcome of a battle. However, by the time they reached Smith, they would have left the child at the orphanage, the papers would have been delivered, and shortly afterward, Barrett would be taking her back to Mercy Flats.

She wasn't sure how she felt about that anymore. In the beginning all she'd wanted was to be back to Anne-Marie and Amelia, but it wasn't so bad having Barrett around. He'd been nice to her, and she felt happy with him—happy and contented.

"You think the baby's getting enough to eat?"

Abby smiled down at the infant sleeping beside her, grateful that his ordeal was nearly over. "Do you realize we don't even know his name?"

"Hattie Mae didn't say?"

"No, she wasn't rational."

Moving closer to the fire, Barrett drew the blanket around himself more tightly as a chill shook him. He glanced up, wondering if Abby had noticed. He had a fever now, but he didn't want her to know. She would try to mother him, and he was having a hard enough time trying to keep his distance from her. Every time he looked at her lately, something else ached other than his head.

"He's got to have a name." Abby thought for a minute. "I'd like to name him something from the Bible."

"Like what?"

"Like Matthew or Mark—something brave and daring. Maybe Daniel."

"I have an Uncle Daniel. He's mean as hell and twice as ornery."

"I don't want to name him something mean. I want a name that he can be proud of. Joshua is nice, or Nebuchadnezzar. He was king of Babylonia and conqueror of Jerusalem, you know."

Barrett looked up. "You will name that child Nebuchadnezzar over my dead body."

"Well, maybe Nebuchadnezzar is a little grandiose."

Coughing again, Barrett leaned closer to the fire.

"If I remember my catechism classes, the biblical Daniel was brave and strong. He was thrown into the lion's den and came out without a scratch."

"Well, there you go. If his namesake can socialize with the lions and come out in one piece, he ought to do all right in life."

"Then Daniel he is."

They sat hunched in blankets, listening to the night sounds—the howl of a coyote, the hoot of an owl, the twittering of a night bird.

"Do you ever think about what you'll do when the war is over?"

"Go home and see what's left."

"Where's home?"

"Georgia."

"Are your parents there?"

"No, they died a few years back. I have a couple of sisters and some nieces and nephews"

"Then you really aren't married." When he'd been posing as Hershall Digman, he'd said he wasn't married, but that, too, could have been a lie.

"No." Bitterness tinged his voice now, and she looked up.

"Have you ever been?"

He reached for a stick and stirred the fire, watching the sparks shoot up, then die away. It was a long time before he answered. "Is it important?"

"I guess not—I was just wondering."

Pitching the stick into the fire, he leaned back against his saddle, studying the stars. "I was married once."

Abby saw the telltale muscle tighten in his jaw. She'd noticed that anytime he was upset about something, a twitch there gave him away.

"Did she die?" Abby didn't like the thought of him with another woman. Maybe he had a child being cared for by someone at home. That would explain why he'd been so patient with Daniel.

He laughed cheerlessly. "She ran off with a circus."

"A circus!" Abby blurted, then seeing the flash of discomfort the confession had brought, she softened her comeback. "A circus?"

But she needn't have worried. Barrett's mind was on Ramona as he stared into the fire. He hadn't thought about those days in a long time, hadn't wanted to think about them. But the hatred that had burned so long and so deep within him then had been replaced over the years with apathy.

"Do you care to talk about it?" Abby asked.

"I don't know what I can tell you."

Abby knew a variety of things he could tell her. "What was her name?"

"Ramona."

"That's pretty."

His lips curved in a wry smile.

"Was she beautiful?"

"Beautiful, self-centered, and spoiled. I knew that when I married her, but when you're nineteen and in lust, those things don't bother you too much. Ramona and I had grown up together, and I guess we kind of fell into marriage."

"It was an arranged marriage?"

"Yes, at first we both thought it was more than that, but it wasn't." He'd carried the resentment of her desertion for a long time, and now, looking back on it, he knew how useless that had been.

"Ramona was seventeen when we married. She loved to sing, and she didn't have a bad voice. She was the apple of her father's eye, and he was good at filling her mind with big dreams, telling her that she was good enough to go to New York and sing in one of those big symphony halls someday."

Abby saw the smile playing about his lips, and she was stung by jealousy. In spite of all he said, she was certain that he was still in love with the beautiful, ambitious Ramona.

"But when her father walked out the door, she'd sing bawdy songs she'd heard from her brothers and dare me to stop her." His voice faded momentarily, and Abby waited for him to go on.

"We'd only been married a few months when a traveling show came to town. They were doing some sort of play, and she wanted to go. We went, and Ramona

was enthralled. All she talked about for days was how
wonderful the music was and how much better she
could have sung the lead role. I thought she was just
excited because the experience had been new and different for her.

"I got tired of hearing about the play and how
she wanted to go see it again. We were in the middle of harvest, and I told her she'd have to wait until the crops were in before we could go. One day I
came to the house for dinner, and she was gone. Just
like that. She left me a note and ran off with the
circus."

"What did the note say?"

"That she loved me, that she didn't want to hurt
me, but she wanted a chance to fulfill her dreams. She
was joining the traveling show, and when she'd made
a name for herself, she'd be back."

They sat for a moment, both lost in thought.

"Barrett?" she finally said.

He looked up. "What?"

"She didn't run off with the circus." She felt obli-
gated to point that out to him. Men could get things
so mixed up.

"She did."

"You said a traveling show—there is a difference,"
she reassured him gently.

He turned to look back into the fire. It had taken
him years to get over the fact that he'd been deserted
for a damned *circus*. It would be a blow to any man's
ego. "What's the difference?" he said in a spiritless
tone. "She left, didn't she?"

"Well, there's a difference. A circus—is a circus,
but a traveling show, well, now, that could turn any
woman's head if she had a dream to sing someday.

And it sounds to me like Ramona was young and full of life, and she didn't stop to think that maybe she'd hurt your feelings so badly that you might not be waiting when she got back.''

''And I wasn't,'' he said as though that somehow purged his part in the whole thing. ''And I'll never marry again.'' That much he knew. Once he'd overcome the hurt, he'd promised himself he was never getting that involved with a woman again.

''So, did she come back?''

''Yes, in a pine box.''

''Oh, Barrett,'' she whispered, appalled by the story's outcome.

''I got word six months later that a brawl had broken out during one of her performances. Shots were fired, and Ramona was hit by a stray bullet.''

The fire popped, sending another spray of sparks through the air in Ramona's honor.

''I'm so sorry.''

''It took a while to get over her,'' he admitted reluctantly. For years now he had kept women at an arm's length, but here he was, spilling his guts to Abigail as if he thought she could change anything.

''But you did . . . get over her?''

He didn't answer at first but continued to stare into the fire, deep in thought.

''Well, guess we better get some sleep,'' she said lamely. She wanted to say more, and she would have, but she couldn't think of a single comforting thing to say to a man whose wife had run away to join a traveling show and gotten her fool self killed.

''I'll be along in a while.''

''Don't sit out here too long.'' *And brood about Ramona*, she added silently. ''It's getting chilly.''

She climbed to her feet and leaned down to take Daniel into her arms. If you asked her, the woman was just plain looney to run off and leave a man like Barrett Drake.

Chapter 16

Just before noon the next day Abby spotted the mission's faded wooden sign that was almost hidden by the overhanging limbs of a spreading walnut tree.

Slowing the horses, Barrett read the sign aloud. "Lady of Our Saints. This is it."

Turning the horse down the narrow lane, they rode toward the house, studying the dwelling that was barely visible through the treetops. It was a large house, and while it seemed solidly built, it appeared to be in need of repairs. There were massive barns in back, and several head of cattle grazed in the fields beyond. A large garden was set off to one side, enclosed by a wire fence. Abby knew from experience that the sisters raised most of their own food.

As the horses drew closer, she saw a large number of children playing in the yard. A nun with a discerning eye stood watch over them.

The sister looked up as the horses approached, but her attention was immediately diverted by a couple of small boys who engaged in a tumbling match.

Barrett dismounted, then took little Daniel while Abby climbed off her horse. Walking slowly toward the house, Barrett sensed a hesitancy in Abby.

"It looks nice enough," he remarked.

"Yes, it looks nice enough."

Abby watched the sister who prowled the playground from the corner of her eye, wondering if she was as tolerant as Sister Lucille had been. She wasn't. She could tell by the tension in her face even from this distance that she wouldn't be as understanding of childish pranks.

Bouncing the infant up and down on her hip, she waited as Barrett knocked on the orphanage door. Daniel had endured all of the tiresome ride he wanted.

A few minutes passed before the door finally opened.

"Yes?" A sister appeared before them, her appearance austere.

Nodding, Barrett said gravely, "Sister, we have a young boy who needs a home."

"Oh, my . . ." The sister's face fell with dismay at the sight of the young Quaker child. "We are so very crowded. . . ."

"Surely there is room for one more." Abby switched Daniel to the opposite hip, trying to quiet his fussing.

Uttering a prayer, Sister ushered them into the darkened foyer. "I am Sister Mary Margaret, Mother Superior of this convent."

"Levi Howard, and my wife, Abigail."

A clatter of feet erupted as several boys half-walked and half-slid down the steps from the upper story.

"Boys, you will walk like gentlemen! Two demerits for each of you!" she reprimanded sharply.

"Yes, Mother Superior," the boys intoned repentantly. They glanced at Abby and Barrett curiously as they tiptoed along the hallway and out the back door.

Sighing, the Mother Superior turned back to the Quaker couple. "They're late for class again, and we're very strict about studies here. At times, the job is so overwhelming. . . ." Her voice faded hopelessly.

Abby hugged Daniel closer to her, picturing him a part of that long, strict, narrow line. "And when the children accumulate too many demerits?"

"A suitable punishment is chosen," Mother Superior assured her. "Each child is aware of the rules. No infractions will be tolerated."

Barrett glanced at Abby, sensing her reluctance. "How many children are here?"

"Oh, my. We've lost count. We do what we can, but the war has left so many orphans." She drew a ragged breath, wondering how they would care for yet another one. "Unfortunately, we have only the same number of staff that we had when we had just twenty children. There must be over eighty now, but none as young as this one. We will make do, however. The Lord has always provided."

Abby felt a sinking feeling in the pit of her stomach. This wasn't what she'd expected. Mother Superior seemed so stern, so puritanical, and her eyes lacked the kindness that was always in evidence in Sister Agnes's.

Mother Superior's eyes roamed puritanically over Barrett and Abby. "You are not the child's parents?"

"No, the boy's parents are dead," Barrett said.

"And you and your wife do not wish to assume responsibility for the child?" There was censure in her tone.

Lowering her eyes, Abby bit back tears. "It isn't that we don't want to keep him," she murmured.

The nun waited, her eyes unreadable now.

"We just can't," Abby finished softly.

"Very well." Her voice was cold, and Daniel

screamed as Mother Superior took him from Abby. "I'll
see that the child is settled. You and your wife are welcome to stay for supper, Mr. Howard," she invited as
she started up the stairway.

Scalding tears rolled from the corners of Abby's eyes
as Daniel's screams grew more hysterical. Holding his
arms out to her, his eyes mutely begged her to rescue
him from the stern stranger.

Whirling, Abby ran for the door, the knot in her
stomach tightening. Gripping the railing, she closed her
eyes, trying to blot out the sound of Daniel's screams
as they echoed up the stairway.

She heard the door open and close a moment later.
Barrett stood behind her, hat in hand, his eyes uncommonly bright.

Without thinking, she went into his arms. "A Quaker
man does not remove his hat," she said, sobbing.

"I know," he soothed, "I know."

He let her cry until the tears no longer came in a
rush. Handing her his handkerchief, he said quietly,
"We'll stay for supper."

"We are so short of time already." She sighed. She
hated that she was making a difficult situation even more
impossible by giving in to her emotions. Shreveport
was still a long ride, and here she was, asking him for
yet another delay when he had been so tolerant with her
almost hourly interruptions.

"Another hour or two won't make any difference,"
he conceded. The past week had been nothing but de-
lays, and time was running out, but if two hours would
make it easier for her to part with the child, they would
stay for supper.

"Thank you." Lifting her head, Abby smiled at him
through a veil of tears. Barrett thought that she had
never looked more beautiful. "I know that we have lit-

tle time. . . . But if we could just make sure Daniel's settled in properly. He's so little . . . and so frightened.''

Barrett returned her gaze soberly. "Abby, Daniel does have to stay. You must understand that. We have no choice.''

"I know—I just want him to adjust—because he's so little, and the sisters are . . . different for him. Please understand.'' She smiled, and he knew that he was beaten.

But he said simply as she returned to his arms, "I understand.''

"Single file, children! Single file,'' a strident voice called from the hallway.

Abby and Barrett sat at the dinner table later that evening, watching the children file through the doorway in a straggling line to take their seats at the three long wooden tables in a dining room adjacent to the kitchen.

The cook carried in large bowls of mashed potatoes and green beans and platters of roast chicken and set them on the tables.

A sister walked slowly up and down the aisles, overseeing the meal. There was none of the laughter and infectious whispering that would normally accompany such a gathering. A strained hush occupied the room as the children's plates were filled and set before them.

After a prayer was said, the children picked up their forks and began to eat.

The cook returned carrying two plates. Setting the food in front of Barrett and Abby, she unceremoniously returned to the kitchen.

Abby stared at the chicken, trying to swallow the lump crowding her throat. She could see Daniel strapped into a makeshift high chair across the room, being fed by a sister, who was hurriedly poking food into his mouth. Abby's appetite, which had seemed so intense only a moment earlier, had completely disappeared now.

Mother Superior entered the room, the hem of her habit brushing softly over the wooden floor. Pausing behind Abby's chair, she viewed her untouched plate and frowned.

"Is there something wrong with the chicken, Mrs. Howard?"

"The chicken is fine, Mother. I seem to have lost my appetite."

"Are you ill?"

"I must be coming down with my husband's cough."

The Mother Superior's eyes focused on Barrett assertively. "Your cough seems to be acute. Is there anything we might do to make you more comfortable?"

"Thank thee, but no. It isn't serious," Barrett insisted.

"We have been traveling in the rain," Abby explained, "and apparently my husband has caught a slight chill."

"Perhaps you should stay the night? Though the rain has let up, there is a dampness in the air."

Abby lowered her eyes. "Thy offer is most kind, but we must be on our way—"

Barrett interrupted. "How far is it to Shreveport?"

"Over a day's ride."

"No more?"

"No, but it is a long and most tiresome day's ride."

"Then I think my wife and I will accept thy generous offer." Meeting Abby's disbelieving look, he said gently, "The rain has worsened my cough. Perhaps a night's rest in a warm bed will hasten my recovery."

"I think you have made a wise choice," Mother Superior agreed. "I will have Sister Louise prepare a mixture for your cough."

"Thou are most kind," he said.

Laying a hand briefly on Abby's shoulder, Mother Superior moved on.

Leaning closer to Barrett, Abby whispered, "Thank you."

Barrett casually lifted the fork of chicken to his mouth. "I'll think of a way you can repay me." Abby poked him sharply in the ribs, and the chicken on his fork flew, nearly hitting the stern-faced sister sitting across from them.

The hem of Mother Superior's habit whispered along the hallway as she led them toward the back of the house.

"I'm sorry we have no provisions for married couples. Your beds are close, but we have nothing large enough for . . ." Sister paused, searching for the proper term, "a man and his wife."

"We don't mind," Abby told her. She looked at Barrett and grinned.

"Sister Mary Rebecca, our former Mother Superior, went to the Lord last month. She was a dear soul," Mother Superior said as she inserted a key into the lock. The door swung open, and Abby and Barrett saw a small room, dimmed by a drawn shade.

The room was Spartan, the bed covered with a thin blanket drawn so tightly that the corners were strained. A square table, the only other piece of furniture in the room, contained a pitcher and bowl and a folded white towel. A crucifix hung on the wall above the bed.

"The bed isn't large, but it will be more comfortable than sleeping on the floor," Mother Superior acknowledged as they entered the room.

Barrett's eyes fixed on the narrow bed, thankful that he wouldn't be subjected to another miserable night in a too-small bed with Abby. "This will do fine. We appreciate thy thoughtfulness."

"We are a service order," Mother Superior explained as she opened an adjoining door where a cot had been set up. "You will sleep here, Mr. Howard."

Mother Superior viewed the arrangement, her hands tucked inside the sleeves of her habit. "Our needs are simple. We have little communication with the people of the area, especially since the war has continued. Whenever help is needed, we are ready and willing to serve. We see to the orphans' spiritual needs, as well as their physical ones, and provide the discipline to make them responsible adults. Sister Mary Rebecca was particularly fond of children. She is sorely missed."

"Would it be possible to have a bath? I'll be happy to carry the water," Abby assured her. She couldn't remember ever feeling so dirty.

"I've requested water to be heated, and I will go through the clothing that has been donated to find a dress that might fit you." Mother Superior paused. "It might not be proper attire for you, but it will be clean."

"I thank thee. What about Daniel?"

"Daniel?" Mother Superior's brows lifted.

"The child," Abby said, realizing that Mother Superior hadn't even asked his name. She guessed there were so many children, names didn't matter. He was just one more mouth to feed. "If you'll permit me, I'll bathe him. Perhaps you might even find him something to wear?" The child had only the bare necessities, and even those were pitiful.

"I'm sure we can find something—it might be large, but it will be warm and dry. The washroom is just off the kitchen. The cook will be glad to show you."

Nodding, Abby smiled at Barrett.

"The cook will bring a remedy for your cough, Mr. Howard. I trust you will sleep well," Mother Superior called as she walked out the door.

Not a chance, Barrett thought wearily, viewing the narrow cot. But it was a nice thought.

When Sister Judith returned carrying Daniel, Abby smiled and eagerly reached for him.

At first he drew back, solemnly staring, then upon recognizing her, he grinned and eagerly held his pudgy arms out.

Laughing, Abby gathered him close, marveling at how much she'd grown to love him in such a short time. It was hard to believe that a week ago she couldn't have found a male that she liked. Now, she had two.

Carrying Daniel to the washroom, she paused at Barrett's door, listening to his muted cough. Was it her imagination, or was there a rattle in his chest now? Fear gripped her, but she pushed it aside, telling herself that his illness wasn't serious. He had just been in the rain too long.

The cook showed her the washroom. The cast-iron tub was filled with steaming water and waiting for her enjoyment. Sitting Daniel on the floor, she tested the temperature and smiled when she found that it was nearly perfect.

She undressed Daniel, then herself. Abby took him into the bath with her. Together they splashed and laughed, getting nearly as much water on the floor as was left in the tub. An hour passed before she finished drying and dressing him, and by then, his eyes were drooping sleepily.

She hurriedly wiped up the water on the floor, then carried the child back to her room. A short candle was burning on the table, revealing a note from Mother Superior that said the child could sleep with Abby if she preferred.

Abby preferred. Before she had Daniel settled beneath the covers, he was fast asleep.

After blowing out the candle, she sat down on the side of the bed, gazing down at him. Moonlight streamed through the small window, beckoning to her. Though she was exhausted, the moonlight was too inviting. There were so many thoughts troubling her tonight: the child . . . and Barrett.

As she slipped outside a few moments later, she drew a deep breath, savoring the smell of the rain-washed air. The night was cool, but the sky was a canopy of twinkling stars.

Strolling along the flagstone walk, she idly wondered if Barrett was sleeping. She'd seen the cook mixing herbs that would ease his cough before she and Daniel had bathed.

It would be nice if he were with her right now. They could walk together and talk about the day and how it hadn't gone as they had expected. Nothing had gone as they'd expected from the day they'd met, but he had been patient with her. Was it possible that she was falling in love with him? Her pulse raced, and that knot formed in the pit of her stomach again. She couldn't. She just couldn't! Her life had been so neatly settled until he had come along. What would she do about all the plans she and Amelia and Anne-Marie had made? And if she were to fall in love with Barrett Drake, it was so painfully clear that his heart still belonged to a dead woman. She shuddered. How could she fight a ghost for the man she loved? Anne-Marie had taught her many things, but she'd never said anything about ghosts.

And what was she to do about Daniel?

Just thinking about riding away and leaving him in the morning brought an ache to her heart. Yet she had to. She couldn't take care of a baby. She didn't know anything about babies.

Perhaps she could take him back with her to Mercy Flats. Anne-Marie and Amelia would help raise him. It wouldn't be so hard on him, and he'd have three mothers instead of one. After all, there was no reason why three grown women couldn't provide for the welfare of one small boy.

The aroma of tobacco drifted to her. Drawn to the familiar smell, her pulse quickened as she saw Barrett standing in the moonlight, one boot propped on a low stone wall as he gazed out at the quiet hillsides.

Drawing a deep breath, she casually sauntered toward him. She didn't want him to think she was happy to see him.

"Hi."

"Hi."

"Lovely night, isn't it?" She drew the shawl closer, aware that the dress the Mother Superior had provided wasn't exactly a "plain" one. The calico hugged her body in all the places that would encourage a man's gaze to linger, but the thought of Barrett's gaze lingering longer than propriety allowed didn't bother her.

"I thought you'd be asleep by now," he said, straightening. He tossed the thin cigar into the darkness, and the breeze caught the sparks and sent them into the night.

"I just put the baby down, and I was too restless to sleep." Edging closer to him, she gazed up at the stars, heaving a sigh of contentment. "It's beautiful tonight."

"Yes, it is, but you should be asleep. We have a long

day tomorrow.'' He effortlessly shifted his stance, putting a little more distance between them.

"I know.''

They gazed at the heavens, sharing a comfortable silence. She wondered at times if he was blind. Couldn't he see how she was beginning to feel about him? It was in her eyes as plain as the nose on her face every time she looked at him.

"How is Daniel?'' he asked.

She leaned against the tree, studying him. He was truly a fine-looking man, all muscles and ridges and mysterious bulges here and there that she found herself longing to explore. Most men would take advantage of a woman alone in the moonlight, but he seemed almost afraid of her. "He's fine,'' she said. "Sound asleep.''

"He can put away the potatoes and chicken.''

Abby laughed. "He's a growing boy.''

Barrett took another fluid step, intensely conscious of her scent and the way the material formed to her breasts. If he could hold out another week, just one more week, seven days, he told himself, he could return her to Mercy Flats as chaste and pure as he'd found her. Until he'd met her, he had been certain that he would never fall in love again, and he meant to hold to that vow. He didn't care how tempting she looked right now.

She pushed away from the tree, and her eyes fixed on his as she moved a step closer. "Did the cook bring you the medicine?''

"Yes, a while ago.''

It might have been the moonlight, or the fact that he hadn't been with a woman in months, but she had never looked more desirable. The sprigged cotton flagged her every curve, and the thought of stripping away the fabric and baring every inch of her slender body for his pleasure alone caused a painful tightening in his loins.

The neckline of her dress, too low for any man's comfort, shadowed her delicate shoulders and the soft curve of her breasts. His blood raced hot as she paused in front of him. Sliding her arms around his neck, she whispered softly, ''It has been a strange five days, hasn't it?''

He mentally groaned, wondering why she was doing this to him.

Her fingers toyed lightly with the tips of his ears as she gazed up at him.

''Is there something you want?'' he prompted.

''Maybe.'' She had never been so brazen in her life, but if he couldn't see that she wanted him to kiss her—well, she didn't know what else to do.

A wisp of hair escaped the loose knot at the nape of her neck, and he resignedly tucked it behind her ear. He would have liked to have kept this simple and uncomplicated. ''You ever kissed a man, Abby?''

Feeling a little fearful but a whole lot willing, she slowly shook her head.

Drawing her closer to him, he gazed down at her. ''Then maybe it's time we remedied that.''

''Are you man enough to kiss me, Barrett Drake?'' she teased.

The hue of his eyes darkened, and she wondered about the wisdom of such teasing. ''I think you'll find me man enough to do anything you'd ask.''

''But you see,'' their mouths drifted perilously close, ''that's my problem. I'm not sure what to ask.''

He chuckled, and it sounded to her as if he found her comment amusing.

''Can you help me?''

''I think I can.''

''Would it be shameful?''

''Oh, yes.''

Her eyes widened, both enchanted and frightened by the expectation. "Most shameful?"

"Most shameful," he concluded as his mouth lowered to take hers.

She suddenly felt hot, then cold, then giddy with desire. She'd never dreamed a man could make her feel so glorious. His lips tasted faintly of tobacco and the night air, and she pressed closer, eager to feel his commanding length against hers.

Pulling her flush against him, Barrett coaxed her mouth to open beneath his. Like a petal opening to the sun, her tongue met his, and a million stars exploded behind her eyes as his tongue stroked, then prodded deeper.

Her arms tightened around his neck as she was caught up in the delicious sensations he had aroused. His desire, bold and magnificent, bore into her middle, firm and unyielding in power. His abdomen muscles contracted as he forgot that she was Abigail McDougal and kissed her the way a man kissed a woman when he wanted her.

Their blood raced hot and unchecked as the kiss deepened to frightening proportions. For a moment, Barrett forgot her innocence. For a moment, passion blinded him as he sensed that when she was schooled in the ways of love, she would be a passionate, responsive lover.

Passion drove him on as his palms covered her breasts, his fingertips gently stroking them.

Gasping softly, she pulled away, her mind racing with indecision. She wanted to let him take such liberties; her heart cried out that he was the one she wanted to teach her things she had only imagined, but she was frightened. His touch was daring and experienced, and though she longed to respond, she was frightened.

It was that fear that made her turn and flee for her room, made her ignore his voice as he called after her.

"Abby, come back here!"

Tears rolled down her cheeks as she blindly ran down the flagstone walk. By taking the initiative and inviting him to kiss her, she had hoped to prove to him that she could be as worldly and refined as any other women he found desirable; instead she had succeeded in showing him what an innocent, brainless twit she really was!

"Abigail!"

Sobbing now with weariness and just plain dismay, she climbed the steps to her room, wondering how she would face him in the morning.

Slamming the door behind her, she told herself that her misery was her own fault, as usual! She should never have fallen in love with him in the first place.

Chapter 17

"Your cough is of great concern to me, Mr. Howard.
Are you certain you feel up to traveling?" Mother Superior inquired during breakfast the next morning.

"We can delay no longer, Sister, but I thank thee for
thy compassion," Barrett said in a hoarse voice.

Abby scrutinized Barrett closely as he picked at his
food, convinced that he was feverish this morning.

Leaning across the table, she whispered, "The cough
does sound worse, Barrett."

"I'm fine. Eat your breakfast."

"But you look terrible," she whispered anxiously.
His forehead was a sickly white, and his cheeks were
flushed. She had heard him cough most of the night.

"Thank you. You've made me feel considerably better."

Abby absently pushed a piece of ham around her
plate, worried about Barrett and Daniel. She knew that
they had to leave that morning, but knowing didn't make
it any easier to accept. She had been awakened that
morning by Daniel lovingly patting her cheek.

She'd watched while he crawled off the bed to try his walking skills. Clinging to the covers, he had cautiously worked his way to the foot of the bed and back, giving her a triumphant grin when he made it back without cracking his head. She had laughed at his charming antics, wishing that Barrett had been there to share them with her. But all too soon, he'd tapped on the door to tell her that breakfast was being served.

Daniel was perched on Sister Judith's lap now, stuffing scrambled eggs into his mouth hungrily.

"Abigail, if thou art not intending to eat thy ham, we must be on our way."

"Oh. Yes, of course." Abby murmured, embarrassed that he'd caught her daydreaming.

Mother Superior followed the couple outside, where the horses were saddled and waiting. Abby hugged Daniel to her tightly, dreading the moment she had to let him go.

"The cook has prepared food for your journey." Sister smiled regretfully. "It isn't much."

"It is more than enough, Sister," Barrett said, accepting the packet she offered. "Would that we had something to offer to thee in return."

She waved her hand dismissively. "When you have the means, remember us."

Kissing Daniel's rosy cheek for the last time, Abby reluctantly handed him to Sister Louise, her heart wrenching when his small hands clung to her hair possessively.

The sun was just painting the sky with pinks and yellows as Abby and Barrett turned the horses down the lane. Swallowing back the lump in her throat, Abby told herself she wasn't going to look back. But by the time they'd reached the end of the lane, she couldn't stand it any longer. Twisting in the saddle, she peered through the leaves at the house.

Sister Louise was standing on the steps, holding Daniel. The austere figure dressed in black blurred as tears blinded Abby. This was so foolish! It hadn't hurt this bad when she'd been separated from Amelia and Anne-Marie.

Tears trickled from the corners of her eyes as she watched Mother Superior try to calm Daniel, who was crying loudly now.

Jerking her head around, Abby held her body erect in the saddle in an effort to hold back her pain. It wasn't fair. A small boy, both parents gone—it just wasn't fair! Even though Daniel had had precious little time to warm to her or Barrett, they both were all he had in the world. And now they were deserting him.

She choked back a sob, but a hiccup escaped her. Averting her face so Barrett wouldn't see, she surreptitiously wiped away the scalding tears.

"He'll be fine." Barrett's quiet reassurance did little to ease her pain.

"I know he will." She breathed raggedly, trying to control her emotions.

"The sisters treated you well, didn't they?"

"Yes." *The sisters had been good, but having a set of parents would have been better.*

A meadowlark called as the horses picked their way down the lane. Tears ran unchecked down Abby's cheeks now as the orphanage gradually faded from sight.

"Damn it." Barrett suddenly stopped his horse and got off. He strode back to her horse and held out his hand to her. "Come here."

Abby slowly dismounted, not certain what he wanted.

But when he opened his arms to her, she went gratefully into them, her tears flowing again.

For the first time in her life she wanted a man to hold her; she wanted a man to make her believe, if only for the moment, that everything would be all right in her life, even though she knew that after having Daniel, it could never be the same again.

Barrett held her against his chest, feeling her slim body racked with sobs. He wished that he could ease her hurt, but he couldn't. Daniel had struck a maternal note in Abigail McDougal that wouldn't be easy to assuage. He'd seen it coming. Every passing hour had drawn her closer to the child, and he should have stopped it before it had reached this point. But he hadn't, and now they were in another fine mess.

Abby's tears dampened his shirt as he rubbed her back consolingly. When her tears finally abated, she lifted her head, finding it hard to look at him. "I'm sorry," she said, sniffing.

Blubbering this way in front of him was dreadful, especially after the way she'd made a fool of herself kissing him last night. She was never going to make him see her as a beautiful, sophisticated woman that a man couldn't live without. Not when her eyes and nose were as pink as radishes!

Wiping away her tears with the pads of his thumbs, Barrett handed her a square of gray linen. "Courtesy of the Mother Superior. She's an amazingly perceptive woman."

Abby offered him a feeble smile as she brought the linen up to dab her watery eyes. "I'm sorry. I'm such a twit at times."

"For once, I think we agree on something." His grin was impertinent, but she forgave him for being a man, for there was a sympathetic light shining in his eyes that touched her. "You're a mess, Abby McDougal."

"I know." She drew a ragged sigh. "I don't know what's gotten into me."

I know what I'd like to, Barrett thought, then wondered why he thought things like that about her. She was beautiful, but a woman and a child were the last things Barrett needed in his life right now.

Yet somehow the memory of her kiss colored his reasoning. Drawing her closer, he kissed her this time, knowing that he was only complicating matters more.

Abby's eyes drifted shut as his lips brushed against hers—once, then twice—then closed over her mouth hungrily.

Very briefly the thought registered that his skin seemed hot, but the thought was so quickly replaced by desire that it never entered her mind again.

"What are we going to do about Daniel?" Abby whispered when their lips finally parted.

"Abby," he chided patiently. "We've settled the question of Daniel."

"I haven't."

"Abby." His tone held a subtle warning, but she didn't care. She didn't know why, but the question wasn't settled. She couldn't leave Daniel in a place with strangers who were too busy and too overburdened to give him the tender love he deserved. "I want to take Daniel with us."

Smothering a curse, Barrett released her abruptly. "That's crazy! I know what you're thinking, but it's impossible. We've got to ride fast—"

"He didn't slow us down before. And if he did, it was only because he was hungry. But with food, he'll be no trouble at all," she argued.

"No."

"Yes."

"No!"

Her eyes locked with his stubbornly. "I'll take care of him," she promised. "You won't have to do a thing. I promise."

When she saw his momentary flicker of hesitancy, it was all the encouragement she needed. Standing on tiptoe, she showered his face with kisses, knowing full well that he was going to give in to her.

"We'll keep him with us until you've finished your business in Shreveport, then we'll bring him back. That way we'll have more time to help him get settled. Please, Barrett? Please?"

Barrett shook his head, sickened that she could work him this way. "It'll only make it harder on you. You'll get more attached to the child, and you'll never want to let him go."

"Nonsense. I simply want to make certain that he gets the proper love and care that any child is due. As soon as you've handed Smith the papers and we've started back to Mercy Flats, I'll be more than ready to turn him over to the sisters." She kissed him again. "And besides, he'll make it easier for us to travel without arousing suspicion. Who would suspect a Quaker family of being spies?"

Her mouth covered his again, smothering any retort he might have been thinking.

"All right," he consented grudgingly, when she finally took mercy on him. "But I'm warning you: *don't* get any more attached to the boy than you already are."

Abby clapped her hands joyfully. "I won't! I promise!"

"Of course not." He knew as well as he was standing there that it was an error in judgment—one of many since he'd met her, but she knew how to work him. It was as simple and as baffling as that. "I'm warning you, Abby—"

But she wasn't listening. She was already riding off, leaving him standing in a boil of dust as she rode back to get Daniel.

"You want the child back?" Mother Superior clearly thought that Abby had lost her mind.

"Only for a few days. Then we'll have to bring him right back."

The nun looked at her, wondering who she was trying hardest to convince, herself or everyone else.

Sister was standing on the porch, shaking her head as Abby rode off, the child in her arms once again.

Squeezing Daniel victoriously, Abby galloped her horse down the lane. She knew that she would only keep him for another twenty-four hours, but that would be enough.

"I've got him," she announced breathlessly as she stopped her horse beside Barrett's.

"You don't mean to say we can finally get on our way?" Barrett asked wryly.

"We're ready!" Abby and Daniel grinned at him.

Barrett shook his head, still marveling at how she'd talked him into this one.

They pushed hard the rest of the day, stopping only briefly to allow Daniel to crawl around freely for a few minutes. The child had become so accustomed to the rocking motion of the saddle that he'd slept most of the afternoon.

But by the time they stopped for the night, the baby was cranky again. Abby noticed that Barrett was unusually subdued. At noon, he had refused the ham and biscuits the sisters had sent, but Daniel demanded so much of her time that Barrett's behavior had slipped her mind.

But when he refused the evening meal, she got downright worried. "Are you all right?" She stood before him, her hands on her hips with a bossy look on her face.

Barrett decided that motherhood had turned her into a shrew. "I'm fine," he returned shortly.

Remembering how hot he'd felt to her touch earlier, she knew that he wasn't being honest. "You don't look 'fine,'" she said sarcastically. She reached out to lay her hand on his forehead, but he averted his head, overcome by a racking spate of coughing.

"Barrett, you're sick. You have a fever. I'm sure of it."

"Don't mother me. I'm fine."

But he wasn't. His feverish tossing that night kept Abby awake most of the time.

Shortly before dawn, he awoke, coughing violently. She sat up and leaned over to feel his forehead again. His skin was hot and dry, and he was muttering incoherently.

Crawling out of the lean-to, she hurried to the stream and filled both canteens. For the next two hours, she bathed his face and chest, but almost as soon as she dampened his skin, the moisture dried up. Her efforts seemed as useless as throwing cold water on a hot cook stove.

Thrashing around on the pallet, Barrett drifted in and out of reality, at times insisting that Abby take the papers and go on to Shreveport without him. Each time she steadfastly refused.

"Abby," he called weakly.

"I'm here, Barrett. Here, you have to drink a little more water. You're burning up with fever."

Cradling his head against her breasts, she trickled water down his throat. He was as hot as Hattie had been—oh, dear Lord, she thought, had he caught whatever had killed Hattie?

Her heart nearly stopped beating.

His dry cough sounded the same as Hattie's had— why hadn't she noticed the similarity before?

He managed a few swallows from the canteen, then fell limply back on the pallet.

"You've got to go on by yourself," he whispered.

"No, I won't leave you."

"Abby, God," he groaned, clasping his head in pain, "don't argue. Those papers have to reach Smith no later than tonight, and I'm too sick to travel."

"No." She forced back rising hysteria. She wasn't going to leave him here, sick and alone! "I can't leave you—"

"Finish this for me, Abby. Find Smith. He'll send men back for me, but the papers have to be in his hands by tonight. Tell him—" he broke into a coughing seizure, and she waited until the spasm had passed. "Tell him he'll have to divert troops to attack Banks's advance unit."

"No, Barrett, no!" She couldn't leave him. She couldn't! Yet she knew how important it was not only to Barrett but to the whole Confederacy that the message reach Smith in time.

"I don't know where to go," she said brokenly. "And I can't leave you alone. You're sick, Barrett, terribly sick."

"There's a small map . . . in my back pocket. . . . Get it."

Her hands trembled as she eased him onto his side, following his request, but even that small effort exhausted him. Quickly locating the map, she gently lowered him back onto the pallet.

"Leave now. . . . You should reach Smith's camp before dark."

"Barrett—"

"Don't argue, Abby. Kirby will send someone back for me."

Daniel's head popped up on the pallet, his blue eyes quizzical as he stared back at them in bewilderment. When he recognized Abby, he grinned.

Hurriedly changing his pinnings, Abby gave him a biscuit, then ran back to the stream to fill the canteens again. When she returned, she laid one within Barrett's reach along with a folded wet cloth.

"I'm scared," she confessed readily.

"No need to be. You'll make it. If anyone should stop you, tell them that your baby is ill and that you're trying to reach the child's father in Smith's camp."

Abby saddled her horse, trying to keep Daniel from crawling underfoot, which wasn't easy with a one-year-old.

She slipped back into the lean-to and pressed her lips to Barrett's feverish forehead.

"I wish I didn't have to leave you!"

"Won't need you, just a little cough." He rolled to his side, bending double as another spasm overtook him.

"A little cough?"

"I'm not dead yet, am I?"

She was at least thankful that he hadn't lost his dry sense of humor. Settling her head on his chest, she choked back tears. "No, but you look like you're close."

"You always could cheer me up," he murmured.

A sob caught in her throat as she held him tightly.

You have to pull through this, Barrett Drake, she agonized. *Damn you, you have to pull through this!*

Abby left shortly after dawn with Daniel tucked in front of her on the saddle.

She pushed the horse hard, galloping across open fields and down dusty roads.

Daniel, seeming to sense the urgency of their mission, contented himself with chewing on a piece of jerky Abby had given him. All day she urged the horse headlong toward Shreveport, stopping only briefly to cool and water him.

As darkness began to fall, she slowed the horse to a walk. He was dripping with heavy lather, and she was worried she was pushing him too hard.

Absently poking pieces of biscuit into Daniel's mouth, she studied the map Barrett had given her.

The drawing wasn't very clear, but there appeared to be a large square through which he'd drawn the trail. There was an alternate route drawn off to the side with the notation: five miles.

Squinting at the disjointed printing, she finally made out the words: Indian Burial Ground.

She looked up, her heart sprinting to her throat.

Silhouetted on the horizon were the wooden platforms the map indicated, platforms made of spindly limbs and laced together with rawhide, gaily festooned with feathers and weapons. Surrounding them were pots of food to help the deceased on his way to meet the Great Spirit.

An Indian burial ground. Goose bumps rose up on her arms like smallpox blisters.

Daniel began to fret, and she absently patted his leg, her eyes fixed on the frightening silhouettes of the platforms.

She suddenly became aware of the wind that had sprung up with the approaching darkness. It moaned through the platforms, the eerie sound sending a shiver up her spine.

"Oh, Lord," she said, breathing. In a few minutes it would be pitch dark, and here she sat on the edge of a burial ground! There might be all sorts of spirits lurking about . . . waiting for her.

She squinted to study the map again. The five miles Barrett had scribbled must be how far it was around the sacred ground. If she went around it, she'd lose too much time.

She glanced up, her eyes resting on the long row of scaffolds suspended in the air. She couldn't go through . . . *that*. Even Barrett wouldn't expect her to go through that!

A burial ground was sacred, guarded by spirits of the dead. Men had been killed for trespassing.

She remembered Anne-Marie saying that if an Indian warrior died in battle, he was generally left where he fell, but if he died in camp, it was customary to wrap his body in robes with his personal belongings and place him on a scaffold or high branch of a tree near the camp—her blood suddenly felt like it had turned to ice. She turned, peering over her shoulder nervously.

Did that mean there were Indians nearby? Maybe even watching her at this very moment?

Daniel squalled, and she slapped her hand over his mouth. He clamped his front teeth on the fleshy part of her palm, and she shrieked as she jerked her hand away. For a long moment, her eyes fixed on the obstacle that lay in her path as she turned the alternatives in her mind.

What would Amelia do? She'd turn around and run.

What about Anne-Marie? The answers came as swiftly as the questions. *She'd ride right through it.*

Abby watched nervously from the corner of her eye, half-expecting to see a tribe of the deceased's relatives bearing down on her.

Swallowing dryly, she shifted Daniel to settle him down.

What would Barrett do?

A picture of him lying so ill in the small lean-to prodded her. Kneeing the horse, she knew what she must do. Barrett was counting on her to get the papers to Smith. And the sooner she reached Smith, the sooner Barrett would get help.

A week ago she couldn't have imagined a man on earth that could make her ride through an Indian burial ground in the dark. A week ago she could never have imagined a man who would inspire her to ride *anywhere* in the dark, but Barrett Drake could and had, and she loved him enough to do anything.

Loved him enough to do anything.

The revelation was almost as startling as the thought of what she was about to do.

"Barrett Drake, you owe me for this," she muttered as she urged the horse to walk faster. "Hail Mary, full of grace . . ."

Her heart was pounding so hard she could hardly breathe. Nudging the horse to a faster gait, she gingerly picked her way through the line of platforms.

Oh, God, this is awful.

"Holy Mother, Mother of God, pray for us sinners now at the hour of our—" she broke off in a shriek as the horse shied, his rump bumping a platform support.

Her heart lodged in her throat as she watched the platform sway, then gradually steady.

"Oh, I'm *sorry*," she agonized, and truly meant it.

Her eyes were as round as Daniel's as darkness closed

in. An owl called, startling Daniel. He screamed, and she thought she was going to faint.

"Shhhh, it's just an owl," she soothed. "It won't hurt us."

Abby felt as if a big hand were encircling her throat, shutting off her air supply. Her heart pounded so hard it drowned out the sound of the horse's hooves, but nothing blotted the whine of the ghostly wind.

Squeezing her eyes shut, she prayed that the horse would find his own way. "Father, I don't know what I've done to deserve this, but I swear I won't ever do it again," she promised.

A strange clicking sound penetrated her terror. Forcing her eyes to open, she saw a grotesque mask staring back at her from the pole of a burial platform. The wind swayed the mask back and forth, then forward and back, banging it against the pole.

"Amazing grace, how sweet the sound," she sang. At this point, she was neither Catholic nor Protestant. She was just plain scared, so she sang the first thing that entered her mind.

Fear told her not to look up, but morbid curiosity made her wonder if it was true that the deceased were buried with their knees pulled close to their bodies.

"That saved a wretch like me!" she howled.

Tilting her head upward, she squinted, trying to make out the robed figure lying atop the scaffold. Was it a man or a woman? She couldn't tell; she no longer cared. It just looked like a lump of robe lying up there.

"I once was lost, but now I'm found—"

She remembered hearing stories of how every twelve years the Indians had a Festival of the Dead ceremony. All of the bodies were taken from the scaffolds and buried in one mass grave. The Indians would sing songs, make speeches, and recount tales of the deeds of the dead. Fixing her eyes straight ahead, she held her breath as she viewed the end of the burial ground ahead. So far, nothing had come out to get her.

It took hours or maybe only minutes to leave the sacred ground. Abby wasn't sure.

As the horse passed the last scaffold, she finished in a rush. "Was blind, but now I see."

Kicking the horse's flanks, she was off again at a full gallop.

Chapter 18

The moon had been up for hours when Abby rode into the outskirts of Shreveport.

She could see a large encampment just over the rise, and she prayed it was Kirby Smith's battalion.

The camp fires looked like tiny candles flickering through the treetops. The horse was lathered, and Abby was dripping with perspiration. Daniel had fallen asleep, and her arms were cramping from supporting his lifeless weight, but she had made it and, hopefully, in time.

Halting the horse in the shadows, she watched the camp, trying to make sure that it was Confederate. When she was able to make out the Confederate red, she breathed a sigh of relief. Even if it wasn't General Smith's camp, they could tell her where he was.

Prompting the horse forward, Abby wondered how her arrival would be met.

"Halt! Who goes there?"

"Is this General Smith's camp?"

The young man, who couldn't have been over sixteen,

stepped out of the shadows, carrying a Mississippi rifle. His voice still changing, it cracked in the midst of his attempt to sound commanding. "Who wants to know?"

Abby hesitated. "I have a message for General Smith."

"I'll pass it on."

"It . . . it's a personal message," she called.

He turned and shouted to someone behind him, "Brown. Tell the general a woman has a message for him."

"Please inform the general that I have word from Hershall Digman."

"Diggon?"

"Digman."

Abby couldn't see the young man's face for the shadows, but she could hear the doubt in his voice. "What's your name?"

"Abigail McDougal."

"Tell the general Abigail McDougal has word from Hershall Digman."

The seconds dragged by. Abby's horse shifted restlessly as she waited. A few minutes later a voice called back.

"Bring her in."

"Follow me." The young man turned and walked toward the fires.

Abby knew that it was late. The few men lounging around the low camp fires watched her curiously as she rode slowly by them.

When they reached a large tent, the young boy held the horse's bridle while Abby dismounted. Daniel murmured in protest when her feet touched the ground, but he quickly drifted back to sleep.

A second soldier led her horse away as a guard at the opening of the tent pulled back the flap.

The man sitting behind a makeshift desk looked up,

frowning at the young Quaker woman. "Miss Mc-Dougal?"

"Yes, sir."

"You want to speak to me?" Kirby Smith stood up, eyeing Daniel inquisitively.

Abby glanced at the man standing just behind the general.

Sensing her hesitancy to speak, Smith said quietly, "Alvin Moore, my aide. He can be trusted."

Abby hesitated, glancing down at Daniel. "May I lay the baby down?"

The general motioned toward a small cot. "Excuse my lack of manners. Lay him on my cot. And please, sit down. You look as if you've had a long journey."

"Thank you. I have."

Abby lay Daniel on the cot, turning his face away from the light. The boy curled bottom up, sighing as he snuggled deeper on the thin blanket.

Pulling a chair from the table, the general offered Abby a seat. A cup of hot coffee appeared in her hand, and she smiled her gratitude at the young corporal.

She brought the cup to her mouth and flinched as the bitter liquid burned a path down her throat.

"Hershall Digman sent you?"

Abby nodded as a wave of fatigue washed over her.

"You're carrying a message from him?"

"How do I know you're Kirby Smith?"

Taken by her unusual beauty, the general smiled. "Ah, a cautious woman." He leaned back in his chair and soberly considered her. "How do I know you are a Quaker?"

Abby shook her head. "I'm not."

"Then Barrett has encountered trouble."

Relief flooded her. He was Kirby Smith. "He's very ill. I'm afraid it may be the fever."

"Yellow jack?"

"I'm not sure. Through an odd set of circumstances, we came into contact with a woman along the way who was very ill. She was coughing continually, and she had a high fever." Abby glanced at Daniel, and the general could clearly see the love in her eyes. "The woman and child died during the birthing, leaving this boy an orphan. I'm not sure if Hattie died from childbirth or from the fever, but a day or two later Barrett developed a cough. He tried to make it here to deliver the papers, but he was so ill this morning he couldn't continue the mission." Reaching under the table, she withdrew from beneath her skirt the packet containing the papers and handed them to him. "Barrett said that you will have to immediately divert troops to head off Banks."

General Smith opened the papers, his features somber as he read the messages.

"Please, Barrett is so ill. . . . You must send someone back for him immediately."

"Sergeant Douglas!" Smith bellowed.

A rough-faced man appeared in the opening of the tent.

"Sir!"

General Smith's eyes pinpointed Abby. "Can you draw a map of where you left him?"

Abby rose and removed her bonnet. "I'll show them the way."

"Nonsense. You're exhausted." She looked ready to collapse, and Kirby couldn't be responsible for the child. "You will remain here in camp. My men will find him." Turning back to the sergeant, he barked, "Take three men and follow the map she draws. A member of my staff needs assistance. I suggest you approach with caution. He's sick with fever and may not be capable of sound judgment, and he's a damned good shot under any circumstance."

"He doesn't have a gun," Abby said wearily. "We were posing as a Quaker couple, and we didn't think it wise to carry one."

The general stared at her for a moment, then broke into a chuckle. "Excuse me," he said, trying to get himself under control, "but the image of Barrett Drake posing as a Quaker confounds my imagination."

"He was unforgettable as Hershall Digman," Abby admitted as she busied herself drawing a map on the paper that he had provided.

The general chuckled again as he handed the map to the sergeant after she'd finished.

"It isn't very clear," she said, looking worried.

Studying the crude drawing, the sergeant tried to ease her fears. "We'll find him."

As the sergeant left the tent, Abby sank back onto the chair, closing her eyes in exhaustion.

"Forgive me, Miss McDougal. I'll have one of my men escort you to your quarters."

"I would be ever so grateful," she admitted.

The general called out again, and a tall, blond man stepped inside.

"Sergeant Dobbs, find a place for Miss McDougal and the baby to sleep."

"Thank you, General."

"Thank you, Miss McDougal. When you're rested, we'll talk again."

"Yes," she returned vaguely, "we'll talk." She was numb with weariness, yet her heart grieved for Barrett. Would they be able to find him using the hopelessly inadequate map that she had drawn? She could only pray that they did . . . and soon.

Sergeant Dobbs picked up Daniel, then escorted Abby out of the tent.

Abby followed him as they walked across the campground toward a long row of tents.

"You'll be sleeping in Lieutenant Bennett's tent. He won't be needin' it for a while," the sergeant said.

"He's not—"

"No, ma'am. He's wounded but doin' fine. Doc's got him over in the hospital tent." Abby followed his gaze to a long tent that was dimly lit. She could see the silhouette of a portly man moving about inside and row after row of occupied cots.

"Here ya' are," the sergeant drawled softly. "You and the boy should be just fine."

"You're very kind, Sergeant."

"If there's anything I can do for you, you call. I'll be close by." He gently lay Daniel in the center of one of the two cots in the tent.

"I'll bring some fresh water. I'm afraid the facilities here aren't the best for a lady—"

"I'll need very little, Sergeant. Thank you again." The sergeant had the nicest smile she had ever seen.

After he'd left, Abby sank onto the edge of the cot and closed her eyes wearily.

"Oh, Barrett," she murmured. She missed him so much her heart ached nearly as much as her body.

Plucking the pins from her hair, she released it to fall over her shoulders. Massaging her scalp for a moment, she leaned over and lowered the lantern flame.

She stretched out on the cot and prayed for Barrett and for the men General Smith had sent to get him. Most of all, she prayed that none of them were squeamish about Indian burial grounds.

Moments later, she was sound asleep.

* * *

Abby awoke with a sudden start. Sitting up, she tried to orient herself. The sounds of the camp confused her for a moment, until she remembered where she was.

Daniel was awake, entertaining himself with a hat that had been hooked on a tent pole, playing peek-a-boo with himself.

"Miss McDougal?"

Sergeant Dobbs's voice came from just outside the tent.

Abby hurriedly raked her fingers through the tangles in her hair before starting to braid the long strands.

"Yes, Sergeant. Come in."

Sergeant Dobbs pushed back the tent flap and bent to step inside. As he straightened, his gaze met Abby's, holding for a moment.

"Thought I'd escort you and your son to breakfast."

"Oh," Abby tried to talk around the pins in her mouth as she twisted her hair into a coil at the nape of her neck, "Daniel isn't my son. Captain Drake and I assumed his care after his parents died."

"Oh." The Sergeant's eyes filled with concern. "Indians?"

"Idiots," Abby muttered, recalling the father's senseless death.

"Then you and the captain are—" He broke off, a flush dotting his fair complexion.

Abby stared back at him a moment before his implication sank in. "Oh, no, nothing like that."

"Well," he released a sigh of relief, "that's nice to know." He grinned broadly. Wasn't often they got a woman in camp, and it'd be a shame if this one was already taken.

"Oh?" She tilted her head teasingly. The sergeant seemed so young. Barrett was so much older and more experienced and more handsome and more . . . She stopped her thoughts. "Why's that, Sergeant?"

Sergeant Dobbs blushed, trying to cover his blunder. "Would you join us for breakfast?"

"I'd love to."

"Can't guarantee how good it'll be, but the cook's pretty good at makin' what little we have taste like food."

Abby quickly changed Daniel's pinnings. As they left the tent, the sergeant insisted on carrying him as they walked to the commissary tent.

The tent, just slightly larger than the hospital, had all four sides rolled up. Several men sat at makeshift tables. Others lounged outside. All had respectful but appreciative looks in their eyes as Abby passed.

She didn't find their glances alarming; it had been some time since they'd seen their wives or sweethearts, and she understood how lonely a person could get when he was separated from his loved one.

Sergeant Dobbs settled Abby and Daniel at a table and went to fill their plates.

"Pardon me, ma'am."

Abby turned to find a young man wearing a gray uniform jacket bearing corporal stripes and a mismatched pair of butternut brown trousers standing beside her.

"I wondered, if the boy took to me, could I hold him a bit? My boy was about his age when I left home. I reckon he must be about four now."

Abby's eyes softened with concern. "You haven't seen your son in three years?"

"Once. But he was asleep and didn't know I was there. We were passing by, and I only got to stay a minute."

"Of course you can hold him, Corporal."

The war had barely touched the lives of the Mc-
Dougal sisters. Abby had never thought about men who
hadn't seen their families in months, sometimes years.
The deplorable conditions in camp made her realize for
the first time how much these men had sacrificed for
their cause.

"I think Daniel would let you help him with his
breakfast."

The corporal bent and began getting acquainted with
Daniel, who, after a moment's shyness, was soon bask-
ing in the attention of the corporal and others who
watched the boy's antics with interest.

"They're lonesome for their own boys." Sergeant
Dobbs set a full plate of gruel and hard tack in front of
her. "Chickory coffee, sorry."

"Are you a family man, Sergeant?"

"No, ma'am. And I'm grateful. The war's hard
enough; I couldn't stand being away if I had a wife and
little ones."

Abby sipped her coffee, watching as the men played
with Daniel. "Do you know Mr. Drake?"

"The captain? Yes, ma'am. Know of him, least
ways."

Abby felt unsettled as she thought about Barrett. Had
the men found him? Was he . . . no, she didn't dare
think the worst for fear that it might come true. "What's
he like?"

"Well, I can't say, ma'am. He keeps to himself most
times."

"Has he been in the service long?"

"Quite a spell. They say he's content with military
life. Rumor had it his great-grandfather fought in the
Revolutionary War and his grandfather in the Mexican
War. Born to it, they say, followin' the men of the Drake
family in graduatin' from the military academy."

"You and Barrett have the same accent. Are you from Georgia?"

"Yes, ma'am. Different ends of the state. How about you?"

"West Texas."

"West Texas, well I'll be darned."

Daniel had quickly discovered that any antic he tried brought boisterous laughter, and he was busy outdoing himself entertaining the growing group of men gathering around him.

Abby was on her feet instantly as a sentry's voice suddenly rang out, "Riders comin' in!"

Abby raced out of the tent to the edge of the camp, her eyes fixed on the three riders approaching. She could see the horses were pulling a travois, and her pulse quickened.

Running beside Barrett's stretcher, Abby started to cry. He looked so very still. Reaching out to touch his hand, she willed him to open his eyes, but he didn't respond. He was unconscious, not even aware that she was there. His lips were cracked, and his breathing was so shallow that she had to lay her head on his chest to make sure that he was breathing at all.

The camp doctor, having been advised of Barrett's arrival, stepped out of the medical tent and waited. The horses stopped, and the men quickly dismounted and carried the stretcher inside the tent, Abby close on their heels.

She was alarmed by Barrett's appearance. Even with the two days' growth of beard covering his face, she could see that his fever was dangerously high.

"How is he?" she asked anxiously.

The doctor glanced at her, bending to his task of unbuttoning Barrett's shirt.

"Bring me that bucket of water," he directed.

Abby complied, dampening a cloth and bathing Barrett's face while the doctor listened to his heartbeat. When she had left him twenty-four hours ago, he'd been tossing with fever. Now he seemed ominously quiet. The doctor felt for a pulse. When he released Barrett's wrist, it fell to the cot limply.

"I think it might be yellow fever," Abby supplied. "What do you think?"

"Good Lord, that's all we need." Dr. Greene walked to the end of the stretcher, removed Barrett's boots, and tossed them at the end of the cot.

While he proceeded to unfasten Barrett's trousers, Abby busied herself with rinsing out the cloth. When she turned around again, Barrett's clothing was piled on top of his boots, and he was covered with a light sheet.

"We have to get his fever down," the doctor said more to himself than to her.

"I want to help."

The doctor glanced up, then went on working. "If it's the fever, you're in danger."

"It doesn't matter. I was around Hattie, too."

The doctor set to work with Abby at his side. It was an hour before they stepped back, wiping their hands on a cloth.

"What happens now?" Abby murmured.

"We wait."

"Wait?" Her face fell. She had hoped that by now Barrett would have responded. But he lay as still as death, his body racked with fever.

"Try to get some water into him. I'll have the cook make a broth. You can spoon it down his throat, as long as he'll swallow it. See that he doesn't choke." The doctor moved on as two more were carried into the tent.

Sergeant Dobbs assumed the full care of Daniel so

that Abby could stay with Barrett. She spent the morning alternately washing Barrett's face, chest, and arms with water, then carefully dribbling teaspoons of water and broth into his mouth.

The day wore on, and darkness fell, but Abby refused to leave his bedside.

Burying her face in her hands, she listened to his racking cough, praying for some small sign that he would live. She offered God everything she had to offer, promised to give up her evil ways and do any novena He wanted, if only He would let Barrett live.

"Miss McDougal?"

She looked up to find Sergeant Dobbs standing in the doorway of the tent.

"Sergeant. I'm sorry, if Daniel—"

"He's just fine. The men are enjoyin' takin' care of him. Helps them feel like they've got a little bit of home." His brow furrowed with compassion. "You must be tired. I'll sit with him while you rest a bit."

"No, I want to stay with him—but thank you."

"You're going to make yourself sick. At least let me bring you somethin' to eat."

For the first time that day she noticed that she was hungry. "I'd be very grateful, Sergeant. Thank you."

"No trouble at all, ma'am."

"Please, call me Abby."

"Yes, ma'am, it would be an honor. I'll be right back."

When he returned, he was carrying a plate of stew, a chunk of bread, and two cups of coffee. Pulling his chair closer to the cot, he drank coffee while she ate.

With half her attention on Barrett and the other half on their conversation, Abby found herself telling him about Anne-Marie and Amelia and how much she missed them.

"That's why I had trouble leaving little Daniel with the nuns," she confided. "I want to make sure he has the best care I can provide for him. At first, I thought I might take him back to Mercy Flats with me, but I'm not sure that's wise. I wonder if there might be a childless couple in Shreveport who would want to adopt him?"

"Might be. I'll tell the men to keep an ear open."

Abby studied the young sergeant's face and found it to be handsome in an aristocratic way. Not rugged and breathtakingly handsome like Barrett's, but infinitely kind. "What did you do before the war, Sergeant?"

"I was a teacher."

Abby was surprised. "A teacher? How strange to find you in a sergeant's stripes."

"I find it so, too," he admitted. "But every ablebodied man has been called to support the cause."

She smiled. "The cause. I guess I'm like a lot of people. I thought the war was about the issue of slavery, but Barrett says it's really over the right to govern yourselves."

"Well, not entirely, but I do believe in selfgovernment. As a teacher, I reported to a school board, most of whom didn't read or write and some of whom didn't see the importance of education at all. In their eyes, a teacher is an expendable item.

"When I tried to explain the importance of a boy knowing how to read and work his sums, the importance of knowin' something about the history of his country and of the world, the board just plain didn't understand. Gettin' money to buy books became a major issue. I guess I was ready to give up teachin' and try somethin' new when the war broke out."

"How do you feel about teaching now?"

"Ignorance is no excuse for anythin'. I'll go back to

teachin', and I'll buy the books and supplies myself if I have to. Children need to be taught not only the basics, but philosophy and literature as well.''

Abby sighed, tucking the blanket closer around Barrett. "My sisters and I were educated by the nuns at the mission. We learned to read from the scriptures and what few books the mission was given.''

"Bein' from Texas, I guess the Spanish influence is very strong.''

"Yes, I knew very little about what was happening in this part of the country." She smiled. Or the world for that matter, she thought. "I know Barrett must think I'm pretty ignorant.''

"Not ignorant. Just unaware," Dobbs corrected. "A pretty woman like you could never be accused of being ignorant.''

Abby returned his smile warmly. "Beauty precludes education?''

"No, but in your case the two are mutually inclusive. Beauty and intelligence, along with courage. I don't know of many women who'd be doin' what you're doin'.''

"Well, seems I've always been long on determination. Stubborn, I believe the sisters at the mission called it.''

"I'm sure determined is more like it. Could I bring you fresh water from the creek?''

"That would be very nice of you.''

"I'd be happy to do it. Is there anything else you need?''

"You can check on Daniel for me." She felt bad about virtually deserting the child. "When the men get tired of playing with him, you can bring him to me.''

"The boy'll be fine. I'll keep an eye on him for you.

I imagine he'll be wantin' to go to bed soon. I'll bed him down in your tent.''

"Thank you, Sergeant."

"Doyle." He smiled. "If I call you Abby."

"Thank you, Doyle," she amended.

The way she'd said his name brought a big smile to his face. "No, thank *you*, ma'am."

Word circulated throughout camp that the Quaker woman wasn't Quaker after all.

Toward morning the second day, Barrett began to toss and moan, rolling around on the cot.

Abby jerked awake and stood up. "Doctor. Doctor!"

Doctor Greene rolled out of his cot, half-asleep. Pushing to his feet, he walked to Barrett's side and began to examine him with his short but competent hands.

"Looks like he's coming around. His temperature's lower."

"But he's still unconscious."

"And he could be for a while. He's not out of the woods yet."

As the sun came up, Barrett's mutterings became more coherent.

"You sure you don't want to go on over to the commissary and have a bite to eat?" Doctor Greene asked Abby as Barrett called out a woman's name again.

"No, thank you." Leaning over him, Abby's lips thinned as she caught the tail end of the name he was calling. It was Mona.

Ramona.

He's actually calling for his ex-wife.

Tossing the cloth into the half-empty bucket, she stepped outside the tent to gain control of her temper.

"Ramona! Oh, Ramona!" she mimicked as she paced back and forth in front of the tent. "I'm sick,

Ramona. Rub my forehead, rub my back.'' No wonder Doctor Greene was so insistent that she go eat. Men. She hated them all!

By afternoon, Barrett seemed worse instead of better. It was all Abby could do to keep the covers on him.

Concern wrinkled her forehead in a perpetual frown, but the doctor seemed to think that it was only a matter of time before the fever broke.

Abby wondered exactly where his experience lay, with animals or people.

''Ramona,'' Barrett murmured. ''Ramona?''

''I'm here, Barrett.'' It galled Abby to appease him this way, but if he lived, she'd see to it that he'd pay. She irritably wrung out the cloth and wiped his feverish face.

''Did you feed the dog?'' he rambled.

''Yes.''

''Did he eat?''

''Yes,'' she returned stoically.

''Ramona . . .''

Glancing over her shoulder to see where the doctor was, she wadded up the cloth and wedged it between his lips.

''Ramooooaaa . . .''

''Miss McDougal.''

Abby jumped and guiltily jerked the cloth out of his mouth and dropped it back into the pan of water. ''Yes, Doctor?''

''You should eat something,'' the doctor called from across the tent. ''You're getting cranky.''

Doyle entered the tent, carrying a tin plate. ''I've brought her dinner, Doctor.''

''Good.'' The doctor looked at her sternly. ''I'll remind Barrett that you're in his debt.''

''Come on, ma'am. Let's go outside,'' Doyle coaxed.

"I can eat right here." Abby dropped onto the chair next to Barrett's cot, holding her hand out for the plate. "I don't mind, really."

Shrugging, he handed it to her. "Never saw a woman so protective," he grumbled.

Doyle sat with her again as she ate. Tonight they talked of gentler times, of his home and his family. Abby was aware that the young sergeant was attracted to her, but she was too tired and too polite to openly discourage his interest.

The sergeant finally left her to stand guard duty, and as darkness fell, Abby continued her bedside vigil.

The lantern's rays bathed Barrett's features in the shadows as she knelt beside his cot. Her eyes filled with love when she noticed how much thinner he'd grown during the past few days. Somehow it made him more handsome, carving his features more finely.

A stubble of beard shadowed his cheeks, and since he was still for the first time in hours, she decided to shave him. She and Amelia had watched Father Luis shave through a crack in the door many times, though he hadn't been aware of the invasion of privacy.

It took a bit of finesse. She carefully anticipated any abrupt movement on his part to keep from cutting his throat, but she managed.

When she was finished, she washed his face and surveyed her handiwork, satisfied that he looked better and must surely feel better whether he realized it or not.

Dr. Greene returned and checked his patients one last time before bedding down at the back of the tent.

Abby's back ached with fatigue, and she seriously considered going to her own tent for the night, but when Barrett coughed, she knew that she couldn't.

Corporal Bower stopped by to assure her that Daniel

was already asleep, exhausted from the big day he'd had. He promised to keep an eye on the boy for her.

Knowing that she couldn't stay awake another night, Abby decided that the best thing to do was to make herself a pallet beside Barrett's cot. That way she'd know if he needed anything during the night and Dr. Greene wouldn't be disturbed. She'd seen the shadows of exhaustion beneath his eyes and the weight of his years stooping his shoulders.

"Mona," Barrett murmured.

"Shut up, Barrett," Abby muttered as she made her pallet.

She lay down, knowing that she would get very little rest, but some was better than none at all.

As Barrett called out Ramona's name again, Abby heaved a sigh and reached out to gently pat his hand. "I'm here, darling," she whispered, "I won't leave you."

He immediately settled down, seeming to rest more quietly now.

Rays of warm sunlight filtered through the tent as Barrett stirred the next morning.

Sitting up, Abby felt a pang of guilt for sleeping so soundly. It must be very late, she realized as she heard the commotion in camp.

"Don't concern yourself," Dr. Greene said from the bedside of a cot near her. "You and he both needed the rest."

"I—I'll get fresh water," she stammered.

"I'll do that for you," Doyle called from the door of the tent.

"Thank you—"

"I've brought your breakfast, and Daniel is playing in the commissary."

"Doyle, really. You don't have to keep doing this for me—"

"But I want to," the sergeant said graciously.

Throughout the day, he carried her meals and brought Daniel to see her for brief intervals before taking him off to play again. The child was glowing from all the food and attention he was getting, so Abby didn't feel so bad about leaving him.

That evening Barrett seemed to be resting comfortably. His forehead wasn't nearly as hot, and Abby was almost tempted to believe the doctor when he said he was getting better.

When Sergeant Dobbs stopped by with her evening meal, he mentioned that several of the men were playing cards over in the commissary.

"Oh?" She was good at cards. She and Amelia used to sit up all night stealing each other's money. "Do they play often?"

"It's the only thing to do, unless we're on patrol or standin' guard. Until the next battle, that is."

"I suppose playing cards does pass a lot of time," she mused.

"It sure does—though it wouldn't be something a lady would understand."

She got to her feet and stretched lazily. "My father used to play cards."

"Did he now?"

"Poker, I believe. He tried to teach us girls before he died, but, of course, the sisters wouldn't let us play. Not at the mission."

"Perhaps you might enjoy watching the game tonight," the sergeant suggested.

Abby studied the sergeant's earnest expression, disappointed that he was so gullible. It wouldn't be fair of her to take advantage of the men, especially considering that they'd all been so nice to her, and yet . . .

"I'd love to watch, but I can't leave the captain."

"I could have the men move a table over here. Why, you might even get to play. Just for fun," he clarified.

"Oh, certainly. Just for fun," she agreed. "Well, if you don't think the men would mind—"

"No, they wouldn't mind a bit. I'll ask when I take our plates back."

"Well, don't insist," she told him. "I don't want to be any trouble."

"It won't be a problem," he assured her.

Thirty minutes later, a table was set up in front of the medical tent. Abby watched four men play poker as Doyle explained the finer points of the game to her all wrong.

"Would you like to sit in on a hand?" one of the men invited.

"Oh, no, I couldn't—"

"Here," another said, springing to his feet, "take my chair. I've got watch in a half hour anyways."

Abby reluctantly sat down and picked up the cards she was dealt. They allotted her a measly amount of matchsticks, but the stakes weren't high, so she wasn't concerned. The men assumed that she was being cautious because of her inexperience, and they had a grand time teaching her the rules during the first two hands.

Then, when it seemed that she was getting the hang of the game, they settled down to more serious play.

"Why, I can't believe my luck!" Abby exclaimed, scooping up the handful of coins they were using now that the men were convinced she was an imbecile.

"Beginner's luck is definitely on your side," one of the sergeants complained, throwing his cards down.

Abby took the pot the next four hands in a row.

"Why, I do declare, gentlemen. Can you believe such a stroke of luck?" She batted her eyes, clearly aghast at her good fortune.

"Yeah. If I didn't know better, I'd say you'd played this game before," one of the men grumbled.

"Me?" Abby smiled as she cut the deck. The McDougal girls had cut their teeth on a deck of cards. Irish had supported his family by drawing strangers into a game with his blarney, then beating their socks off.

When she won the next two hands, two of the men gave up, but another two were waiting to take their places.

She was careful to let one or the other win a pot now and then, but she saved the big ones for herself.

One surly corporal watched her from the corner of his eye like a hawk, convinced that she was dealing from the bottom of the deck. By midnight there were more than a few disgruntled players at the table.

"Don't that beat all you ever seen!" The corporal threw his hand on the table as Abby laid down a royal flush.

"Well, it has been delightful, gentlemen, but it's getting late." She yawned delicately, feigning exhaustion.

"Yeah, real delightful," Sergeant Stredevant mocked. The witch had taken him for over three dollars!

Abby smiled back at the sergeant nicely. "Thank you ever so much for teaching me the finer points of the game. It's been an experience. Don't you agree, gentlemen?"

Doyle shot the men a swift visual reprimand. "Our pleasure, ma'am. It isn't often we're whipped by someone so pretty."

"Why, Sergeant Dobbs, how you do turn a phrase,"

Abby replied modestly. "Thank you again, sirs, but I must bid you a good evening now."

"You got a feeling that woman just slickered us?" Sergeant Stredevant asked Corporal Mason as they walked away.

Corporal Mason not only felt it, he knew it, but he damned sure wasn't gonna admit it!

Chapter 19

By the third day, Abby began to notice increased activity about the camp. It was obvious that the men were preparing for a coming battle.

"How's your patient today?" Dr. Greene asked that morning.

"Better, I think."

The doctor checked Barrett over, then drew the sheet back over him. "I don't think it's yellow jack."

Abby sagged with relief. "Are you sure?"

"About as sure as I can be. I think you'll begin to see an improvement any day now."

"I'm still worried that he hasn't regained consciousness."

"It'll be soon, I think," the doctor encouraged. "If he doesn't, it won't be for lack of care. Wish I had a dozen like you." He smiled at her, then moved on to the next bed.

Sitting down on her stool, Abby folded her hands and waited. That's all she'd done lately, but she didn't mind.

As the heat began to build in the tent, she found

herself nodding off. An annoying fly buzzed overhead, darting on and off her cheek. Brushing the pesky insect away, she tried to keep her eyes open, but they felt as heavy as weights.

Swiping the fly away again, she was vaguely aware of the moans surrounding her. There was so much pain and suffering inside the tent and so little anyone could do to ease the agony.

She nodded off, waking with a start a moment later. Forcing her eyes open, she glanced down at Barrett, and her heart nearly stopped.

His eyelids were moving. As she stared at him, one eye flickered open, blinking as he tried to adjust to the bright sunlight streaming through the opening of the tent.

"Barrett? Can you hear me?" Abby clasped his face between her hands, leaning closer. "It's me, Abby. Can you hear me?"

"Abby?" he asked in more of a croak than a whisper.

She grinned. "Yes! We're at General Smith's camp. He has the messages, Barrett. We got them to him in time."

"In time?"

"Yes, oh, darling, you've been so sick." She hurriedly reached for the cloth and wrung it out. Though he kept his eyes closed, he seemed conscious. Abby's heart filled with joy as she bathed his face with the cool water. He was going to be fine. He was going to be fine!

"Where are we?"

"Kirby Smith's camp. Just outside Shreveport. We've been here three days."

"Three days?"

"Yes."

He tried to sit up, but Abby pushed him back. "No. You must rest. Everything's fine. The general came by this morning to tell me that without your efforts, the army would have been unprepared for General Banks's advancing troops."

Barrett seemed to relax after that and fell asleep again. This time his rest seemed more peaceful.

Abby sat on the stool, watching him for a long time. When she was certain that he was comfortable, she decided that she could take the opportunity to check on Daniel.

As she walked through camp, she smiled, exchanging pleasantries with the men. She'd come to know many of them in such a short time.

She was struck by the bonhomie the Johnnie Rebs shared. Their uniforms were ragged, half wearing gray, the other half wearing butternut brown, with a goodly number wearing both colors. She had listened to their dry, racy humor that seemed to break out at the least provocation. Though they seemed like soldier boys, they were obviously grown men who knew their responsibilities.

Many were homesick, and the songs they sang around the camp fire were of home and girlfriends and wives left behind. They sang lustily and with abandon, and she'd discovered that many of them had very good voices. One song she particularly favored was called "Gay and Happy"—"So let the wide world wag as it will. We'll be gay and happy still. . . ."

Tents and camp equipment seemed worn. Spades and axes were a luxury. One of the main jobs assigned to a detail was the task of gathering wood for the fires each morning, especially the cook fire. Another detail was sent to scour the countryside for food, butchering any animals they could command from farmers and bringing in "donations" of flour and staples from others. The war had gone on so long that there just wasn't much food left for anyone, even an army supporting a cause that most in the area considered just.

Besides poker, the men played seven-up and vingt-et-un. Others spent their free time polishing their muskets and bayonets with well-moistened wood ashes. What a contrast—bright muskets and tattered uniforms. Abby knew now why Barrett had chosen the role of a shoe salesman for his guise. Many of the men had completely worn out the soles of their shoes, and more than a few were entirely barefoot.

"Howdy, ma'am," a redheaded, freckle-faced soldier greeted Abby warmly.

"Hello. How are you?"

"Fair to middlin', I'd say."

She smiled, entering her own tent for the first time in days. She found Daniel playing with Doyle, the two having a grand time.

"How's the captain this morning?" Doyle asked as he caught Daniel by the seat of his pants as he tried to shinny out of the tent.

"He's awake," Abby said, relief evident in her voice.

Doyle looked at her, the smile fading from his lips. "You think a whole lot of the captain, don't you?"

"I try not to think about the captain any more than necessary," she conceded, because she knew how hopeless it was.

Now that Barrett was on his way to recovery, he'd be taking her back to Mercy Flats before long, and then she'd never see him again.

"What day is it?" Abby asked.

"Well, I'd say it's April." Doctor Greene finished examining Barrett the next morning, looking pleased by his progress. "I would imagine somewhere about the sixth or seventh."

"April sixth," Abby mused. So much had happened in the last week and a half that even thinking about it made her mind whirl. "Is Barrett improving?"

"He's doing fine. He should be staying awake for longer spells now."

That evening Abby stood outside the medical tent and watched as most of the men in camp were called to company. They marched out to the accompaniment of a muffled drum. Something about the sight made Abby uneasy.

"Where are they going?"

"To Mansfield, I hear," Dr. Greene said, as he stood watching with her.

"Where's that?"

"Some forty miles south of Shreveport."

Apprehension filled her voice as she whispered, "Will they engage in battle?"

"Rumor says General Banks is movin' troops clear across Louisiana. Could be as many as twenty thousand or more."

"General Smith can't seriously be thinking of trying to fight that large a force with our men—"

"No, General Taylor and General Smith are looking to combine forces in Mansfield."

Abby's eyes closed with relief. "Good. We'll give them blue bellies a run for their money," she murmured.

The doctor glanced at her. "You support the cause, Miss McDougal?"

Abby watched the men marching out of camp, many of whom had treated her like family. "Well, I'm not sure that anything can be settled by fighting, Doctor

Greene, but I guess maybe for now I support the cause.''

"Well, I think I'll get some rest," the doctor said, wearily turning away. "We'll have casualties by tomorrow noon."

Abby slept poorly that night. Although she was back in her own tent with Daniel, her thoughts were on Barrett and on the men who were marching to meet Banks's troops at Mansfield.

The men's faces drifted before her eyes, both young and old. She wondered if young Corporal Howard would ever see his infant daughter, or if Sergeant Miller would come back to marry his Suzanne, or if nice Lieutenant Madison would ever get to hold his new grandbaby.

She didn't believe in fighting, and she didn't know much about the cause, but she knew those men, and she wondered if anything could be worth the loss of even a single one of them.

Barrett was awake when she returned to the medical tent the next morning. Though he was weak, she was encouraged to see that he was improving every hour.

"I hear there's a battle."

"Yes. I'm afraid so."

"Well, the men are well trained," he murmured. "And Smith's a damn good general."

She could tell by the tone of his voice that he was angry because he wasn't marching with them.

"It makes me sad to think that some won't be coming back."

Barrett saw the sorrow in her eyes and wondered if there was anyone in particular she was worried about. Dr. Greene had told him of her refusal to leave him and of her constant care, but he'd mentioned that a certain

Sergeant Dobbs had been very solicitous of Abby, making sure she'd rested and eaten properly, as well as seeing to it that Daniel had been well taken care of.

"You worried about anyone in particular?"

She noticed that he deliberately kept his tone casual.

"Yes," she admitted. "Sergeant Dobbs, among others. All the men in camp have been exceptionally good to Daniel—"

"Miss McDougal."

Abby turned to see a young corporal standing nervously in the tent opening.

"Yes?"

"Lieutenant Moore has sent me to invite you to join the general for supper tonight."

"But . . . I thought the general had left with—"

"General Smith will be joining his men immediately after supper," the corporal assured her.

"Oh, I see. Then please tell the general that I'll be happy to dine with him."

"Thank you, ma'am." He saluted automatically, then flushed with embarrassment at Abby's smile.

"Seems you've made a few conquests since you arrived," Barrett grumbled.

"Don't be silly," Abby said, unconsciously smoothing her hair.

"Suppose I can't blame them," he muttered, more to himself than her. "Most of them haven't even seen a woman in months. Anything in skirts would look good to them."

Stung by his implication that any woman, no matter how ugly she was, would have sparked the same courtesies, Abby flung the washcloth at the pan of water and stalked out of the tent. Barrett's wicked chuckle followed her.

Oh, he's getting better all right. Too frisky!

* * *

That evening, Abby was dressed and waiting when the corporal came to escort her to the general's tent.

"You look real nice, ma'am," the boy complimented.

"Corporal," Abby looked at him chidingly, Barrett's earlier observation still bedeviling her, "this is the same dress I've worn since I got here." It was the only one she had.

"Yes, ma'am." The boy's face colored painfully. "But somehow a man don't seem to notice."

Though the food was exactly the same as they served in the commissary, the general had managed to unearth a red wine that, while it wasn't the best, was palatable.

All in all, it was a pleasant evening, and Abby strolled back to the medical tent later, humming a tune that she'd heard the men singing earlier.

"So, you've enchanted the general," Barrett commented dryly from the shadows.

"Since you're so sarcastic, I take that to mean you're feeling better tonight?" she returned as she walked right past him.

"No, I feel like hell. Maybe a sponge bath—hey!"

"Hey, what?" She kept right on walking.

"Aren't you even going to check on me tonight?"

"You sound like you're doing fine to me." She continued on, disappearing into her tent a moment later.

"Well I'll be damned." Barrett stared after her, wondering when she'd gotten so uppity.

She slept fitfully that night, her dreams consumed by pictures of a battle, bodies of men she knew falling on the fields, blood splashing across the fronts of their uniforms. She awoke almost as tired as when she'd gone to bed.

There were few men at breakfast the next morning, and Abby was surprised when Sergeant Dobbs sat down beside her.

"I thought you'd be gone with the others," she exclaimed, relieved to see him.

"Someone has to stay," he stated.

She wasn't sure how he felt about being left behind, and she didn't ask. Some men would be sensitive about staying at the fort. Others, like Doyle, she suspected, might be just as glad they weren't involved in the killing. Abby couldn't fault him for that. War, she decided, was an inhumane business, no matter what side a man was on.

Barrett was sitting outside the medical tent as Sergeant Dobbs walked Abby back to her tent.

The sergeant was carrying Daniel, who was obviously enamored of him, and Abby was laughing up into the officer's face like an old friend. Jealousy nearly ate Barrett alive. She might have been damned attentive to him when he was ill, he thought, but it looked like she preferred the sergeant's company now.

He watched them as they sauntered through camp, laughing and talking like they were a typical young family out for a morning stroll.

When Abby stopped by to check on Barrett that afternoon, she found him in a foul temper. He was gaining strength rapidly, but his scowl didn't indicate it.

"Aren't you in the wrong tent?" he growled as she entered the tent. "Dobbs's is three on down."

"I thought you might need something."

"Not from you, I don't."

Abby let it pass. He'd been sick, and the doctor said he'd be cranky for a few days. "That's nice to hear, especially since Daniel keeps me so busy."

"Looks to me like you've got plenty of help with

Daniel. From what I hear, you've hardly seen the boy since you got here.''

Now sick or not, he was becoming unreasonable, and she wasn't sure that she was going to let him get away with it, although she had to admit that what he'd said was true in part.

"The men have enjoyed playing with Daniel. You wouldn't believe how much he's changed. He's chattering like a magpie now—"

"I don't want to hear about it."

"Why, Barrett Drake!" Abby bit back an angry retort. "Maybe you need a nap," she said instead.

"I don't want a damned nap."

Her eyes narrowed on him warningly. "Take one anyway."

"Léave me alone."

"Fine. I'll do just that."

Barrett, clenching his teeth, lay back on the cot and cursed his weakness. If he could convince himself that he was able, he'd be on a horse in the morning, taking her back to Mercy Flats.

True to her word, Abby stayed away from the medical tent all afternoon. Doyle carried Daniel and escorted her to dinner that evening. There she enjoyed the attention of the few men left in camp, who wound up laughing at Daniel's antics. He was a typical one-year-old now, trying to learn how to walk. He'd taken his first unbalanced steps from one soldier to another that evening, and Abby had clapped her hands with praise. Daniel's two front teeth had shined at the accolades everyone piled on him, and he'd gleefully toddled from one man to the other. Even the few falls he'd taken hadn't wiped the grin from his face.

Abby had watched him, realizing why women were so proud of their children. Seeing him achieve just that small accomplishment, watching him change in personality from a sad-faced infant to a smiling little boy made her beam with pride.

After a long game of seven-up, Sergeant Dobbs walked Abby back to her tent, carrying a sleepy Daniel. When Dobbs placed the boy on the middle of his cot, he was already fast asleep.

Abby stepped outside with Doyle to tell him good night. When the sergeant bent down to kiss her, she wasn't surprised. In fact, she'd expected his kiss and found it mildly pleasant. Not exciting like Barrett's, but pleasant.

Barrett sat outside the medical tent, watching the nauseating spectacle. His lips firmed, and the muscle in his jaw twitched.

She wasn't bothering him, not at all.

Barrett saw little of Abby the next day. Only from a distance, and always in the company of Sergeant Dobbs.

That evening, when she finally came to the hospital tent, she found Barrett exercising. Intent on regaining strength, he ignored her, going on with his work.

"You'll be good as new in a couple of days," she encouraged.

"I'll be riding out of here in three," he stated, disregarding the tremble in his legs.

"Perhaps." He was stubborn as a mule, she decided, and twice as cantankerous.

"You still wanting to go back to Mercy Flats?" he asked gruffly.

"Of course." She blinked in surprise. Grabbing his arm, she pulled him around to face her. "As soon as you're able. You're not trying to back out on our agreement, are you?"

"No, I just thought you might have found another escort," he returned coolly.

She frowned. "Who?"

"Sergeant Dobbs. You and he seem pretty friendly lately."

"He's nice to me." *And you're not,* she added silently.

"From what I've seen, he's been more than 'nice.' Looks to me like you have all the men panting at your feet."

Her cheeks burned at his innuendo. "And it looks to me like you better get back in bed. You're talking gibberish again."

Before he could reply, she disappeared out the door of the tent. If she made it through the next week with him, they'd have to name a mission after her.

Chapter 20

"All right," Barrett announced. "If you're looking to make me mad, you have."

Abby glanced up later to find Barrett filling the doorway of her tent. Her first thought was to reach for her dress, but on second thought she decided not to. Her near state of undress didn't appear to bother him, so she chose to ignore it, too. Seeing her in nothing but her chemise just might make him aware that she was a woman! Snatching the pins from her hair, she freed the thick mass to fall to her waist. Reaching for her hairbrush, she ignored him, exactly the way he'd ignored her earlier. Obviously, something was bothering him, but she wasn't going to get into a shouting match to find out what it was.

"Answer me!" he demanded.

"I assume you're referring to Doyle's innocent kiss the other night?"

He laughed. "It didn't look so innocent to me."

Pulling the brush through her hair, Abby vowed to hold her tongue. He'd been spoiling for a fight all day, so she wasn't about to give him one. "Were you spying on me?"

"Spying on you! The whole camp saw it!"

"I hardly think the 'whole' camp saw it, and even if they did, what's so bad about one innocent kiss?"

"You made a spectacle of yourself."

"You're exaggerating." Circus, traveling show, spectacle, innocuous kiss. He viewed things differently than she.

The muscle in his jaw twitched. "But you did enjoy his kiss."

She shrugged. "Doyle is an attractive man."

Barrett's eyes moved to Daniel's cot, which was noticeably empty. "Where's the boy?"

Abby closed her eyes and jerked the brush through her hair resentfully. "The 'boy's' name is Daniel."

"I know his name."

"Then use it when you refer to him."

Brushing back the flap of the tent, Barrett entered and dropped the canvas back into place.

"Do come in," she mocked.

"I suppose Daniel's with that damned Doyle?"

Abby smiled, pleased that his jealousy was barely controlled, yet seared by his arrogance. If he cared for Daniel and her, why didn't he simply say so? She'd certainly had no trouble making her feelings for him appallingly apparent lately.

"Daniel is with Corporal Maddix tonight."

"Corporal Maddix. Well, that's just dandy." She saw the flash of the all too familiar impatience in his eyes.

"Corporal Maddix asked permission to keep him for the night."

Abby had been hesitant at first about the corporal's request, until she recalled a prior conversation she'd had with Doyle. Corporal Maddix's wife and two sons had perished in a raid on Maddix's hometown a few months earlier. He'd withdrawn into a shell, preferring to keep to himself since the tragedy. But when he'd seen Daniel, he'd smiled and lowered his defenses.

When Abby had recalled the tragedy, she'd readily agreed to share Daniel. It was comforting to see how such a small boy could bring happiness to so many people.

The last she'd seen of the two, the corporal had been busy whittling the boy a toy soldier from a stick of birch with Daniel raptly watching from the corporal's lap.

"Yes, it's sinful how I've bewitched every man in the Confederate Army, isn't it?" She pitched the brush onto the cot as she rose to her feet. "Did you just come here to insult me, or was there something you specifically wanted, Barrett?"

An almost dangerous light entered his eyes as he lazily assessed her in a way she'd never seen him do before. "Well, now, Abigail, since I'm the one who's dragged you all over the country, perhaps I just want my fair share of your favors."

She kept her features deceptively composed. "And what 'favors' are we speaking of, Captain?"

She found his suggestive tone insulting and unwarranted. For the first time in her life, she was more interested in the thoughts and feelings of someone other than herself, and she didn't like him spoiling that for her. It was obvious that after she'd carried his message to General Smith, she'd ceased to be of use to him, yet for some reason he found his male ego mortally endangered when other men found her desirable.

Although he claimed to have his wife's memory in proper perspective, it was plain to her that he didn't.

As uncaring and spoiled as Ramona had been, in spite of all the hurt she'd caused him, it was still her name that he'd called when he lay delirious with fever.

Her name he called in his darkest moment.

If that didn't prove where his loyalties were, nothing did.

"My, my, we're touchy tonight, aren't we?"

"It depends on who is asking to do the touching," she returned coolly.

Their gazes refused to yield to each other. The icy contempt in his tone should have warned her that he was in no mood for compromise, and he had her clearly at a disadvantage. She felt naked in nothing but her petticoat, but she refused to give in to his mocking scrutiny.

"Well, well, this is a side of Abigail McDougal that intrigues me." His gaze moved insolently to the swell of her breasts, and she felt herself growing warm under his perusal.

She would not be intimidated by his patronage. Lifting her chin, Barrett once again found himself confronted by the spunky defiance he should have known better than to challenge. "There are many things about me that you have not, nor will you ever see, Captain Drake."

"Tsk, tsk, tsk, Miss McDougal. You sound upset— am I upsetting you?" he inquired innocently.

"Leave, Barrett."

"No."

"Why are you doing this to me?" She suddenly felt ill-equipped to spar with him. She didn't know what he wanted, but it obviously wasn't her, so why was he intent on antagonizing her?

His face sobered. "Why are you doing this to me?"

he mocked. "If you want a man so bad, I'm available."

She turned away. "You're disgusting."

"How do you know? I've never shown you how irresistible I can be, Abigail."

Resentment stung her. His tone implied that she was cheap and only using the men in camp to gratify her pride, when all she wanted was one man: Barrett Drake.

"Go back to your tent, Barrett," she said wearily.

"Are you in love with Doyle Dobbs?" he demanded.

"That is none of your business."

"You're leading him on."

"I'm not leading him on. Maybe I just enjoy knowing that I'm desirable in his eyes."

"Are you in love with Dobbs?" he repeated. His tone demanded an answer that she was not prepared to give. In love with Doyle? She'd never given it a thought. She respected and admired what he stood for, but was she in love with him? Could she have fallen in love with any man in so short a time?

The second answer was clearer than the first. Hadn't she fallen in love with Barrett in less than a week? Even when she had thought he was Hershall Digman, pitiful, bumbling Hershall Digman, he had struck a responsive cord in her that no other man had ever tapped before.

"Answer me, Abby." His voice was husky now, more uncertain.

"I—I enjoy being with Doyle," she admitted.

"And when he kisses you? What do you feel when he kisses you, Abby? Does he tie your stomach in knots, make you want to kiss him back, make you want to do a whole lot more than just kiss?"

"Sometimes." She didn't know why it mattered; it would only take one miniscule indication from Barrett that he wanted her, and these questions would be pointless.

His tone softened deceptively. "And what about the way my kisses make you feel? Do you enjoy them as well?"

She thought it was pretty low of him to bring that up. Though her behavior with him had been shameless, he didn't have to remind her of it.

"Maybe I just like kissing in general."

"Kiss a man, then leave him standing. Right?" The muscle in his jaw worked angrily.

"I believe you have me confused with Ramona," she snapped.

"You're nothing like Ramona," he snapped back.

Her voice was calm, and her eyes were steady as she gazed back at him. "I'm not the one you need to convince, Barrett."

Something entered his eyes, something dark and forbidden. "You think I'm still in love with my dead wife?"

"Yes."

"You think I could never love another woman, don't you?"

"Yes."

Taking her hand, he carted her out of the tent and started dragging her through the center of the camp.

"Barrett, stop this," she warned, dreading this mood that had turned even fouler. "You're making a scene."

Ignoring the men's catcalls and friendly jeers, he hauled her along, defying her protests.

Abby saw how dark his face was with anger, and it occurred to her that maybe he had decided to take her off and shoot her after all. She thought about screaming for Doyle, then realized that it would only serve to incite Barrett more.

Doctor Greene stepped outside the medical tent, surprised to see Barrett dragging Abby behind him.

Smiling lamely, Abby waved as Barrett dragged her by the tent. "Evening, Doctor Greene."

The doctor removed his pipe from his mouth slowly. "Evenin', Abigail."

Through the camp, by the creek, and up a wooded thicket Barrett strode with Abby struggling to free herself from his steely grasp, but he held her firmly in hand.

"I'm yelling for Doyle!"

"Go ahead."

"Barrett!" She stumbled along behind him, trying to keep her balance. She felt so humiliated that she could die! He had dragged her through camp in front of all those men in her petticoat!

Parting a thick growth of bushes, he dragged her through an opening of a small cave, refusing to release his painful grip until they were inside.

Wrenching free of his hold, she glared at him, rubbing her wrists resentfully. Looking around her, she was surprised to see that the cave was large. Water dripped overhead, and she saw several pairs of yellow eyes peering back at her from within a black crevice.

'What is the meaning of this?" she demanded in a tight voice.

"You want to be admired by a man?" He stripped out of his shirt and tossed it aside.

Abby could only stare at the broad expanse of hairy chest, her pulse quickening. He was in a dangerous mood.

"I—shouldn't have taunted you," she murmured,

her eyes mesmerized by all the muscle and brawn he was exposing.

His hand calmly moved to his belt, and she took a precautionary step backward. "Barrett," she warned, feeling hot, then cold all at the same time.

"You want to know what it's like to be with a man, Abigail?" The belt came off, and he threw it aside.

"Now, Barrett, I know you're not the kind of man to do anything against a woman's will—"

"How do you know that, Abigail?" he said in a dangerously low voice.

"Well, I don't." She swallowed dryly as she saw his hand move to the buttons on the front of his trousers. "You wouldn't. . . . Stop this, Barrett."

He smiled, calmly stepping out of his trousers. His fingers slipped down to unbutton his long johns as his eyes fixed with hers.

"Yes, I would."

"But it would be against my will."

His eyes taunted her. "Would it, Abby?"

His long johns fell away, and he stood before her, magnificent and proud. Her mouth went dry as her eyes fixed on the part that made him so uniquely male.

In her heart, she knew that she could no longer lie to him. Not now, not at the moment she only realized now that she had been dreaming of for weeks. "I don't want it to be this way," she agonized. She wanted him to tenderly teach her the ways of love, not in anger and spite.

She was barely aware of a low groan as he moved toward her and took her hand. Slowly, he drew her to him. He felt her fingers tremble as he lifted her hand to his mouth. His eyes held hers in a trance when he gently kissed the smooth back of her hand. "How do you want me, sweet, sweet Abigail?" he asked in an

unsteady voice as he turned her hand over and leisurely pressed his lips to her palm, catapulting sensations through her. "You have only to tell me, my
love."

She closed her eyes, and her stomach tightened into
a knot as his tongue sensuously toyed with her sensitive palm, sending waves of exquisite pleasure through
her. He was so experienced, and she was innocent.
She'd never imagined that the flick of his tongue
against her palm could make her throat close up, make
her forget to breathe, make her knees feel weak. He
had been married; he obviously knew the ways to
please a woman.

"I don't know anything," she whispered, embarrassed that she knew none of the ways to bring pleasure to a man. "I only know that this . . . this
shouldn't be done in anger."

"And it won't," he said in a quiet voice as he released her hand. The last thing he'd wanted her to believe was that he would take her against her will. The
thought that in his jealous rage he'd almost done just
that made him stop and take stock of the situation.

He was waiting for a signal from her, some sign that
she wanted him or some sign that she didn't. It was
her decision; he knew it, and he wanted to be sure that
she knew it, too.

She felt a keen disappointment as she saw him move
away and stand very still, gazing at her, his expression
unreadable. She was seized by a sudden panic that
perhaps this was all over before it began. She began
to agonize that she'd probably said absolutely the
wrong thing again.

A moment ago she had been afraid of what he might
do to her; now she was afraid that he would do nothing

at all, that he might be ready to give up on her entirely, that he might be ready to walk away for good.

"Oh, Barrett," she said brokenly.

He pulled her against his chest. It was as if something had suddenly burst within him. "God, Abby, you're driving me crazy."

His mouth took hers roughly, kissing her so hard that she tasted blood. She had thought he was a passionate man, but his kiss warned of a darker frenzy.

"I won't hurt you," he whispered in a voice thick with passion. "I won't hurt you." He groaned as she whispered his name. Their mouths came together in a kiss that deepened as desire raged hot and unbridled.

"I don't know what to do," she agonized, "you must teach me." She wanted so badly to please him, but she didn't know how.

"It is natural," he whispered into her ear, "and nothing to be afraid of." Taking her hand, he guided her to him, where he lay rigid against her stomach. The exploration made her weak with longing, and his mouth returned to ravage hers again. Her arms slid around his neck, and they kissed, their tongues meeting hungrily.

His mouth moved slowly down her throat, kissing her bare shoulders as his fingers pushed the straps of her chemise aside. Lifting his face, he locked his eyes with hers as his hands worked deftly, masterfully, but gently, considering her innocence, holding a tight rein on needs that were driving him to the brink of madness.

Easing the chemise over her head, he bared her firm breasts, his breathing growing ragged as he gazed at her, finding her beauty even more than he'd imagined. She stared back at him, her eyes round and ques-

tioning, but in their depths he could see a need that
might have surpassed even his own.

"A woman should be married—" she whispered in
confusion.

"Abby . . ." He was in agony, yet he knew that if
she asked, he would force himself to stop.

"No, go on," she whispered. "and may God forgive me."

He drew her back to him, their bodies meshing, and
she gloried in the feel of his bare flesh against hers.
He was majestic, not only in body, but in soul. And
as for marriage, she had done that in her heart many
days ago.

He knelt on one knee to draw her petticoat and pan-
taloons down. His hands molded her slender hips; his
fingers skimmed the long curves of her legs, sending
sensations through her like a shower of sparks stirred
from a fire. He looked up into her eyes, gauging her
reaction as his hand moved to touch her in dark, intimate places, doing things she had never dreamed could
elicit such feelings. She settled her hands on his shoulders, no longer afraid.

"Barrett, there's no blanket," she said as her knees
began to tremble. The floor of the cave was cold and
damp.

"Ah, there are other ways, my love," he whispered,
guiding her down to rest on his knee. His tongue darted
inside her ear as she looped her arms around his neck.

"Really?"

He rose to his feet, carrying her slender weight.
Then he wrapped her legs around his waist and held
her tight.

Her mouth opened, then closed as a tiny smile of
wonderment settled on her lips.

"Barrett," she gasped as the wondrous things he

was doing to her filled her with awe, "Sister Agnes would die!"

Abby awoke the next morning on the cot inside her tent. There was a song in her heart. Her first thought was to go to Barrett, but she suppressed the urge, knowing that if the hours they'd spent in the cave together last night meant anything to him, he would come to her. She needed to know that what had happened was as special to him as it was to her, and she could not be certain of that unless he told her. So now, as in the past, she waited.

She could no longer imagine her life without him, yet he had said nothing about being in love with her. The word "love" hadn't been spoken, while many others had come so easily.

Around midmorning, she grew restless. Daniel was napping, so she decided to stroll to the commissary in hopes that she might bump into a certain handsome captain. The memory of his kisses still made her blood race, and she longed for just a brief glimpse of him.

She asked a lieutenant who was hanging around outside her tent to peek in on Daniel occasionally. He said that he would, and she set off.

Casually ambling past the medical tent, she glanced inside and felt a letdown when she discovered Barrett's empty cot.

"Mornin', Abigail."

"Good morning, Doctor Greene," she said in a rush, hoping that he wouldn't mention his seeing her dragged through camp in her underthings the night before.

"Looking for your captain?" There was thinly disguised amusement twinkling in the doctor's eye.

"No," she lied, wanting to get away quickly. "Just getting a breath of fresh air while Daniel's napping."

Feeling acutely disappointed, she meandered toward the stream. It was a lovely day. The sun's rays nestled warmly upon her shoulders, and for the first time in a long time, she wasn't preoccupied with thoughts of Amelia and Anne-Marie.

Strolling along the bank of the stream, she idly brushed her fingers across the blooming weeds, sending their frilly tops spiraling into the air. Birds chattered back and forth as the creek gurgled lazily through the rocks and logs strewn in the water.

"Hello, love."

Turning sharply, Abby saw Barrett sunning lazily on a log in the middle of the stream.

Suppressing her elation at seeing him, she made her smile as casual as a woman could when she was with the man she loved. "Oh, Captain Drake. How nice to see you again."

Their gazes met, and the intimate undercurrent threading through his made her stomach curl with warmth. The things he'd done to her last night—well, Amelia and Anne-Marie would never believe it when she told them. In fact, it dawned on her that she might not tell them at all, because those special moments belonged to just Barrett and herself.

"Sunning yourself?" she inquired in a most detached observation.

His mouth curved with an unconscious smile as he crossed his arms behind his head and stretched out more fully on the log. Patting the empty spot beside him, he beckoned to her. "Come sit with me."

"Well," she pretended to think about it for propriety's sake. She owed the good sisters that much. "I suppose I could—for a moment." Lifting the hem of her dress, she quickly shinnied out of her shoes and stockings then holding her slippers above her head, she waded out to the log to join him.

"You look mighty fetching this morning," he observed lazily. "Sleep well last night?"

"Very nice, thank you." She stepped into the water, gasping softly at the icy temperature. "And you?"

"Very well, thank you." His grin was decidedly smug, she decided.

Casually pulling a cheroot from his shirt pocket, he lit it. A moment later, the smell of tobacco filtered pleasantly through the air.

Lifting her face to the sun, Abby closed her eyes, wishing that the moment could last forever. Whenever they spent an hour together, it only seemed like a minute to her.

Barrett's health was improving so readily that they were bound to be leaving any day now, she thought, as she studied a passing cloud. That prospect was painful, yet she knew she couldn't complain. The extra days she had been granted with Daniel were a treat, one she hadn't anticipated.

But giving up both Daniel and Barrett . . . at the same time . . . was more than she thought her heart could bear.

She studied Barrett's handsome profile from the corner of her eye. If she'd changed on the inside during the past week, he'd changed on the outside. It was hard to remember when she'd thought that he was a persnickety little old shoe salesman, more concerned with his spectacles and white spats than her welfare.

She smiled as she recalled how she'd considered him to be short and frumpy and an insult to the male gender.

Now, just looking at him made her weak with desire.

He wasn't particularly tall, hardly taller than she. But he had a commanding presence about him. How had she missed that in the beginning? How any woman could resist him, no matter who he was pretending to be, seemed beyond her comprehension now.

Leaning back on her hands, Abby skimmed her toes through the water. The creek was cold, but the water felt wonderfully refreshing.

"Out here, like this, it's hard to believe there's a war going on," she observed, thinking about the men who had ridden out of camp yesterday. "General Smith will meet the Northern forces today—I heard talk at breakfast this morning."

"He expects to engage Banks's advance unit today," Barrett observed lazily.

"How very sad."

She caught him studying her, and she turned to meet his gaze. "What?"

"I don't think I've thanked you. You did a good job getting the messages through. It couldn't have been easy, with the baby and all."

"No." The thought of the Indian burial ground brought an involuntary shudder. "It wasn't easy."

He grinned. "You're afraid of the dark, aren't you?"

She exhaled softly, wondering how he had discovered that. "How did you know?"

He chuckled as he brought the cheroot back to his mouth. "How did you know?" he mocked. "Let me see, it might be from the way your eyes grow round as silver dollars once the sun goes down."

She accepted his teasing graciously because she was in an acceptable mood this morning. Sometimes he could look so stern, but when he laughed like this, his eyes reminded her of a sunny summer day.

In fact, he looked uncommonly handsome this morning. His hair, though longer now, curled over his shirt collar and over his forehead, giving him a roguish look.

"You plan on getting married someday?" he asked her as causally as if he were conducting a survey.

Abby's pulse skittered at the question. It seemed odd, coming from him. They could pretend that nothing unusual had happened last night, but they both knew better. And they both knew he didn't want to marry again.

"I have never planned on it," she admitted softly.

Drawing on the cheroot, he studied a bird in flight. "I suppose, like all women, you dream of marrying a tall man."

Now that seemed a peculiar observation. Was the tough Barrett Drake sensitive about his height? "I don't know." She shrugged. "I've never thought about it."

"A tall man who'd give you tall children," he mused.

"And a tall house with a tall tree in front and a nice, tall picket fence around the tall grass that grew in the yard," she teased. He *was* sensitive about his height!

"I'm serious."

"So am I."

"Be honest with me, wouldn't you want your husband to be tall?"

Sighing, she leaned forward to catch a leaf floating by. "How tall are you?"

The telltale muscle above his jaw began to twitch. "Tall enough."

"That's exactly how tall I'd want my husband to be." She looked directly into his eyes. "Tall enough."

They sat for a moment sharing the silence, and she glanced away as a disturbing thought occurred to her. "Would you want a tall wife?" She wasn't exactly a giant herself. Perhaps he preferred tall women—maybe Ramona had been six foot.

"No, I like runts about your size."

"I'm not a 'runt,' " she scoffed.

"No, but you are quite a lady, Abigail."

She didn't know why that should make her feel so heady, but it did—oh, how it did.

"And you've turned out to be an acceptable man, Mr. Digman."

She looked at him and love shone in her eyes, but Barrett's gaze wasn't quite as readable. "Acceptable, huh?"

"Acceptable," she confirmed.

They turned their faces upward to enjoy the sunshine.

"Abby, we'll have to leave soon. I've neglected my duties as long as I can," Barrett told her quietly.

A sadness came over her. Though she'd expected the announcement, she'd dreaded this moment. "I thought we might."

"I plan to keep my promise to see you safely back to Mercy Flats. We'll leave Daniel at the orphanage, and with any luck you'll be back with your sisters in a few days."

"All right." Plucking a floating flower petal from the water, she twirled it between her fingers. "Will we travel as Quakers?"

When the silence stretched, she finally glanced at him. His eyes were closed as if he were in deep thought.

"No," he said finally. "I'll request a troop escort."

She hated logic. It was so inflexible.

Rolling onto his side, he idly trailed a blade of grass down her arm, and she laughed, pushing his hand away.

"We won't be able to pose as Mr. and Mrs. Levi Howard," he teased in a voice that intimately reminded her of the night before.

"I know."

"You don't mind?"

"No."

"You're mighty obliging all of a sudden."

Twirling the flower between her fingers, she gave him one of those mysterious smiles that made a man wonder what a woman was up to. "When my sisters and I were young and full of fancy, we used to pick flowers and make necklaces out of them, or we'd pick the petals to try and find out if a certain boy liked us."

"A test that I'd stake my life on," he said dryly.

Abby calculatingly plucked one of the petals, her eyes locked with his teasingly. "He loves me." She plucked another. "He loves me not. He loves me. . . . He loves me not."

"You're cheating. That flower has fifteen petals on it," he accused. "Aren't you supposed to use a daisy?"

She shook her head and gave him a sly smile. "When it comes to the man I want, I need all the extra petals I can get."

He shook his head, marveling at her optimism. "Always looking for a bluebird, aren't you?" he chided.

"And I'll find one someday," she promised.

"Well," his voice grew lazy again, "maybe you underestimate yourself, Abigail McDougal." He dipped the blade of grass provocatively into the crevice between her breasts.

"Barrett." Abby paused, reluctant to broach the painful subject, but it had been on her mind a lot lately. "You called for Ramona when you were ill."

"Did I?" He chuckled. "Must have been quite a nightmare."

"You still think about her, don't you?"

"She's dead, Abby."

"Is she, Barrett?"

The need in her voice touched him. His eyes deepened to the color of smoke, and where his gaze touched her, she felt a weakness much like the one that had consumed her the night before.

"You worry too much," he admonished her softly. His fingers wrapped around her wrist and pulled her gently toward him.

"I know, but—" He silenced her with a long, heady kiss.

"Come with me," he whispered against her lips. "I know a cave where we can be alone. We'll spend the day making love—"

"Barrett," Abby glanced toward the bank, afraid that someone would see them. The scene they'd caused last night was embarrassing enough.

The teasing light in his eyes brought a rush of color to her cheeks. "Shall I get a blanket?"

"No!" she said quickly, too quickly. Lowering her eyes guiltily, she amended her hasty refusal. "No need for that."

She looked up and found him grinning at her.

"Oh, you."

Pulling her to him, he kissed her, his tongue teasing hers. "Well, since you nearly wore me out last night, I'll trust your judgment." None to his surprise, he'd found Abigail McDougal, as he'd always suspected, an ardent, insatiable lover.

"Race you to the cave," she challenged.

His brow lifted arrogantly. "Anxious?"

She nodded, grinning. "Can't wait."

Sliding off the log, he chased her to the bank, splashing her with water and laughing when she splashed him back.

As they disappeared into the thicket, they were holding hands like lovers.

Chapter 21

When Abby and Barrett returned to camp, they exchanged glances as they saw the activity going on in the camp.

The wounded were arriving, and the stench of tar filled the camp, a gruesome reminder that the war was still going on. There would be human limbs piled high in back of the medical tent by morning.

The battle was engaged at Mansfield, and the first reports filtering back to camp were encouraging. Instead of capitalizing fully on the fall of Vicksburg, the North had diverted over twenty-five thousand troops for General Banks to lead across Louisiana with the intent of capturing Shreveport before moving on to invade Texas from the northeast.

General Magruder rushed as many men north as he could spare to oppose them, while General Richard Taylor and General J. Kirby Smith took almost nine thousand men to attack Banks's advance unit of some eight thousand. But once again the South was taking a heavy toll in human suffering.

Abby and Barrett pitched in, offering what help they could to the doctor.

Late that afternoon, Abby went to retrieve Daniel. As the evening wore on, he toddled in and out of the tent as Abby and every other able-bodied person in camp worked beside the doctor to save what lives could be saved.

When Abby entered the commissary late that night, she was near collapse. Her dress was slick with blood, and she had witnessed so many deaths and amputations in the past few hours that she was numb. But Daniel had to be fed, and there was no one else to do it.

Moving through the serving line, she was barely aware when Doyle approached and took Daniel from her arms.

Handing the child to a corporal, Doyle guided Abby to a table, where he sat her down and pressed a cup of coffee between her hands. "Drink this."

Nodding dazedly, she brought the cup to her lips, barely aware as the raw liquid spilled down her throat.

"You shouldn't be seein' this," Doyle said angrily.

"No," she caught his hand, trying to ease his agony, "it's all right. I'll be fine after I've rested a moment."

He brought her a plate, and she tried to eat. Doyle sat with her, brooding and pensive. Abby sensed that something besides the battle was troubling him.

"Take a walk with me," he said when they were finished. The corporal had left with Daniel with a promise to put him to bed.

She glanced at the row upon row of bodies lying on the ground, moaning. "I'm needed—"

"Just walk with me a ways."

She saw the pained look in his eyes and wondered how life could be so cruel. Doyle was a gentle man, sickened by the ravages of war. It was a war he'd neither started nor wanted, and yet he'd been asked to give up all that he held dear to fight it.

"All right."

Barrett glanced up as she walked past the tent with Doyle. Their eyes met, and the hours of ecstasy they'd shared in the cave flooded through her.

Turning his head away, Barrett continued to wrap a bandage around an injured man's leg. Jealousy filled him, as bitter as bile. The sergeant had made himself indispensable to Abby and the child. Barrett knew that if the battle continued, Dobbs would be sent in as a replacement. Anger had a way of altering a man's perception. For the first time in his life, he hoped that a man wouldn't return.

It was obvious to Abby that something was bothering Doyle. She wondered if he was being sent to join the battle. He'd been so good to her and had helped her so much that saying good-bye to him was going to be difficult.

Ironically enough, Doyle walked toward the opening of the cave where she and Barrett had made love only a few short hours before. He strode beside her, more like a man who was intent on walking instead of talking. When they reached the opening to the cave, Doyle paused and turned to face her.

"I saw you with him today."

Abby blushed and glanced away, wondering exactly what Doyle had seen.

"It doesn't matter," Doyle admitted as if he could read her thoughts. "I just wanted you to know."

"I'm sorry." Abby lay her hand on his arm to comfort him.

"I didn't see anything I shouldn't have—but a man can guess about those things."

"I'm sorry," she offered again simply. She didn't want to hurt him.

"Rumor has it you and the captain plan to leave soon."

"Yes, Barrett feels he has to return to his duties."

"Does he still plan to take you back to Mercy Flats?"

"Yes."

His eyes met her evenly. "He hasn't offered to marry you?"

"No." Averting her eyes, she wondered if her willingness to let Barrett take advantage of her was that obvious to everyone. If Doyle had been witness to her folly this afternoon, then perhaps it was.

"I know this isn't the time or the place, but I might not have another opportunity," Doyle said quietly.

Abby glanced up.

"I know you'll be leaving soon, and I may have to join the company at any time," he went on.

"Maybe not—"

"I will, if the battle continues."

Laying her hand on his arm again, she told him quietly, "I'll pray for you."

"Thank you, I'd be much obliged, but that's not what I'm needin' to say. Abigail, I don't know how you feel about me, but I'm in love with you and the boy."

Abby's mouth dropped open, but he stopped her.

"Even if you don't love me right now, you could grow to care for me."

"Doyle—"

"Just hear me out. Please." He caught her hands in his and studied them for a long moment before going on. "I know how much you care about Daniel. I know you love him and how you would like to see him have a real mother and father. I'd be a good father to him, Abby. If you'll marry me, we can be a real family."

"Oh, Doyle." Abby didn't know what to say. Doyle was so good, so kind, but she didn't love him. "You've only known me a short while."

"That doesn't matter to me, and we wouldn't have to marry right away. I know you're worried about your sisters."

"Doyle, I . . . I don't know what to say." Her mind raced. What he was offering had never occurred to her, and oh, how she longed to keep Daniel with her. Marrying him would solve her problem, and under other circumstances she might even consider it, but—

"All I want is for you to promise you'll consider my proposal." He saw the indecision in her eyes, and it lent him hope. The men in camp said that she was in love with Barrett Drake, but Barrett Drake would never make a commitment to her. Dobbs wanted her and the child, and he was willing to fight to get her.

"Doyle," she said softly. "I don't love you. The captain and I—"

"I know. You're in love with the captain, but that doesn't matter to me. I don't mean any disrespect, but he'll never ask you to marry him. The men say he's still in love with the memory of his first wife, and no other woman will ever take her place."

Her eyes clouded with hurt. "Captain Drake will never marry me. I'm aware of that."

"Then permit me to earn your love and respect."

"That would be unfair, Doyle. I want to keep Daniel so badly I ache—"

"Then marry me." Grasping her shoulders, he held her solidly between his large hands. "I'm offering you the chance to keep the child and marry a man who loves you, Abby. I can't do any better than that. I'm not Drake, and I never will be, but I promise, you'll never want for anything."

She shook her head, sorely tempted to accept his offer. Though her heart belonged to Barrett, this way she could at least keep Daniel. But he would have to know about last night, and today—

"Doyle, the captain and I—"

His eyes met her stringently. "It doesn't matter, Abby. If you'll marry me, I promise I'll never ask any questions about the past."

Pulling her close, he murmured her name and continued to plead with her as she rested her head on his chest. It was a good, solid chest, worthy of so much more than she could offer him.

"Go back to Mercy Flats and see about your sisters, Abby. Think about what we could have together, and when the war is over, I'll come for you, if that's what you decide," he promised.

Dazed, she closed her eyes wearily. "All right, Doyle. I'll think about it."

Squeezing her to him tightly, his voice trembled with gratitude. "Good girl. Just you, me, and our babies. As God is my witness, Abby, I'll make you happy."

Chapter 22

By the end of the battle, General Kirby Smith had captured one hundred fifty loaded supply wagons, twenty-two cannon and took twenty-five hundred prisoners before falling back to Pleasant Hill, some thirty miles west of Natchitoches, Louisiana, to regroup.

Twelve thousand Confederates had fought savagely to cut off the Union escape route, but they were driven off with a loss of some fifteen hundred.

Although Union losses were not as heavy, Banks's campaign to move into Texas was broken and the scheme abandoned.

When General Smith and his troops returned to camp, Abby worked by Dr. Greene's side until the last casualty was treated. Collapsing on her cot that night, she stared at the ceiling, too exhausted to move.

"Are you hungry?"

She opened her eyes to find Barrett standing over her, holding out a cup of coffee and a plate of stew.

"I have never been so tired in all my life."

His eyes shone with what she would like to think

was admiration, but on closer examination, she decided it was only appreciation.

"I'm proud of you. You've grown up in the last two weeks."

"Really? Is this what being a grown-up is all about?" She closed her eyes, sick at heart from the sights and smells and sounds going on around her.

Setting the plate and cup on the ground, he lifted her up and held her close to his chest. Sighing, she let her eyes drift closed again as she savored the moment of closeness.

"The bluebird is getting more elusive," she admitted as fatigue washed over her.

"We've done all we can do, Abby."

"But Doctor Greene—"

"We've done all we can do," he repeated softly. "We leave at first light."

As his mouth lowered to hers, she pushed aside all thoughts of tomorrow. If these were to be their last hours alone together, she wanted them to be ones he could always cherish.

Sunrise found Abby in the commissary, coaxing Daniel through breakfast. Some of the men sat at the long table watching with long faces as Barrett led the horses to the front of the tent. Barrett had said little to Abby that morning, except to tell her that the general had assigned a small contingency to escort them to the border. Once there, the contingency would turn south and ride for another camp.

Barrett heaved the saddle onto her horse, tightened the cinch, then dropped the stirrup back into place. "You about ready?"

"All ready."

Daniel held his arms out to Barrett, and Barrett took him.

"Thank you again for all your help, Abby." Doctor Greene walked beside her as she prepared to mount up.

"I wish I could have done more."

His eyes met hers as he took her hand and graciously lifted it to kiss her fingertips. "It has been an extraordinary pleasure, madam, having you in camp."

With a smile, Abby nodded graciously. "The pleasure has indeed been mine, kind sir."

"Captain." The two men shook hands. "Take good care of her. She's a rare find."

Barrett's gaze was solemnly affectionate as he looked at her. "That she is, Doctor."

After mounting up, Abby reached for Daniel, refusing to look at the soldiers who stood in the doorway of the tent. Some wore bandages around their heads, while others supported their weight on crudely fashioned crutches.

Barrett swung into the saddle, then turned to salute the men. The troop straightened and briskly returned the salute.

The small contingency quietly closed ranks. "Forward, ho." The horses began to trot out of camp, and Abby refused to look back.

Abby and Barrett rode side by side during the morning. She concentrated on keeping Daniel entertained by pointing out the various birds and animals they saw along the way.

Barrett coaxed him to repeat the sounds, then laughed along with the other men at his fractured pronunciations. Daniel laughed delightedly with them, unaware that he sounded silly.

During noon break, Barrett fed the child while Abby

ate. She picked at her food, choosing to distance herself from the men. She sat by the stream, staring dispiritedly into the water. Barrett knew that she was grieving over having to give up the child; he just didn't know what to do about it.

He could only hope that being reunited with her sisters would ease her loss.

Abby sat by the stream, watching Barrett play with Daniel. Though he seemed to love the child, she knew how foolish it was for her to hope that he returned *her* love. His lovemaking had been provocative and exhilarating, but logic told her that their time together had only been a pleasant diversion for him. Soon she would be with Anne-Marie and Amelia again, and they would help her sort the hurt that was in her heart.

It was close to noon the following day when the small company halted in front of the lane leading to Lady of Our Saints orphanage. Abby's eyes blurred with tears as she read the weathered sign. Forcing back the painful lump in her throat, she dropped back to ride behind Corporal Nelson. She didn't know why she felt so resentful toward Barrett—yes, she did know why. In her opinion, he was the only one who could prevent what was about to happen.

"Looks like a peaceful place," the corporal commented encouragingly as they rode along the lane.

Barrett moved up beside her, a concerned look in his eye. "Do you want me to do this?"

"No, I'll do it." She kept her eyes fixed stoically ahead of her.

"Are you sure?"

"I'm sure."

Mother Superior spotted the group of riders approaching and stepped out onto the orphanage porch. She watched as the riders drew closer, her eyes showing her puzzlement over Levi Howard's dress. He was wearing confederate blue this morning.

The horses halted, and the dust settled. Abby met the sister's quizzical gaze evenly. "Mother Superior."

The nun nodded. "We were beginning to wonder if you'd changed your mind about leaving the child."

"No, we were only delayed." Taking a deep breath, she dismounted and handed Daniel to the sister. "He's walking everywhere now, and he eats almost anything. He's learned a few words—some you might not be thrilled about," she added, "but he doesn't have the slightest idea what they mean, so please don't give him extra demerits."

Sister nodded, trying to hold on to the squirming child. "We were about to sit down to the noon meal. Will you join us?"

"Thank you. We can't stay." She stood for a moment, then said stoically, "Captain Drake, is there anything you'd like—" she bit her lip, modifying her choice of words "—is there anything you have to say before we go?"

The men exchanged uncomfortable looks. Clearing his throat, Barrett said softly, "Take good care of him, Sister."

"We do the best we can, Mr. Howard."

"I'm sorry we had to be dishonest with you, Sister. My name is Drake. Captain Barrett Drake, and Abigail McDougal."

The Sister's eyes held understanding. "We do what we must, Captain."

Abby quickly climbed onto her horse and reined him in a circle, refusing to look back as she galloped back down the lane.

Barrett handed her a square of gray linen as he rode

past her a moment later. Abby accepted it but refused to look at him as she kicked her horse into a faster gait.

The pace quickened during the afternoon. By night, they'd reached the Texas-Louisiana border.

As they made camp, Abby sat by herself, listening to the men discuss plans to head south the next morning. She ignored their chatter as she rolled into her blanket early and tried to sleep. She was numb now; nothing penetrated her thoughts.

The company rode out early the next morning, and for the first time in days, Abby and Barrett found themselves alone.

"I'm ready if you are." Barrett wouldn't meet her eyes as he saddled the horses.

Abby pitched the remains of her coffee into the fire, then silently packed the cup back into her pack before mounting up.

Dawn streaked the sky as they started off again. Abby knew that she should break the silence that hung between them like a shroud, but she didn't know what to say. Should she beg Barrett to marry her? Should she plead with him to go back for Daniel, or should she remain silent and keep her promise to free him of any further obligation to her once he returned her safely to Mercy Flats?

She decided on the latter, since his continuing silence appeared to indicate his preference.

They made camp that night, speaking only when spoken to. After supper, Abby rolled up in her blanket and turned her back to him.

By tomorrow night, she'd be in Mercy Flats. One more day, and Barrett Drake would be rid of her. Tears stung her eyes. One more day, and she'd be rid of Barrett Drake.

"Are you warm enough?"

His voice came to her, low and sensuous from the darkness. Other than asking her if she wanted more coffee, he hadn't spoken to her at all that night.

"Fine, thank you."

"I wish you'd quit being so damned polite," he snapped. She either talked too much, or she didn't talk at all. She was driving him crazy! He guessed that she wanted him to say that he was in love with her. Well, maybe he was. But the only other woman he'd told that to had run off and joined the damned circus!

Gritting her teeth, Abby spat back, "And I wish—" She caught herself before she could express her wish. She was through wishing for bluebirds, it didn't do her any good anyway. Clamping her eyes shut, she focused on a more pleasant subject: Doyle Dobbs. Maybe she *would* marry him. Barrett didn't want her; Barrett didn't want Daniel, either. If he had, he would have stopped her from giving Daniel to the orphanage that morning.

Oh, it was a bitter pill to swallow when she thought of how she had allowed a man to disrupt her life the way she'd allowed Barrett Drake to do. Her lips trembled, and she was appalled to feel hot tears rolling down her cheeks again.

If you marry Doyle, you can go back and get Daniel. Rolling to her side, she tried to blot out the tempting thought.

It was foolish to wish she could keep Daniel, but she did wish it. On one hand, she told herself that she could raise him with the help of Amelia and Anne-Marie, but on the other hand, logic argued that motherhood would be a staggering task.

Sister Agnes and Sister Lucille might agree to assume responsibility for Daniel's care, but they were so old now, and he would still be an orphan. Abby wanted so much more for him. She wanted him to have a real father, and Doyle could be that for him. Yet it wouldn't be fair to marry a man she didn't love for the sake of one small boy. Would it?

I'm not in love with Doyle, her heart cried out. He'd pledged his love to her, but it would be a lie to pledge hers in return. Weeks ago she hadn't cared how many lies she had to tell, but Barrett had changed that, and she resented him for it.

And what would she do if Amelia and Anne-Marie weren't at the cemetery? What if they never returned? What if they were—dead? The thought was so painful that she couldn't bear to think it. Could she live without knowing what had happened to them? And if they were awaiting her return, could she leave them again to marry Doyle, sharing her hopes and her dreams with them only through infrequent letters?

Morning dawned, and camp was broken in strained silence. Abby wasn't sure why Barrett was so subdued. Was it possible that he was plagued by as many doubts and so few answers as she? His eyes, so expressive when he'd made love to her, were unreadable now.

The countryside gradually began to be familiar to Abby. She and her sisters had spent their lives riding these hills and valleys they were traveling now.

When they were within three miles of Mercy Flats, Abby urged her horse into a full gallop. Giving their horses free rein, they rode side by side as they raced toward the border town.

As they topped a small rise, they slowed, and a smile broke across Abby's face as she gazed at the town that had been the only home she'd ever known. Mercy Flats wasn't much. Just a few adobe buildings that looked as if they had been around for a long time.

A dust devil was the only sign of life this afternoon.

It was siesta time, and not even the old dog that lay in front of the trading post bothered to stir.

"It's not much, is it?" Abby said softly. "Over there," she pointed to a small dwelling on the outskirts of the town, "that's the Mission San Miguel, where I was raised."

They sat on the horses, looking at Father Juan's apple orchard and the sisters' vegetable garden, and tears misted Abby's eyes again. "Over there is Church Rock, the cemetery where my parents are buried."

Resting against the saddle pommel, Barrett centered his gaze on the small cemetery beside the mission. The graves lay in the shade of tall oaks, and wildflowers bloomed in riotous colors around the headstones.

"It looks real peaceful, Abby."

Flies buzzed around the horses, and their bridles jingled as the animals shook their heads to rid themselves of the pesky insects.

"My parents are buried beneath that tree just to the left—see it?"

Barrett's eyes located the two graves, and he nodded.

Side by side, they sat, gazing down on the tranquil scene. The cemetery appeared deserted, but that didn't mean that Amelia and Anne-Marie weren't there, Abby told herself. It didn't mean that at all. They were probably at the mission this minute, having tea with Sister Agnes.

"Well, I guess this is where we say good-bye," she acknowledged, trying to speak above the lump crowding her throat.

"Yeah, guess it is." The horses rippled their hides as the people on their backs waited. "You think Amelia and Anne-Marie are waiting for you?"

"Oh, yes. They're there."

"Yeah, expect they are."

The moment stretched, both feeling reluctant to say good-bye. They'd shared a lot the past two weeks.

"Barrett?"

"Yes?"

She sighed. "Nothing, I guess."

The horses grew restless and stamped as the flies buzzed around their fetlocks.

"What do you think you'll do when the war's over?" she asked suddenly, unaware until that moment that she would ask. The second the words were out of her mouth, she wished that she'd kept silent.

Gazing at the valley below, he said softly, "I've got a hundred acres of prime farmland in Georgia. Once the war's over, I'm going home."

"That sounds real nice."

Their heads turned, and their eyes met.

"What about you?" he asked.

She looked away. "Doyle asked me to marry him."

Pain flickered briefly in his eyes. "Are you going to accept his proposal?"

"He's a good man, Barrett. He wants to adopt Daniel."

"I know." They sat in silence another moment. "Are you in love with him?"

Abby hesitated. "I could grow to love him."

He straightened, almost angrily. "I thought you weren't in the market for a husband."

Love shone so clearly in her eyes that she didn't see how he could fail to see it. "Well, I thought I wasn't either," she said defensively.

They sat for another moment, neither one knowing what to say now.

"Well, I've been thinking. Once the war's over, I might settle down."

Abby's heart leaped to her throat. "I thought you weren't in the market for a wife."

His eyes met hers again. "I didn't think I was either."

She waited, hoping he'd ask. Moments ticked by.

When he said nothing, she thumped her heels against her horse's sides, sending him down the hill.

"Hey!" Barrett called after her in a stunned tone. "Where are you going?"

"To find me a bluebird!" she called back.

He watched her go, a grin spreading across his face. *Well, hell, Drake,* he thought, spurring his horse forward.

Maybe he was looking for a wife and baby boy after all.

Watch for the next book in The Sisters of Mercy Flats saga. . . .